MISSION IMPRACTICAL
DAVID A. McINTEE

BBC BOOKS

For Gina and Chris

Published by BBC Worldwide Ltd,
Woodlands, 80 Wood Lane
London W12 0TT

First published 1998
Copyright © David A. McIntee 1998
The moral right of the author has been asserted

Original series broadcast on the BBC
Format © BBC 1963
Doctor Who and TARDIS are trademarks of the BBC

ISBN 0 563 40592 9
Imaging by Black Sheep, copyright © BBC 1998

Printed and bound in Great Britain by Mackays of Chatham
Cover printed by Belmont Press Ltd, Northampton

Introduction

With the appearance of Glitz and Frobisher here, I've now pretty much done all the continuity I really wanted to in *Who*... So, do I simply fade the continuity away with grace to please the critics, or go out with a grand finale?

Hmm. Grand finale it is.

To those of you who will find this book shallow – damn right. After two grimmer, more downbeat books, I need something to cheer me up, and this is it. So, for now, check your brains at the door, 'cos you probably won't need them.

Thanks, credits and acknowledgements this time go especially to Gary Gillatt and Stephen Cole, for enabling Frobisher's appearance – not forgetting Steve Parkhouse and John Ridgway, who created the little feller in the first place – and Kate Orman.

This story takes place between the Marvel *Doctor Who Magazine* comic strips *War Game* and *Fun House*.

Prologue

The sun was a distant patch of gold which barely showed through the warm clouds. The landscape itself was like a mound of spaghetti bolognese: all time-worn rocks and tangled fungoid jungle. Clouds of sweet steam floated between the fungal boles, drifting in a timeless dance.

'Watch your timing carefully – the shot isn't permanent. You got yourself maybe ninety minutes before it wears off. After that the poppers should fool automated sensors, but if you run into a live guard, you're dead meat.'

Chat caught herself about to nod in response to the message in her ear. 'I can tell time,' she murmured under her breath. That was loud enough to be picked up by the mike built into her filter mask. The mask might filter out any natural toxins, but Chat wasn't very impressed with its record when it came to filtering out the putrescent stench of this place.

'Just letting you know. I mean, *I* don't have to worry about getting trapped in there,' Monty's gruff voice came back. Chat was about to reply, when she heard the squelching of feet on the spongy ground. She ducked behind a fleshy root as thick as an oak's trunk. As she watched, two reptilian Veltrochni strolled past, talking animatedly. Young ones, judging by the whiteness of their quills, but still big enough to tear her apart with one hand.

They wore tabards and ceremonial axes, but no powered armour. That made them more likely to be staff apprentices than guards or military personnel. They didn't look in Chat's direction, which was a considerable relief to her.

3

She stepped out from behind the root once they had passed, and finished her trek discreetly. A circular vent was set into the rock floor, and clouds of condensation flowed steadily up from the grille. It was the work of mere moments to slice through the retaining bolts with a small laser cutter from her pack, and then lever off the grille.

Attaching a monofilament cable to one of the bolts that was still embedded in the rock, Chat lowered herself into the vent. She was slim and athletic, but it was still a tight squeeze. The tricky part was switching from her vertical position to a crawl when she reached the base of the shaft, which opened on to a junction of eighteen-inch-high tunnels. With a bit of contortionism, she managed it, and paused to consult a small electronic map. The faint glow of its display screen showed that the vault was quite close now.

A grille stood before her, and she could make out the twinkling lights of computer banks in the room beyond. A Veltrochni technician with ochre mottling was tending the equipment directly below. The engineer was unarmed, but any struggle he made, or shots she fired, would make noise that would bring the rest of them down on her. Her mother had told her there would be days like this.

Luckily his back was turned, so she eased the grille open with agonising slowness. Veltrochni had notoriously sensitive noses, and she just hoped he wouldn't be too concerned about sensing another Veltrochni in the vault. She also hoped that the pheromone shot was sending out the right signals; she just wanted to blend in with the other Veltrochni, not seem like she was on heat. She lowered herself head-first out of the vent, silently palming a hypo. Her shadow fell across the technician, and he looked up in surprise.

Chat plunged down, shoving the hypo into the engineer's neck. The engineer spasmed as the sedative took hold, and she caught him under the arms as he started to fall. Still hanging from the ceiling by her feet, she swung him round and propped him up against a console. Even with him in the room, the floor alarms would still be triggered by the pressure of an unauthorised extra person.

She swung herself back to a position directly over the complex electronic cradle which held her goal. In the midst of an array of bizarre equipment was a stubby yet exquisitely beautiful cylinder about two feet long. Partly crystalline and partly metallic, it was gilded and filigreed with expensive-looking ornamentation. She had no idea what it was made of, and didn't care. All that mattered was that some people were willing to pay a lot for it.

It took several minutes to neutralise the alarms and remove the cylinder, which she stowed away in her toolbag. Then she slid an apparently identical cylinder into its place, and reset the alarms.

Her next instinct was, naturally, to retrace her steps and make a quick getaway. Instead she unclipped herself from the monofilament cable and dropped to the floor. Out of curiosity, she started working on the alarms again. She had undone two of the seven when she heard the door open and booted feet surround her.

Two Veltrochni warriors in powered armour were covering her with their KEM rifles. The kinetic energy missiles that the rifles launched would probably be polycarbide darts, but Chat had no particular desire to find out for certain.

Chat raised her hands wearily as the Veltrochni motioned her away from the computer core. The two warriors stepped aside as an older Veltrochni, her quills dark with age, moved between them and into the room.

She hissed softly, 'Bravely done, *Iirdmon*, but quite futile.' She glanced pointedly at the cylinder in its electronic cradle. 'I am afraid the alarms would take rather longer to disable.' She looked back at Chat, and gestured to the two troopers. 'Take her to the security cells for indictment.'

Monty, a pugnacious-looking man in his fifties, was safely ensconced in an electronic womb, lit only by the glow of the screens and holograms. He didn't see them, however, since he was jacked into the system personally, and kept his eyes closed to avoid confusion. His mind knew exactly where they all were, and what they were doing, every step of the way.

'Liang, rendezvous in three minutes. Jack, you're about to receive delivery.'

The door slid open in front of Chat, revealing a wide indoor plaza. Thick metal doors were set into the polished stone walls at regular intervals. An unarmoured Veltrochni rose from his work station at the security console to greet them, and an armoured guard also came over to view the new arrival.

'Remand this prisoner,' one of her escorts growled. 'She will be indicted for burglary.' He handed over her satchel. 'She was carrying this.'

'It will be thoroughly searched,' the jailer promised. The two warriors exchanged a glance, and left. As the jailer punched a door button on the console, the armoured guard pushed Chat roughly across the plaza.

'Watch it,' she warned. 'I'm an Earth citizen.'

'You are a prisoner,' the guard snapped, shoving her towards the open cell door. From the corner of her eye, Chat could see the jailer working at the security monitor panel, but then the door slammed shut behind her, trapping her in the spartan cell.

The Hunters on guard at the Council Chambers' auxiliary landing platform didn't take much notice of the shuttle that descended from the matt sky. To have got through the defence grid at all, it must have had the proper clearances. They checked it on their hand-held scanners as it alighted on a platform carved from an immense limb of vegetation. The scan confirmed it had the proper clearances, and that there were no contraband materials on board.

In truth, of course, the guards were rather bored; they saw dozens of shuttles belonging to various Packs, as well as the Self Defence Force, arrive and depart every day. This one bore Self Defence Force markings: one of their own. When the occupants emerged, their passes would be checked, of course, but for the moment it sufficed that the shuttle was neither armed nor a bomb.

Chat blinked in the sudden light as the cell door opened after only a few moments. The armoured guard beckoned her out. 'Out you come, my little beauty. That look suits you.'

She glanced at her reflection in a deactivated console screen. The image of a Veltrochni warrior looked back at her, courtesy of the holosuit that had been left in her cell. 'I hope this isn't going to be another new fetish, Jack.'

The guard gave a most un-Veltrochni laugh. 'Now that you mention it, that extendable jaw could have its moments. Come on, we'd better get moving – the security monitors will hold the loop indefinitely, but sooner or later somebody's going to come in here.'

'Here,' the jailer – in reality another conspirator, named Oskar – pressed a hypo to her neck. 'Now the biosensors – and guards' noses – won't know the difference either.'

'I would have been happier if I could have got in and out without being caught.'

'But what a catch you are,' Jack said. 'Once you set off the biosensors, you'd have been met at the vent exterior by one of their patrols and caught anyway. This was the only way to make sure they assumed you were caught *before* you could take the prize.' He hesitated. 'You *did* grab it, didn't you?'

'Yes,' Chat said coldly. Innuendo she could stand, but questioning her professionalism was something else.

'Hey, just checking,' Jack said defensively. 'We didn't get a live feed here in the calaboose.' He tossed a KEM rifle from the weapons locker to Oskar, and handed another to Chat. 'Time we were gone.'

Pack-Leader Lothkash of the Self Defence Force was keen to interrogate the new prisoner. Human visitors to Veltroch were rare enough, and it was surprising that one would choose to attempt a crime. Surely the human must have known that that was impossible here?

Her choice of target was also intriguing. In terms of monetary value, it was not the most desirable thing in the building. Nor was it particularly attractive in any aesthetic sense – though Lothkash reminded himself that human aesthetics were probably very alien. He suspected that there must be something more to this, and was determined to find out what, before the thief was returned to the humans' Galactic Security for trial.

Flanked by two armed guards, the Pack-Leader marched into the security section, and looked around for the jailer. There was no sign of any jailer or guards. His dorsal spines flattened with the feeling that something was very wrong here, and he cast an eye over the security console. The monitors showed the jailer and guard at their duty stations, but no sign of Lothkash and his escort.

'Pack-Leader,' one of the warriors called. He pointed a claw at the nearest scanner. 'Look.'

Lothkash looked, and saw a small device attached to the scanner. He pulled it off, then glanced back at the console, where one monitor now showed himself and his escort. 'She has escaped with accomplices!' He triggered the alarm. 'All Hunters, this is Pack-Leader Lothkash in security. Locate and apprehend human fugitive accompanied by two Veltrochni accomplices.' He looked at the recorded image of the jailer and guard, both of whom had faint ochre mottling on their leathery skin. 'Both are from Pack Hysoth.'

Jack Chance didn't hesitate in his stride up to the landing area, even though the alarm bells were ringing. He wouldn't have much of a tale to tell the eager girls back home if there wasn't at least some chance of getting caught. Now his blood really pumped through his veins, giving a pleasant adrenalin buzz.

'Liang, get the engines red hot and ready to go, just like my women.'

Chat groaned slightly.

'That's the idea, baby,' grinned Jack.

The guards on duty at the landing platform exchanged glances when the alarms rang. 'Should we go?'

'If they are trying to escape, they may come this way.'

'You wait here, then. I will tell the shuttle pilot to take off, in case they try to hijack it.' He started towards the shuttle, but its drives were already whining into life. The guard hadn't really expected any less from a well-trained pilot.

He had only taken a few steps when the door into the building opened, and three Hysoth warriors emerged. The warrior hesitated, but then recalled that the alert was for two Hysoths and a human.

The first Hysoth approached, gesturing to them, while the other two Hysoths entered the shuttle. 'Guard the platform. We will search this shuttle in case it is to be used as an escape vehicle, and take it off the platform to prevent that.'

'Yes sir,' the guard agreed. Nodding to his partner, he took up position watching the entrance to the landing platform. Meanwhile, the Hysoth disappeared into the shuttle.

With a roar, the shuttle blasted straight up and into the clouds. The guard thought that was perhaps a little overzealous, when a simple hover off the platform would have sufficed. Perhaps, he thought, the pilot was unused to alerts.

A chorus of delighted whoops and yells filled the shuttle's cabin as it burst from the atmosphere and arced away.

Looking round from the pilot's seat, Liang could see his sister hold up the cylinder like an athlete showing off a trophy. Along with Jack and Oskar, she had switched off her holosuit. 'We'll rendezvous with Monty and the ship in ten minutes,' Liang called back from the cockpit.

'Good,' Jack said approvingly. 'No sense in hanging around when there's wine, women and song waiting on the nearest GalSec planet, eh?'

'Who said anything about women?' Chat muttered.

Chapter One

A circular bar was in the centre of the single ground-floor room. Little cubicles with card tables and gaming machines encircled the walls. A wide and rusted staircase led up to the next floor. Despite the early hour, quite a few people were in, huddled over their drinks in the dim light. The barman was bored, but couldn't complain about his business. It was the only going concern in town, and at least there was no particular legal authority to kowtow to on such a backwater planet.

The door opened, admitting a shaft of light that dazzled the barman's eyes. He turned to curse the newcomer, but the words stuck in his throat. The new arrival was visibly not to be trifled with. It was a brown reptilian with red and black mottling, almost eight feet tall, whose knee joints were at the back of his legs. Gently wavering quills ran from the crown of his head, down his neck, and formed a ridge down his back. A bulky KEM rifle was slung across his back.

The barman tried to utter some sort of greeting, but his throat was unaccountably dry.

'Tirdmon,' the new arrival said, the voice starting somewhere in his boots, 'where is Travis Crowe?'

The barman shrugged, his profession's instinctive reaction to questions from authority-figures. 'Never heard of him.' Innkeepers, he thought, had a bond of confidentiality with their guests.

The visitor's jaw extruded forward, baring marble fangs. 'His flier is parked outside.'

The barman winced inwardly. 'A lot of people park their

fliers here. It's a less troublesome spot than some places.'

One powerful arm flicked out, grabbed the barman's beard, and pulled him close across the bar-top. A claw slid out from the forefinger, touching the barman's jawline. The barman tried not to think about how easily that claw could slide through the skin and into an artery. This creature might even do that by accident, without noticing, he thought.

'Not any more, *Iirdmon*.' Warm and acrid breath stung the barman's eyes. 'I want to ask him questions.'

'You GalSec?'

'No. Galactic Security would not flatten this building if you refused to answer.'

The barman swallowed hard, far too easily envisioning further unpleasantness being inflicted on his valuable person. Tossing drunks out was one thing, but this Veltrochni obviously wouldn't go so quietly. Better to give him what he wanted and be rid of him. 'Room 12. Top of the stairs and turn left.'

'That was easy, was it not?' The Veltrochni ripped his clawed hand away, and the barkeeper felt as if half his face had gone with it. The alien let the strands of beard fall from his claws, and went to the stairs. He had ascended only a couple of steps when he paused and turned. 'Do not allow anyone to come up these stairs while I am here, *Iirdmon*. Anyone who does so is dead.' Without waiting for a reply, he turned and ascended.

The barman steadied himself against the bar, and poured himself a drink. It was unusual for him to drink the slop he usually doled out to the poor marks who stumbled in here, but on this occasion it would have to do.

The Veltrochni trod warily along the first-floor corridor, examining the numbered cards on the doors. He paused at

14

the door labelled '12', and listened carefully. Laboured breathing and a distinct squeaking of springs was emanating from within. The Veltrochni slipped the KEM rifle from his shoulder, and used his free arm to shatter the door with a massive punch.

The barman winced as a crash reverberated down the stairs, accompanied by a female scream. There was a cacophony of breaking glass, and something hurtled down past the windows to land in the street with a thud. After a moment, the Veltrochni descended the stairs, rifle in hand.

A woman was staggering behind him, unsuccessfully trying to hold a towel round her naked body and screaming at him, but he ignored her.

The barman started reaching for something under the counter, but pulled up short when the Veltrochni's eyes fell on him. 'I wouldn't, if I were you.'

The barman went ahead anyway, bringing out an old laser rifle. The Veltrochni shot him without even aiming properly, and left as the barman hit the floor. A polycarbide bolt had passed clear through him to embed itself in the wall.

Travis Crowe was trying to pick himself up from the dirt street. Half his scrawny body was already starting to discolour with bruising, and he paused painfully on all fours, just long enough to spit out some blood. It was also just long enough for a vague figure to stride over and touch his back with a crystalline rod. Crowe rolled away into a sprawl, every nerve-ending on fire.

He struggled to his feet as the rod was touched to his neck. This time the pain didn't come. 'Resistance was a foolish act, certain only to inspire reprisals,' a dry voice told him. 'If you

15

make any further attempt to escape, physical disablement will be necessary.' Crowe froze, tempted to mention that it was surely just luck which prevented any permanent disablement when he came through the window. He thought better of it when he opened his eyes and saw who had spoken.

The diminutive figure was poised beside him in well-tailored spacer garb. A waistcoat was draped over his tight-fitting coveralls. Long and spindly fingers were wrapped around the crystalline weapon. It was his eyes that chilled Crowe the most, though. They were almond-shaped expanses of impenetrable blackness, set against the oversized, mushroom-coloured head. No white, no iris; just jet black. 'Sha'ol,' he muttered. The Veltrochni who had pitched him through the window now turned the corner and loomed behind Sha'ol. 'Karthakh,' Crowe groaned, as much to himself as to them. 'If I'd known it was you –'

'The bounty is larger for your return unharmed,' Sha'ol went on, a translator implant flickering red at his throat. 'It would be in your best interests to co-operate with us.'

'Look, Sha'ol,' Crowe said hopefully, 'you know me. Whatever they told you was wrong –'

'The accuracy of our employer's beliefs is not relevant to your situation,' the S'Raph Tzun interrupted coldly. 'The bounty has been placed, and we have accepted the contract; that is our only concern.'

Crowe's mind raced. If Sha'ol and Karthakh were only in it for the money, maybe he could cut a deal with them... 'Look, guys, what if I was to offer you double?' Yes, that was the approach to take, he was sure. He picked himself up. 'Whatever they're paying you, I'll double it.' He grinned, sure that greed must appeal to them.

Karthakh's jaw edged forward, baring the tips of fangs. 'We cannot dishonour our contract,' he rumbled.

Crowe felt the last of his confidence evaporate. 'Look, Sha'ol, whatever it is you want, I can get. Money, a ship, vrax…' They weren't going for it. It was damn near impossible to read alien faces at the best of times, but their silence was more than enough of an answer.

Crowe dodged sideways, grabbing Sha'ol's arm, and swinging him round before bolting for his flier. There was a faint slapping sound, and Crowe saw the ground rise to block his path to the flier. There was something different about the flier ahead of him too. A protuberance was buried in the door. It looked like a metal rod, a couple of feet long and slick with blood. It hadn't been there a moment ago, and he was sure he should be thinking more about it.

Instead he found himself wondering why he couldn't seem to rise from the dirt street. He was surprised at how comfortable the street was; it was relaxing, and made him forget his fears…

Karthakh lowered his KEM rifle, as Sha'ol glanced up at the faces which were beginning to appear in the surrounding windows. The human had been foolish, but had scored a minor point against the pair, ensuring that their reward would be a few thousand less than if they had delivered him alive.

Each alien took hold of one of the corpse's arms, and Sha'ol tapped the hard spot on his neck, where a subcutaneous communicator was implanted. '*H'shar moch*,' he hissed, and a red glow swept the trio from the face of the planet.

There was a faint rustling sound from the darkness. No, Karthakh decided, confused, not darkness, but not light

17

either. The void in which he found himself was cloaked in the absence of either. Looking down, Karthakh found that he couldn't even see himself. He waved his hand in front of his eyes, saw nothing. He must be here, though, as he was standing, and could feel the muscles move his arm.

This wasn't the ship, however… Where was he? Was Sha'ol with him? Who had brought them here? It must have been with hostile intent, or else why not hail them first?

The rustling sound came again, and Karthakh turned on the spot, trying to work out where it was coming from. If he had to guess what the sound was, he would say it was like heavy cloth, with a rasp of brocade.

'Sha'ol?' His partner's eyes worked on a slightly different wavelength; perhaps he could see better, if he was here.

'I am here.' The voice came from about three feet to his left. 'The transport has been disrupted.'

'Can you see where we are?' Karthakh's mind briefly threw up the possibility that they were in fact dead from a transmat malfunction. But this was not the Great Forest of Atroch. He was still alive, he decided. Alive, but definitely in the wrong place.

'No. The void is complete.'

Karthakh unshipped his KEM rifle just in case, but privately doubted that it would do any good if he couldn't see to aim. At least the weight of it reminded him that he was still real; that seemed comforting somehow.

'I apologise for the unexpected nature of this detour,' a crisp new voice said. It seemed to come from all around them. Or even, Karthakh thought with a shudder, from within him. 'Our meeting, however, has to be rather covert.'

'Hidden even from the participants?' Sha'ol asked.

'Let us just say that we would like to maintain an air of

plausible deniability, Sha'ol. But, if a reference point would make things easier for yourself and Karthakh…' the chilly tone seemed to suggest that this was an example of inferiority that was to be humoured. Karthakh didn't much like the idea that the mystery voice knew who they were. They had many enemies.

A number of figures coalesced around them, and now Karthakh could see Sha'ol and the body of Crowe quite clearly. The figures around them were indistinct, as if viewed through smoke or murky water. They were just visible enough to make out that they were humanoids. Half a dozen or so were arrayed around them. 'Is this better?'

'Who are you?' Karthakh demanded. 'And what is this place?'

'To take your questions in reverse order, this place is merely a convenient conference area. We are, as it were, concerned citizens, with an offer for you.' The leading figure tossed a flat disc, which Karthakh deftly caught. One massive paw enclosed it with incongruous delicacy.

Immediately, a hologram flicked out from the disc. It was a rather tall and burly humanoid male, with curly blond hair. He wore clothes odd even by humanoid standards. Striped yellow trousers clashed with a long patchwork coat, which was mostly red and pink, with a partly green back. 'Who is this *Iirdmon*?' Karthakh asked.

'He likes to call himself "the Doctor",' the leader said, his voice dripping with disdain. 'He is not a human, though.'

'Why should we do anything for someone who just abducted us?' Karthakh growled. 'It is not so difficult for those who know of us to make contact.'

'We have better things to do than visit the haunts of criminals or bounty hunters. But you will be well paid for your efforts.'

19

'How well?'

Karthakh could almost feel the satisfaction emanating from the figure. 'Name your price.'

'A hundred million credit-bars,' Karthakh said, plucking the figure out of the air. If they wouldn't be serious, then why should he listen?

'Very well, one hundred million,' the leader agreed matter-of-factly. Karthakh's quills stiffened. Had he heard correctly? 'The money payable upon proof of the Doctor's demise.'

'What?'

'You specified one hundred million,' the leader said icily. 'I have agreed to these terms. That is how one does business with freelance operators, is it not?'

They must want this Doctor very badly, Karthakh thought. Or else they were planning on not paying up. Karthakh didn't mind people planning that, since one way or the other, they always paid their dues in the end. Beside him, Sha'ol's head tilted curiously. 'The Doctor is known to us by reputation,' the Tzun said. 'He is a Time Lord. There is no guarantee that he will choose to visit this era.'

There was a faint suggestion of a laugh from the dark figures. 'His travelling habits are somewhat cosmopolitan to say the least, but we will enable you to find your way to him. Now, do you accept the contract or not?'

The Doctor himself – the flesh and blood original from which the hologram had been derived – was in fact currently relaxing, watching the twin suns set over the Tatooine desert.

'Why you couldn't have just watched the video, I have no idea,' he murmured to his companion, prompting a loud

'Shh!' from someone in a nearby seat.

'Hey, with access to a TARDIS, I gotta see the seven hundred wonders of the universe. The walking mountains on Haskor, the great Sphinx on Mars, and *Star Wars* on the big screen. Tales of what it was like to see it in a theatre have been passed down for generations in my family. You're just sour because you've seen it before.'

'I happen to prefer the Special Editions,' the Doctor said huffily.

'Why am I not surprised?'

The Doctor fell silent, much to the relief of the rest of the audience. By the time the film reached the Death Star trench run, even he had got into the spirit of things, cheering with the rest of the audience. He shook his head sadly when Princess Leia presented the heroes with their medals.

'Some people have no sense of reality,' he commented to his companion as they stepped on to the street outside Mann's Chinese Theater. There was a long queue of curious cinema-goers snaking around the block in the mild May evening. All of them were probably wishing that they had made it into the first showing, instead of the second. 'Believe me, Frobisher, when you save the planet from destruction, nobody queues up to hand out medals.'

His companion retrieved the last few pieces of popcorn from the box with his beak, and used one flipper to bat it accurately into a waste bin. In contrast to the Doctor's burly six-foot explosion of colour, Frobisher was half his height and thoroughly monochrome. In fact, he was a penguin.

There was something very mellow and calming about being a penguin. He had half expected that a man dressed in what looked like a patchwork quilt, accompanied by a penguin, would get some funny looks in Hollywood, but this had not proved to be the case. People probably assumed that they were an act.

A large blue police telephone box sat under a set of traffic signals on the corner. It was a booth of a type common to Britain in the third quarter of the twentieth century, but was decidedly uncommon in Los Angeles in 1977. Just as Frobisher wasn't an ordinary penguin, so too the police box was no mere phone booth. In fact it was a cunningly - and often embarrassingly - disguised space-time craft called the TARDIS, and it belonged to the Doctor. Frobisher occasionally speculated, though, that maybe the Doctor belonged to the TARDIS, which had a knack of depositing him wherever he might be most useful.

The Doctor strode into the TARDIS, while Frobisher paused to look at a little coin-operated newspaper box containing the *LA Times*. Frobisher liked to collect newspapers - or the local equivalent - from the places he visited. The reportage helped give him a larger sense of what was going on in other parts of the planet than the one he was in. He didn't want to fall into the trap of thinking that the little piece of ground where he stood was all there was to a world. It was amazing how many travellers in his own time thought of some planets as being just a spaceport with a piece of city around it. Some maybe noticed a bit of countryside attached like a conservatory, but hardly anybody really though about what else went on on a planet.

Frobisher prided himself on maintaining a sense of scale; that there was a whole world out there, no matter which world it was. He dropped a local coin in the box, and extracted a paper before following the Doctor into the TARDIS.

Inside was a spacious white room, decorated with circular

indentations. The Doctor was busying himself at a very complex hexagonal console in the middle of the room. A few other pieces of furniture were scattered around: a hatstand, a sun-lounger, a small table with some games set up on it… It was a very odd mixture indeed.

'Admit it, though, Doc; you had fun, right?'

'Fun?' the Doctor echoed, as if this was something to be avoided – but Frobisher could see the twinkle in his eyes. 'Well, yes. I must confess, it was rather entertaining. That Tarkin chap looked vaguely familiar, though. I think I met his granddaughter once…' He finished his work at the console, and the transparent column at the centre of the console began to slowly rise and fall. Frobisher idly wondered what the sci-fi fans standing in line thought of that.

He waddled over to the interior door that led deeper into the TARDIS. 'I hope there are still some chocolate pilchards left in the food machine…'

'Are you still hungry, after all that popcorn?' the Doctor asked in mild astonishment.

'Having variable mass and cellular composition does some freaky things to your metabolic rate, Doc,' Frobisher explained patiently.

'It can't be good for you. There was a moment in that cinema when I thought you weren't going to get into the seat.'

Frobisher's head rocked back. 'I am not getting fat. I've just changed shape.'

'That I can see,' the Doctor said pointedly.

Frobisher gave him a beady glare. 'I mean I used to be a King penguin, and now I'm an Emperor penguin. Anyway, isn't there something about pots and kettles here?' He prodded the Doctor's torso with the tip of one flipper.

'You're a bit more grab a slab than pinch an inch. At nine hundred years, you can hardly call it puppy fat.'

The Doctor straightened huffily. 'I'll have you know I'm the very figure of Gallifreyan health.' His features took on the lecturing expression that Frobisher knew so well. 'When you've been locked up without food as often as I have, you'll learn to appreciate a little... safety margin!'

'I always kinda tried to avoid the "getting locked up" part myself. It's a union thing among detectives, you know – job demarcation. We don't go getting locked up, and lowlifes don't go detecting.' Well, technically, at least. There had always been a bit of crossover, in Frobisher's experience. Not that he was exactly the pride of the police force, or even a member of one; he'd mostly handled messy divorces and petty thefts.

Not quite the stuff that dreams were made of, or that he had taken the job for. Travelling with the Doctor might be a bit more dangerous than following an unfaithful drunkard, but at least it was more interesting.

Chapter Two

The Vandorian cutter *Thornton* was a small and angular reddish-painted vessel. It was vaguely wedge-shaped, with a large sensor array mounted amidships.

Captain Handley had taken his shift-break five minutes early. He needed the coffee if he was to be any use at all. Like any good captain, he was never really off duty. Even when regulations said he should be relaxing, he was running duty rosters and course changes through his mind.

However, he tried to relax as dutifully as he was able, putting a holovid of *The Black Belt Of Kung Fu* on the viewer. He'd seen only a few minutes of action before the intercom burst into life.

'Ops to Captain: possible sensor contact, bearing two-seven-five mark one-one-four.'

Handley straightened, his eyes turning from the holo player to the intercom. 'Aspect heading?'

'Paralleling our own course.' It was possible they had accidentally taken up a course identical to that of a drifting asteroid but, if so, it wasn't on any of the charts in the tank. 'Come port ten degrees, mark two.' Handley left his cabin, and went through to the bridge.

The helmsman nudged the controlling joystick, and the cutter *Thornton* rose slightly as it banked left. Handley, a fit-looking officer in his early forties, glanced at the chart tank as he came in. Nothing was showing up there, so it wasn't likely to be an asteroid, unless it was very small indeed. Perhaps a speck of dark matter, or a naked singularity, he thought hopefully.

The bridge of the *Thornton* wasn't very large; it contained just enough room for a navigational station, engine monitor, tactical station, and helm. The dog-watch's dim lights made it seem even more cramped. Unlike most spaceship crew, Handley liked the cramped conditions; it made the ship cosier, and more homely.

The intercom buzzed again. 'Ops to bridge: confirmed sensor contact.'

'Same aspect heading?' Handley hoped so. Then there would at least be a chance that it was just a hunk of rock. He tried not to think that it could also mean a smarter helmsman.

'Yes, sir. Shall I scan it?'

'No.' If it was another ship shadowing them, he didn't want to let whoever it was know that he was on to them. And if it was just a rock, then it didn't matter anyway. 'Filter out as many other energy traces as you can from the passive receptors, and watch for any change from your contact.'

'Aye, sir.'

Handley turned back to the chart tank. Whether they had a shadow or not, he still had to mark out their patrol course, as he had done so many times over the past fifteen years.

'Ops to Captain,' the intercom suddenly said. 'Sensor contact bearing three-four-four mark ten.'

Different from before, he realised. 'What's it doing?'

'It's maintaining a steady course. Seems to be drifting.'

Handley directed the sensor displays into the chart tank. 'Over a mile across... Asteroid?'

Nausch, the science officer, looked at it, then shook her head. 'Not dense enough for a refugee from the local belt. Some energy signatures, but not enough for a ship.'

'Scan it.' Whatever it was, it was clearly worth investigating, seeing as it was headed through Vandorian space. At the very least it had to be plotted for navigational purposes.

Nausch settled into her chair, operating the sensor controls. 'Two and a half miles long, one mile wide… Composition largely duralinium alloy. Definitely a ship.' She looked up. 'I'm getting a transponder signal,' she said in surprise. 'It's a colony ship, the *Speculator*.'

'Any sign of our shadow?'

'Still there. They're keeping very quiet. Definitely under a camo field, I would say. It fits with the recent Veltrochni activity. For some reason they're keeping tabs on Vandorian shipping.'

'Damn.' Somebody was definitely up to something, and Handley didn't like not knowing what it was. Out here, not knowing things was what got people killed. 'All right, call it in to VP. Tell them we're tagging an old colony ship, and we've got a probable Veltrochni Dragon keeping an eye on us.' It wasn't that unusual. They sent a few Dragons to watch Vandorian space, and Vandor Prime sent the occasional drone to shadow their visiting ships. It seemed to be happening a lot more these days. Politics, Handley supposed.

'Scan them. Let them know the fun's over.' Once they knew their point had been made, the Veltrochni tended to consider the job done.

Pack-Leader Hyskanth of the Dragon *Thazrakh* watched the Vandorian patrol craft bank away towards the larger derelict at the edges of sensor range. The prospector in the crew's work pit had already identified that as an ancient human craft. Hyskanth's Flight Director hopped up ~~to join him on~~ the command balcony of the triangular flight deck. 'They're scanning us now, Pack-Leader.'

Hyskanth wasn't impressed. 'I imagine they detected us some time ago. This is merely our dismissal.' He let his claws slip out a little at the thought of being dismissed by humans. 'But… our orders are clear. Let them know we can reach them anywhere at any time. Now they know, so…'

'New course?'

'Vandor Prime. We are to join the escort for the conference delegation.'

'At once, Pack-Leader.'

Frobisher had retired for the evening to his room in the TARDIS. Although the walls were indented with the ever-present circles, this room had curved walls, the way Frobisher liked them. Curves and the like seemed more flowing, and therefore definitely more natural to him.

He had swum about in his pool for a few minutes, then decided to read the paper he had picked up on Earth. It seemed to be full of politics and sport, with a little entertainment gossip in between.

He had started to theorise about how these three subjects were a natural progression, when there was a sudden bizarre howling from outside.

Frobisher hurried from his room, quickly ascertaining that the noise was coming from a storeroom just down the corridor. He considered going to fetch the Doctor, but decided otherwise. He was a grown Whifferdill, which meant he could look after himself. Besides, he thought, as the sound roared through the corridor again, the Doctor would have to be deaf not to hear that. He was surely already on his way.

Apart from that, Frobisher was curious. He was an investigator by nature as well as profession, so of course he should investigate. He waddled down towards the storeroom door.

* * *

28

Sha'ol could feel the destination trying to reject him. Whatever energies encased it must be slightly out of phase with the device on his wrist, he realised. It must be adjusted if another attempt to board the TARDIS proved necessary.

Energy sparked, screaming out into the heated air, as a large white room coalesced around him. There were circles patterned into the walls, and a faint hum pervaded the air. Sha'ol was satisfied; clearly he had indeed managed to board the Doctor's TARDIS.

The local continuum continued to howl, as Karthakh pushed his way through the fabric of reality and into the TARDIS. Sha'ol scanned the room quickly. It was huge and empty, apart from a purposeless pair of shoes in the centre of the floor.

'This is the Doctor's TARDIS?' Karthakh asked.

'Yes.' Sha'ol regretted that none of his forefathers had boarded a TARDIS before. Their knowledge of the size and layout of the vessel would be invaluable to him now. At the very least he and Karthakh must identify the control centre. Even if the Doctor was not there now, he must go there at some point. Since the TARDIS was currently in flight, it was reasonable to assume that he must at least be in the control area for landing procedures.

Sha'ol took up a position to cover the door, while Karthakh moved to open it. Before he could do so, it opened from the outside. It would be most convenient if it was the Doctor himself. However, it was merely a terrestrial avian of the genus *Aptenodytes*. Perhaps a non-sentient companion or pet.

'Hey,' it suddenly yelled. 'What are you guys doing in the TAR–' Karthakh grabbed the avian, while Sha'ol checked the corridor in both directions to make sure there were no hostiles in sight.

Sha'ol turned to the avian, curious that it could speak. Perhaps his identification was in error, and it was a species that merely resembled the Earth *Aptenodytes*. 'This vessel is the TARDIS belonging to the Time Lord known as the Doctor, is that correct?'

'The Doc isn't partial to stowaways –'

'That answers my question. You will now take us to the Doctor.'

'Not a chance, bub.' The avian raised its beak defiantly.

Sha'ol pointed his disruptor at its head. 'You will take us to the Doctor.' It was a simple tactic, but generally effective when dealing with civilians or amateurs.

'Well, if you put it like that...'

Sha'ol motioned to his comrade to put the avian down. He knew most beings would refer to such a comrade as their friend, but somehow he had not been comfortable with that designation.

As soon as the avian's feet touched the ground, it leapt back up, slithering neatly out of Karthakh's grasp. Karthakh watched it bolt down the corridor. When it was gone, he took a small device from his belt. It beeped rapidly. 'If it is frightened, it will try to warn the Doctor,' Karthakh rumbled. 'We can follow it.'

The Doctor was still in the console room when Frobisher dived in through the door, sliding to a halt on his chest. 'Doc! Doc! We got company.'

The Doctor blinked. 'Company?' he asked uncertainly.

'Didn't you hear that noise?'

'What noise?'

Frobisher shook his head at that. The Doctor might be a Time Lord, but Frobisher did sometimes wonder whether he was a few hours short of a full day. 'Someone has broken into the TARDIS.'

'That is impossible,' the Doctor said severely. 'Nothing short of an Osiran or a Guardian could breach the TARDIS' defence shields while in flight.'

Frobisher folded his flippers on what, for want of a better word, could be called his hips. 'Well, tell that to the two gun-toting maniacs heading this way looking for you. Maybe they'll disappear in a puff of logic.'

The Doctor hesitated, then took his coat from the stand, and put it on. He always seemed to want to be at his best when meeting new folks, Frobisher had long since noticed. 'All right. Keep an eye on the console. I'll go and talk to these... "maniacs" of yours.' With that he left the console room.

Frobisher watched the door swing closed behind him, and felt rather guilty. He was the professional, after all; it should be him who faced down the bad guys, shouldn't it?

Karthakh was concentrating more on the tracker, so Sha'ol was paying even more attention than normal to the corridor ahead. A humanoid emerged from a door at the end, and Sha'ol held up a hand for Karthakh to stop. 'The tracker is no longer necessary.' There was no mistaking the mop of curly blond hair, or the distinctive multicoloured coat.

The Doctor saw the pair, and frowned. Then he stepped forward with a bright smile. 'And what can I do for you... gentlemen? Or were you just looking for a lift somewhere?'

'You are the Time Lord known as the Doctor?' Sha'ol asked. He believed in thoroughness. Every care must be taken to make sure they had the right person.

'I am,' the Doctor replied, clearly puzzled. 'And you are...?'

'Here to kill you,' Sha'ol completed the sentence for him.

31

Both bounty hunters raised their weapons.

'And you're wasting your time with those,' the Doctor told the pair a little smugly. He sounded as if he was trying to educate them. An interesting attitude, Sha'ol thought. Not that it mattered.

The Doctor continued. 'The TARDIS exists in a state of temporal grace. Weapons won't work in here.'

Sha'ol fired his disruptor. Nothing happened.

Karthakh growled faintly. 'That is not a problem.' He flexed his hands, his claws sliding from the fingertips. The Doctor backed off.

Suddenly the door behind him burst open, and a full-grown Kastrian leapt out, bearing right down on Karthakh. The Veltrochni tumbled to the floor, his claws striking sparks on the Kastrian's stone skin.

Sha'ol didn't waste time theorising about how a member of another extinct species could be here. The Doctor was a Time Lord, so why couldn't he have visited Kastria? Instead, he darted after the Doctor, who had slipped back through the door.

Sha'ol had no other weapons, but if he could disable the Doctor with the neural inhibitor from his field medical kit, then they could work out a proper permanent solution later.

A smothering sheet was flung across Sha'ol's face as he came through the door. The Doctor's coat, he realised as he struggled free. The Doctor was working furiously at the console, and Sha'ol paused only long enough to pull the medical kit from his jumpsuit pocket.

It must have been long enough, however, because the TARDIS lurched sideways, and Sha'ol slid across the console room floor to crash, stunned, into the main doors.

Frobisher felt himself topple over when the TARDIS tilted.

The intruder went flying overhead, crashing through the door and into the console room. Though the crystalline body he had formed wasn't built for lightning reactions, Frobisher managed to follow him in before he could regain his balance and go after the Doctor.

'Keep him busy,' the Doctor shouted, hanging on to the console.'Just a few more seconds...'

The TARDIS' drives screamed out an echoing wave of sound, and the two intruders were ripped out of sight faster than they could react. The TARDIS straightened immediately, and the Doctor and Frobisher fell heavily to the floor.

The Doctor leapt to his feet, stabbing furiously at the console, while Frobisher shrank back into the comforting penguin shape and shook his head.'Hey, they've gone.'

'Luckily I thought to dematerialise from around them,' the Doctor explained.'Now that usually doesn't work, but since they somehow got in by breaching the defence shields, I thought it would be more likely that they weren't fully in phase with the interior dimensions.'

'So the TARDIS rejected them?' Frobisher had learned to live with the Doctor's propensity for technobabble.

'Precisely.' The Doctor finished his programming with a flourish, and stood back to admire his handiwork. 'There. They won't find it so easy to follow us.' He allowed himself a small smile.'In fact I imagine they'll find it impossible; I've set the TARDIS to make a series of random jumps.'

Frobisher could see that something was still bothering the Doctor. Being both a private investigator and a shapechanger, he had long since learned to read the expressions of members of other races. He had had to.

'What's eating at you, Doc? You look like you're sitting a test.'

The Doctor's brow furrowed. 'Those two miscreants whom we just ejected from the premises were a S'Raph Tzun and a Veltrochni warrior. Given that the one race was wiped out by the other, it's very odd that two of them should be working together.'

'Maybe that hasn't happened yet. Wherever they came from, I mean.' This time-travel business was fun, but certainly had its difficult moments. Or maybe they were just confused. Frobisher could empathise with confusion.

'Possibly,' the Doctor said slowly, 'but then there is also the question of their getting in here. Neither of those races should have the ability to penetrate the TARDIS defence barrier, or survive in the vortex.' He nodded to himself. 'You know, I think there's more to this than meets the eye,' he pronounced. Frobisher could have sworn he sounded happy about that. The Doctor had never been able to resist a mystery. 'Now that's odd…'

'What is?'

The Doctor tapped a read-out. 'Anything that travels through the vortex leaves a temporal trace. That disreputable pair's trace originates from a human world…'

'You think they came from there?'

The Doctor pursed his lips. 'Not necessarily… But whatever means they had of travelling through time certainly originated there.' He flicked a few switches. 'So that's where we're going next.'

Frobisher cleared his throat. 'Isn't there a saying about lions and dens?'

The Doctor looked at him coolly. 'Whoever sent those two did so from the Gamma Delphinus system. I don't know about you, but if someone wants to kill me that badly, I'd rather like to know who and why. Or would you prefer to simply fly around, waiting for more assassins to find us?'

'Well, if you put it that way...' Frobisher said aloud, though his first thought was 'Yes!'

'I do,' the Doctor said with an air of finality. 'In situations like this, it's initiative that decides the outcome, Frobisher, and I'm not going to leave that to a Tzun and Veltrochni who want me dead.'

Chapter Three

Vandor Prime was the fourth planet out from the star Gamma Delphinus. Its capital, Neo Delphi, was a crusted mass of shifting rockcrete and metal that covered a chunk of the southern continent like a scab.

Most people called it the Jewelled City, because they had no imagination of their own and just picked up on what some down-market visnews journalist correctly thought would make a catchy slogan. The planet had originally been colonised as a source of jethryk, but the mining boom had long since died out, and it reverted to being just another human world. Nowadays there were no more jewels around than there were in any other colonial capital.

Wide streets and narrow alleys were cut deep into the high-rise flesh of the city. Transit tubes and roadways draped the enormous buildings like tinsel on a Christmas tree. Between the uppermost buildings that grew from the roofs of those below, the floating malls and apartment blocks dodged each other at a snail's pace. Immensely long transit elevators tethered the exclusive geostationary asteroid neighbourhoods to the sprawling body of the surface city.

In the deeper and darker areas of the city it sometimes didn't get fully light at all. It was not so much the shadows cast by the surrounding buildings that kept it dark, but a sort of omnipresent cloud of twilight. It was almost as if the population's thoughts were psychokinetically warping reality itself. Either that or no one had properly programmed weather control.

Niccolo Mandell wouldn't have been surprised in either

case. As far as he was concerned it was impossible to underestimate the intelligence of the average person. Even as he kept his beard in trim, he could imagine how impressive this exclusive quarter of the city must look to the masses.

He grinned into the bathroom mirror at the thought. The face that looked back at him was intelligent, cultured, and a very good mask for his emotions at any given moment. The black hair and neat, squared-off beard gave him just enough of a sinister air to encourage fear and respect; his piercing eyes under straight brows offered just enough casual openness to be trusted – or at least tolerated – by those who should know better. In short, exactly the impression he wished to project.

He straightened, his moustache also suitably trimmed. 'Everyone hates you,' he told his reflection quietly. 'They hate what they fear, and they fear what has power over them.' It was simple logic. He liked to remind himself of it every day when he got to the office. He had a reputation to uphold, and it wouldn't last long if he was as sweet here as he was at home with his newly pregnant wife. People would think he'd gone soft, and not think he could handle the job any more. He didn't mind that people feared and hated him. So long as Kala still loved him, the rest of the galaxy's population didn't really matter.

He dabbed on a touch of scent, and drained a mug of the strongest coffee that could be legally imported. It was time for another conference with his employers. Employers... It was an amusing thought, to which the President and his Cabinet no doubt subscribed. They were the government, and he worked for them. Mandell saw it a rather different way, of course. Governments came and went every few years, but he would still be here.

The seat of Vandor Prime's government resided in the plush chairs of the Forum at the heart of the formerly Jewelled City. The actual legislative council sat in a large circular debating chamber halfway up a gilded spire.

At the foot of the spire, the marbled outer halls of the Forum were filled with milling politicians and diplomats from various GalSec worlds. Niccolo Mandell ignored them, since they were ineffective as far as governing this planet was concerned. These were the ones who would sort out what happened after the crisis. They would decide which world should be blacklisted, and which deserved reparations. They would decide who to accuse of taking which sides afterwards.

But they wouldn't do a damned thing to actually alter the course of events. They were political vultures, waiting to feast on the expense accounts that came with the duty of forging belated treaties and settlements.

Parasites, Mandell thought, bloodsucking leeches... He wished he was one of them. Not that he didn't love his own job, but the chance to play the great game across the whole galaxy was, well... his guts tightened. The chance to dig into a deeper cash reserve couldn't be bad either.

'Am I looking...?'

'Affable, sir,' the press secretary told the President. 'As affable as the public expect.' He was struggling to keep up with the President's entourage as they moved though the marbled and gilded hallway of the Forum.

'Good,' President Klein said happily. Thin white hair and a broad smiley face lent itself well to the image of a concerned schoolmaster or the like. Klein had always felt that such an appearance was the one described as affable, and had since striven to be affable in word and deed. 'Are the snipers placed – just in case of need?'

'They are,' Mandell said, before the press secretary could say anything. 'I don't imagine they'll be needed.'

'The Veltrochni have been saying some pretty strong things, Mandell. Accusing this administration of theft is not exactly the height of diplomacy.' In fact, Klein suspected, they were just trying to set up an advance justification for whatever it was they were up to. He'd never liked the Veltrochni much; give him a dialogue with a real political race like the Alpha Centauri any day of the week.

'Their words are a mere bagatelle, Mr President. They simply wish to make those who would like to see relations between us deteriorate think that we're not close enough to bother taking action against.'

Klein stopped, nodding thoughtfully. 'Now that's an interesting thought. I trust you're doing the same thing from our end?'

'Naturally.'

'Good.'

The very rich and the very poor in every city have one thing in common – they live with one foot in the past. The élite have ancient buildings faithfully restored at great expense, while the poorest scrape a living in the original buildings that are dwarfed by more modern neighbours, and often falling apart with age.

Every city on every planet in the galaxy had a region with the reek of poverty: a decrepit hive of crime and despair where even the proverbial muggers went in pairs. Or they would do, if there was anybody worth mugging there. The one thing visitors and residents alike could trust was that everyone there was out to get you. Naturally, since it was the one place where you knew exactly where you stood with everybody, it was just about the safest place in the city if you knew what you were doing, and didn't look too closely at the activities around you.

In one of the city's more lived-in bars down in the area known as Methuselah Town, a man of stocky build was looking for someone. He wasn't exactly fat, but certainly had plenty of meat on his bones. A roguish face was surmounted by tightly curled black hair, and surrounded by a neat but full beard. His britches and knee-high boots were rather shabby, and his silk tunic rather faded from its original garish pattern. A bandolier of energy cells for a blaster was tied over one shoulder, and he wore odd fingerless gloves. Odd in the sense that while one was black, the other was red.

He had certainly come to the right place, if the semi-dressed girls draping themselves over men in the smoky booths was anything to go by. After six months in a rehabilitation colony he'd have to test that his charm was still working, and in fashion. Unlike most visitors to such places, however, Sabalom Glitz was seeking a particular individual. Through air that was thick and rancid due to inefficient atmospheric cycling, he spotted the face in question in a booth in a rear corner. That face was also bearded and topped with curly hair, but was rather longer and thinner than Glitz's. Its eyes were focused somewhat dreamily on a row of dusty bottles behind the bar.

Glitz settled into the booth.

'Wake up, Dibber, it's nearly noon.'

Dibber blinked and grinned. 'Good to see you again, Mr Glitz. Just thinking about what to drink next.'

'Thinking? Stick to doing, Dibber, you're better at it. And talking of doing, get me a drink, will you?'

When Dibber came back with a couple of bottles, Glitz stretched out his legs and breathed deeply.

'Even more than a drink, tasting the free air is the first priority for me, Dibber. You know how I hate those rehabilitation centres. It's like being on holiday with a bunch of art students.'

Dibber nodded solemnly. 'Definitely something to be avoided, Mr Glitz. The rehab colonies on this planet sure aren't very good – can you believe they were serving low-calorie foods? There weren't even any fights in the whole six months.'

'Psychological torture, lad. They were trying to confuse us.'

'It worked. I dunno, if that's how rotten the rehabs are on this planet, I might as well go straight.'

'Go straight?' Glitz echoed disbelievingly. 'You must be joking.' People who had known other lives went straight, Glitz thought; not the likes of him and Dibber.

'I always wondered what it would be like to do a proper job,' Dibber went on. 'Get paid regularly… that sort of thing.'

Glitz briefly considered trying a mock heart attack on Dibber – he was beginning to sound serious. 'You don't know what it's like out there. Believe me, the employment market is very overrated. Go straight, and the next thing you know you're paying taxes, and no longer your own boss.' The problem with the straight and narrow, Glitz had often noticed, was that it didn't leave much room for manoeuvre, any interesting detours.

'But I ain't my own boss now, am I?'

Ah, Glitz thought, so that's what this is about.

'That, my lad, is because you are still undergoing your

apprenticeship. Once you strike out on your own, you'd really have to redouble all your efforts.'

Dibber frowned. 'But I already work an eighteen-hour day for you... How am I supposed to work a thirty-six-hour day?'

Glitz wondered why Dibber had started trying to argue technicalities with him. 'How should I know? I'm an entrepreneur, not a mathematical prodigy!'

'I suppose you're right,' Dibber agreed sullenly. He looked around the bar uncertainly. 'So what do we do now that we're out of rehab?'

Glitz smiled, hoping to dampen the worry he knew Dibber would feel. He was a good lad most of the time, but a while ago he'd started trying to think for himself. Glitz was sure that was what had got them locked up for the past six months. The skin cell traces he himself had left on the safe were obviously just a technicality that would never been considered otherwise. 'Maybe you're right about one thing, Dibber. We need to make a quick profit, which we can then invest. Trade, in other words.'

'We'd have to sell something first,' Dibber said slowly. 'But the last of the siligtone went ages ago.'

'We don't need to waste our time hawking scrap metal,' Glitz reminded him encouragingly. 'They never found the crystals that went missing from that shipyard, did they?'

'You mean the ones we nicked from their safe?'

Glitz winced. Dibber had such a simplistic view of the cut and thrust nature of their business. 'I mean the navigation crystals which we were accused of appropriating.' But which, Glitz recalled with relief, the prosecution had never been able to prove were in that safe to start with. At least the sentence for cracking an empty safe was rather less than they would have got if the loot had still been on them. Glitz took a swig of something wet and alcoholic to help his throat along. 'As luck would have it, I do believe I know where we might find them.'

Dibber shrugged. 'Still in that wrecked ship where you hid them, I suppose.'

Glitz couldn't deny that. Well, he could, but there wouldn't be much point in denying it to his own partner in crime. 'Exactly. Where, since nobody knows they don't belong there, they're merely treasure trove. Finders keepers, Dibber. We go to the breakers' yard, find the crystals, and keep 'em perfectly legally.' Glitz couldn't resist a laugh. He'd certainly outsmarted the law this time!

The standard trade negotiations had gone well, Mandell thought. He had expected the Veltrochni to hold out for better shipping routes, but they didn't. They were too clever to be so petty, he reminded himself sourly.

The Veltrochni Ambassador and her entourage all had a blue and red mottled highlight to their leathery skin, showing that they were all from the same clan. Blood is thicker than water, people said. It seemed to be a universal constant among sentient species that they trusted family most.

'Madam Ambassador,' Klein said. 'I believe that concludes the business for today. If you'd care to join me, I believe the news media will be waiting outside with a few questions.' Most normal people hated that part of the job but, being President, Klein loved the attention. Except, Mandell recalled fondly, for the time someone innocently asked him about his secretary's baby. Mandell had nearly burst a blood vessel trying not to laugh.

'If that is the custom here,' Ambassador Brokhal replied,

not sounding too happy at the prospect. She and Klein rose, followed by the assorted bodyguards, civil servants and lawyers. 'One moment,' she added, surprisingly smoothly for a being with a voice that sounded like it gargled with pebbles. 'My government has instructed me to ask about the whereabouts of a relic that was stolen from Veltroch a decade ago.'

'Why should we on Vandor Prime know?' Klein asked, more surprised than he had a right to be.

'Our intelligence reported it had been brought here. Several recent communications we sent have remained unanswered.'

Klein looked baffled, but recovered, and smiled sympathetically. Remember your image, Mandell thought. 'I was not aware of any such message –'

'Then your staff is incompetent,' Brokhal said bluntly. 'You should replace them.'

'There is always a constant review of performance going on… But as to this theft, I'll have my own intelligence services look into it. If there is some Veltrochni property here, they'll find it.' Klein turned back to Mandell. 'You think your people are up to it?'

'I'll see to it at once, sir. You can rely on me.'

Brokhal snorted. 'You mentioned your media…?' President Klein gestured towards the door, and both human and Veltrochni entourages filtered out into the Forum.

Mandell remained standing at the side of the conference table, as the others left, surrounded by their own groups of bodyguards. He had spent a long time learning to read aliens' body language and psychology; he had felt it was necessary if he was to be the best negotiator he could be. Knowing how others thought meant he was negotiating from the position of strength, and that was what made him the best he could be. Negotiating from strength had always been best, and always would be.

Reading Veltrochni non-verbal signals was difficult, but certainly within his capabilities. The flattened dorsal spines were definitely a bad sign. That meant they were not in the mood for any nonsense, and made him a little jittery. It probably wasn't going to be possible to just brush this under the carpet and be done with it.

Left alone in the conference room, he helped himself to the dregs of the coffee pot. Why couldn't they just write it off as experience? 'Felchin' troublemakers,' he muttered, stabbing at the communications panel on the desk. 'Get me the Justice Division.'

The *Speculator* was vast, dating from a century when bigger had been considered not just better, but essential. It was a jumbled collection of massive structures; several city blocks built around each other. The gargantuan size had once been deemed necessary to support the hundreds, or even thousands, of people who would need accommodation and workshops in which to begin the work of terraforming their destination planets.

Now fewer than half the viewports set into the scarred hull were still lit. A couple of the building-sized protrusions on the hull were torn open and rimmed with frost. The hollow pit that ran deep into the length of the ship was webbed with immense chains and metal cable. Sections of scaffolding and rails disappeared down into the blackness of that pit.

'What the fipe is this?' Handley asked more aloud than he probably should have. 'Noah's Ark?'

'It's just about old enough,' Nausch answered. She joined him at the chart tank, which was now displaying a view of the derelict ship. 'Records list the *Speculator* as a terraformer ship launched from Earth's LaGrange shipyards over a thousand years ago.'

'It's been out here that long?'

Nausch's heart-shaped face shifted into a vague facial shrug. 'She was a sleeper ship. Sublight all the way.'

Things were certainly built to last in those days, Handley thought. This was the first time he had actually encountered a sleeper ship. There were standing orders for all GalSec colony worlds about how to deal with sleeper ships or generation ships. The latter were to be contacted and gently repatriated as if it was a first contact situation. The former were to be inspected for malfunctions and safety. If they were still operational, they should be allowed to carry on undisturbed to their destination, where a contact team would meet them. In cases where the destination had since been colonised or found to be unusable for some reason, the navigation computer could be reprogrammed to a more suitable landing point.

Still, it should be interesting to have a look round such an antiquated vessel. The novelty should do his crew's morale some good as well. 'Alter course to intercept. Standard inspection.'

'Ops to bridge: new contact, bearing zero-zero-zero.'

'What's happening?' he asked, swinging on to his feet.

'Something coming out from the *Speculator*,' Nausch said. She checked the chart tank. 'Somebody must be awake over there – there's a shuttle coming to meet us.'

Handley was both thrilled and chilled. This would be the first contact with people who been asleep for a thousand years. There was so much they could learn from each other... 'Have they hailed us?'

'No, but that's not surprising, since their shuttle is a thousand years old. Half their systems probably don't work.'

'All right,' said Handley. 'Contact base and tell them what's happen-' There was a distant booming sound, and the floor vibrated. 'What was that?'

'Particle beam impact,' someone shouted. Handley couldn't believe it. Who was firing on them? 'Raise shields!'

A tremendous blast of sound suddenly exploded around the control crew. The lighting died, but for the sparks from exploding consoles and power lines. The instrumentation tore itself apart with sharp cracks. A distant booming howl echoed through the corridors. 'Damage report!' Handley yelled.

'The communications antennae have been destroyed. Engines are going critical. We have to shut down or blow up!'

'Cut engine power. Who the hell is out there?'

'It's the shuttle, sir,' Nausch said disbelievingly. Handley realised that they must think his ship was hostile. After all, he hadn't hailed them before turning to intercept.

Everyone staggered as the deck shook. 'That was no weapon shot,' muttered Handley.

'They're trying to dock,' announced Nausch. 'I've disengaged the automatics. That should keep them out for a few minutes longer.'

Handley nodded. He had just been about to give that order. 'You take the conn, and try to figure out a way to call for help. I want everyone who's able to meet me at the main hold.' Maybe, he thought, if he could just keep making plans and giving orders quickly enough, he wouldn't have time to be scared.

'Yes, sir.'

Handley grabbed a laser pistol from the weapons locker, and ran to the main hold. There, he took up a position by the inner doors to the main airlock. The remainder of the crew, with one or two exceptions, were squeezing themselves behind any available pillars or equipment here in the hold.

Another impact made the floor quiver as Handley checked his pistol. He had been under fire before, so he knew how to cope with the strain. At least, he knew how to cope with it as well as anybody could. However, being trapped while the very environment was being destroyed around you was quite a different matter. At this rate the attackers would destroy the ship with their obvious bungling before they could even get in.

The floor rocked again, and this time he could hear the thuds of catches taking hold, and the hiss of air flowing. The enemy had managed to dock. There were muffled grunts and footfalls from the other side of the airlock, but nothing that gave any clue as to who they were or why they were attacking.

A dull clang came from the door, as if something had been attached to the metal. Handley momentarily froze, then, realizing what the attachment must be, leapt for better cover.

He was still in mid-air when the shrapnel suddenly ripped outwards. Handley felt hot claws rake his back, and then a sickening crunch as he landed badly. The pain hadn't caught up with him yet, though it would be just a matter of moments until it did. That gave him time to roll to his feet, and recover his gun.

Handley felt himself pale as the first visitor loomed in the hatchway. This was no colonist recently awakened from hibernation, but a towering beast that had the look of coming straight from the dawn of time. Formed not entirely unlike a strategically shaved gorilla whose forehead could be used as a snowplough, it was dressed in rough clothes, hobnailed boots, and a thick leather jerkin. It also carried an alarmingly large hand-blaster.

'Ogrons!' The terrified realisation was the last one of Handley's life.

Chapter Four

The roars and howls of spacecraft drives tore the air apart for miles around the Jewelled City's spaceport. Sonic booms were the least of the problem, but the din did make it relatively easy to walk around without being discovered. Glitz found out, by heart-stopping accident, that it was quite possible to walk right past a security guard who was facing the other way, without him hearing anything.

'There's a nice Solardyne 200 over there, Mr Glitz,' Dibber said, not needing to worry about being overheard among all this noise. It was a beautiful ship, Dibber thought. Sleek, fast and very flash.

'Business before pleasure,' Glitz replied, in a tone that suggested he was just as keen to try out the Solardyne. Dibber knew they wouldn't be taking that ship today. If they were going to a scrap planet, even the most stupid criminal knew to go in a grotty-looking ship.

In fact they sought transport to the third moon, which was small and settled centuries ago by miners. The place had long since been mined out, and the inhabitants almost starved, never getting back above the poverty line. For the moment, however, the government subsidised them by sending ships so old that their scrap value exceeded their profit margin, and allowing the populace to dismantle them and sell the scrap.

'That's more like it,' Glitz said approvingly, pointing to a squat short-haul freighter that was slumped in a tie-down area at the edge of the landing field. It was chunky, with stubby wings to help stability in atmospheric flight. It looked

51

as if it hadn't been moved in months, which meant it wasn't likely that the owner would come round to move it for another few months.

'That'll never fly,' Dibber opined. It wasn't that he wanted to be a pessimist, but his old mum had always told him that it was better to expect the worst and get nice surprises from time to time, than the other way round.

''Course it will,' Glitz retorted. 'It's got engines, hasn't it? There aren't any holes in it that I can see.'

'It looks pretty old to me, Mr Glitz. Probably on its last legs.'

'Well, so long as they can still move it, who cares? We *are* going to a scrapyard after all; we can always claim we're bringing the ship in for a quick payoff. Then we just nick another one from there to come back.' That made a certain amount of sense, Dibber noted; Glitz's schemes usually did, at first. It was later on that they tended to fall apart.

Pack-Mother Brokhal of Pack Zanchyth was the Ambassador to the whole Delphinus group of star systems, and thus travelled between them rather than adopt an official residence on one of the planets. Although there were larger, more powerful and, above all, newer ships available to her, she preferred to reside aboard the Dragon *Zathakh*. It was an older model Dragon, but still serviceable. She chose it for a much simpler reason, though: it was, in a manner of speaking, a family heirloom.

This ship had served Pack Zanchyth for generations, and had become something of a fixture to the whole clan. Comfortable on the command couch which she had played on as a cub, she waited as her son brought her the transcript of the message from the humans' central GalSec government. Both she and Klein had petitioned them: Klein for their support, Brokhal for their agreement to let the two sides work out the problem themselves.

Flight Director Trelokh, her son, handed her the message cube. She scanned it quickly, picking out the pertinent bits with ease. As she had hoped, the GalSec government overall was looking on this as a private matter between the two planets. 'Excellent,' she murmured.

It was a good thing that the rest of galactic society wouldn't interfere, since no one in the Veltrochni government wanted the stolen cylinder to be discussed anywhere else in the galaxy. It was too big a threat to her people for that to be allowed. She knew that the humans didn't understand that, but their understanding wasn't necessary. Just their co-operation.

Glitz looked around the freighter cockpit in wonder, as Dibber took the ship into an escape orbit. Whatever gods had tossed him into that rehab colony must have decided he'd earned a change of luck. Although the freighter had looked like an antiquated pile of junk from the outside, the interior was clean and sophisticated. The owner was probably either a smuggler trying to look inconspicuous, or a legitimate mark trying not to attract the attention of thieves.

Ah well, Glitz reflected; if the owner cared that much about the ship, then no doubt he would have it insured. Everyone's a winner, he thought happily. His luck was definitely taking a turn for the better.

Mind you, he was still lumbered with Dibber for an assistant. He wasn't a bad lad – and he was a much better shot than Glitz, too. A good trigger man was always handy in a tight spot... but Glitz couldn't decide whether he was too smart for his own good, or a couple of fingers short of being a full right-hand man. Still, for some reason he had stood by Glitz for the past few years. Glitz sometimes felt a little pang of guilt at the way he treated Dibber, but not for long. That's what the chain of command was for, after all; to pass on woes.

He was interrupted in his pleasant thoughts by Dibber's coarse tones. 'Does this ship have a name?'

'What?' Glitz was thinking of schemes and what passed for deep personal quirks here; he didn't want to be bothered with trivia.

'A name. All ships gotta have names, haven't they? But I don't see any name for this one.'

He had a point, Glitz supposed. He glanced around at the paperwork on the various clipboards that were dotted around the cockpit. '*Nosferatu*, it says here.'

'What's a Nosferatu, then?'

Glitz had no idea. 'Some sort of old Earth reference, I suppose. People round here are into that sort of th–'

He broke off as a loud mechanical trumpeting echoed from somewhere deeper in the ship. He hadn't heard anything like it before. Perhaps it was some sort of anti-theft device switching on… He exchanged a look with Dibber, and could see that he was thinking similar thoughts. They both pulled guns from their belt pouches, and went towards the door aft.

'After you, Dibber – I'll watch your back.' Glitz doubted that his attempt at giving a good reason for sending Dibber through first actually made any impression. It didn't have to, anyway, as Dibber was through the door before he'd got all the words out.

There was a small crew section just behind the cockpit,

with four tiny cabins and a small galley. Beyond that was the main hold, with the engines at the far end of the ship. The noise had stopped with a resounding crunch, and there was nothing untoward in the cabins or galley.

There was something very untoward in the hold, though. It had been empty when Glitz first came on board - he had checked in case there was anything extra worth stealing - but now contained a large blue capsule garnished with the unwelcome phrase 'POLICE BOX' in prominent letters.

'They didn't waste any time, did they?' Dibber whispered.

'This ship must be more valuable than I thought.' The unpleasant thought occurred to Glitz that it might in fact be an undercover police vessel. That would explain why they transmatted a capsule full of… whatever, on board.

The door opened, and Glitz affected a somewhat strained smile that he often used in attempts to disarm upholders of the law. He stepped forward with his hand extended in friendship, hoping the new arrival wouldn't notice the gun behind his back until it was too late. 'Officer, what a pleasant -' He stopped, blinking, as an imposing man with a ludicrous patchwork coat emerged. Somewhere in Glitz's brain, a couple of synapses sparked. 'Half a millisecond, you're not the law.'

'It's the Doctor,' Dibber exclaimed. 'You remember - the Time Lord geezer from -'

'Ravolox! Of course. I remember now.' And that courthouse… This box had been there too. He realised belatedly that it must be the Doctor's TARDIS. He leaned aside to greet the Doctor's companion. 'And Mel, of -' He broke off. Instead of the slim and bubbly red-headed girl he remembered from the last time he met the Doctor, there was… well, a penguin.

'What are you gawping at?' the penguin asked, in defiance of not having lips with which to form proper words. 'Don't tell me you're one of those people who thinks black and white is old hat, and nothing beats the full Technicolor glory?'

Glitz puffed himself up to retort, but the Doctor hastily interceded. 'Sabalom Glitz!' He shook Glitz's hand heartily, and Glitz wondered what he was so cheery about. 'It's always good to see a familiar face.' He looked at Dibber, and pointed. 'And it's young Dibber, if my memory doesn't deceive me.'

'Er, hi, Doc,' Dibber mumbled in a confused manner, which was nothing unusual.

'You three haven't met, have you? This is Frobisher. Frobisher, meet Sabalom Glitz and Dibber.'

'Pleased to meet ya, bub.'

'Er, likewise,' Glitz managed to say. 'Where is Mel, then?'

The Doctor affected a rather strained look. 'Still at home in Pease Pottage, I sincerely hope. I haven't actually met her yet, you see.'

'Eh?' To Glitz, temporal mechanics was something that involved turning back the clocks on used spaceships.

'The last time we met, at my trial, Mel had been plucked out of the future of my timestream. Once we left, she was returned to her rightful place.' The Doctor's eyes narrowed suspiciously. 'Which reminds me, what are you doing in this time period? We're a couple of million years too early for you, surely?'

Glitz shrugged it off. 'Told you last time, didn't I? Your old mate with the beard of evil arranged the transport for our little tickles.'

The Doctor winced. 'I presume by that you mean the Master? Last I saw, you and he were caught in a limbo atrophier.'

'Yeah. Well, the Time Lords got us out eventually. Your old mate did in the technicians and did a runner in his TARDIS. After that, the Time Lords sent me back to my rightful time, the ungrateful screeds.' And after he'd helped save them and the Doctor, all free of charge. It was criminal, that's what it was…'

'Here, we'll be coming up on the landing site in a minute,' Dibber reminded him.

'Right, lad. You'd better come and strap yourselves in. We're about to land.'

'Oh, anywhere interesting, perchance?'

'Not really. It's just a junkyard.'

'Doesn't sound like your sort of stamping ground,' the Doctor said, with a questioning tone.

Glitz wasn't going to be drawn. The Doctor was all right by him, but he was honest, so it'd be better for all concerned if they just did their business without fuss. 'I dunno. You never know what you might find in a junkyard.' He went up to the cockpit, where Dibber had started the landing cycle.

'What are we going to do with them?' Dibber asked.

'Why, buy them a drink, of course,' Glitz announced expansively. 'It's the least we can do, seeing as they'll make such good scapegoats if anything goes wrong.' This was business, after all, and he couldn't let personal regards get in the way. 'You just concentrate on getting us down in one piece – under their scanning umbrella, if you don't mind.'

'But won't they notice us when we reach the landing pad?'

Glitz sighed. 'We're not going to land at the landing pad, Dibber. We're going to land beside the tanker where I hid those crystals. Otherwise it might look a tiny bit suspicious when we leave the landing pad to go and look for them.'

'Right you are, Mr Glitz,' Dibber agreed.

* * *

The word junkyard was something of a misnomer, of course. Much of the settlement's population had actually set up home within the gargantuan hulks of rusting metal that they were slowly consuming. This meant they were essentially working to destroy their own homes.

Grounded starships each as long as a city block loomed high over the network of landing grounds and breakers' yards. The streets were mud, walled by the hulls of the ships' carcasses. People scurried among them like maggots in a corpse.

Watching through the port in the *Nosferatu*'s crew room, Frobisher thought that in many ways it was the saddest sight he had ever seen. People scraping a living by tearing apart rusted hulks that were no use to anyone... He couldn't imagine what it must be like to be reduced to living like that.

'There it is,' Glitz said, pointing at a massive steel skeleton. 'Right where we left it.'

'What if some of the locals have found the crystals?'

Glitz was losing patience with this lack of faith in his criminal genius. 'Dibber, do you think I would be so stupid as to stash them in a ship which was still being worked on? This one's been left to rot – all the good stuff is long gone. Nobody comes here any more.' So he hoped, anyway. Fate had a habit of making a liar out of him in these situations. Well, he'd brought the multi-blasters when they stole the ship, so if any of the local pack-rats had had it away on their toes with his crystals, they'd regret it.

Dibber brought the ship in for a perfect landing in the shadow of the stripped starship. It was like a metal whale, but a thousand times larger. The sun had set, but there was a permanent twilight cast by reflections from Vandor Prime's atmosphere.

'All ashore that's going ashore,' Glitz said cheerily as he returned to the crew section. He certainly wasn't going to let the Doctor and his… friend stay in here; how could he frame them if they did that? Of course, he hoped that wouldn't be necessary, but it was best to be prepared.

'This way…' Glitz ushered the Doctor and Frobisher out, Dibber subtly bringing up the rear while trying not to look like he was keeping an eye on them. 'I need a few spare parts for my new ship,' Glitz lied fluidly. 'This looks like just the sort of place to pick them up.'

The side of the hulk rose into the sky, but there was a number of gaping holes in the side. Glitz led the way though one of them, into an empty hold the size of a large sports stadium. The air was filled with the tang of rusting metal, but to Glitz it smelled like freshly minted coins.

'Hello, Sabalom Glitz,' someone said from the centre of the room. The speaker stepped into one of many pools of light that shone through the roof. He was of average height and build. A neat black beard squared off his average face, and he wore a dark suit of the latest fashion. 'Glad you could join us,' he said dryly. 'Allow me to introduce myself – Niccolo Mandell: Vandorian Security and Intelligence Division.' Glitz felt the run of luck he'd been so happy about stumble and smash face-first into a brick wall. For the briefest moment, he considered trying to fight his way out but, as his eyes grew accustomed to the gloom, he could make out armed men surrounding them. 'Stopped by to look for a good, honest job, did you?'

'Yes,' Glitz said hastily. 'Being reputable citizens, we felt we ought to do our part for the community.'

'I thought it might be something like that,' Mandell agreed.

'Most new job applicants report to the personnel office –'

'We got lost –'

'– having turned up during working hours –'

'Our ship broke down –'

'– and entered through the landing area rather than dodging the scanners to set down in a prohibited area.'

Glitz squirmed mentally. 'Isn't this a public area…?'

'Ah,' Mandell nodded with a smile. 'Then you weren't, in fact, looking for these navigation crystals which were hidden in the reactor core?' He held up an insulated case.

'Well, we were sort of looking for that type of thing,' Glitz admitted slowly. 'I mean, that is what people get into the scrap business for, isn't it? The hope of finding some nice piece of kit that's worth more than a few grotzis.'

'Well, I pity the poor salvager who finds these. By an amazing, nay, miraculous, coincidence, they happen to precisely match the particulars of a set of crystals stolen from the orbital shipyards seven months ago.'

'Do they really?' Glitz asked with exaggerated innocence. 'Then we're lucky you got here first…'

Mandell's face finally went serious. 'Not really, because they still have skin cell traces from your fingertips on them.' Glitz was about to protest further, but stopped when he saw the glint in Mandell's eyes. As a career criminal, Glitz had become quite adept at recognising when a cause was lost. Mandell nodded, reinforcing that opinion. 'I understand you just finished a six-month sentence for breaking into the shipyards…' He consulted a datapad. 'The judge said it was the maximum you could get without the evidence. If the crystals had been entered into evidence, you would have got fifteen years.' He hefted the case meaningfully.

'The jig's up, then?' Glitz was glad he'd brought the Doctor and Frobisher out of the ship. If he could just think of a way to pin this one on them… The Doctor was a stowaway, after all, and his TARDIS said Police, so he could claim the Doctor forced him to come here under threat of jail…

Mandell grinned.'Not quite.' Glitz blinked, wondering what that could mean.'I could very easily turn this in, and put you away for fifteen years…'

'Or?'

'Or I could claim the crystals were found as the result of an anonymous tip, and let you go free.' He took Glitz aside, so that the others couldn't hear.'If you do a little something to make it worth my while.'

Glitz grabbed at the chance.'You mean cut a deal?'

'Well, sort of. You see, you already owe me, Glitz. It was me who arranged your early parole. It's me who compensated the owner of that ship you stole today…' Glitz knew that whatever was coming was going to be unpleasant.'Do the names Chance, Chat, Monty, Oskar and Liang mean anything to you?'

Glitz had a brief flash of *déjà vu*: meeting them all for the first time. He wondered if this was what was meant by the belief that your life flashed before your eyes when death was near.'Maybe…' This Mandell knew enough that lying to him would be a waste of breath. It still took considerable willpower on Glitz's part to overcome the innate instinct to do so.

'I know you knew them,' Mandell went on.'Ten years ago, they stole a cylinder - a relic of sorts - from the Council of Houses on Veltroch. You fenced it for them.' Glitz nodded dumbly. How could Mandell possibly know this stuff? Mandell leaned in closer with a conspiratorial smile.'I bought it.'

'What?' This took Glitz totally off-guard. Something weird was going on here, and it couldn't be good for his personal safety. He almost wished he'd listened to Dibber about going straight.

Mandell grinned. 'Through intermediaries, of course. The Security and Intelligence Division bought it, and it currently resides in the Thor Orbital Facility on Vandor Prime.' He handed over a datapad from his pocket. 'All the relevant details are in here.'

'Why are you telling me this?' Glitz doubted they could possibly let him walk out of here alive knowing all this.

'Because you are going to reassemble the team who stole it from Veltroch, and you are going to steal it back. You will then take it to Elchur, where you and I will return it to its rightful owners.'

'Do I have a choice in any of this?'

'Of course! If you prefer, I could just kill you here and now.'

'Just curious,' Glitz said hastily. 'I mean, the chance to do something for the benefit of –'

'Just settle for the benefit of your continued existence.'

Frobisher didn't like the way Glitz and Mandell were acting so pally. He didn't know either of them, but he had come to the conclusion that Glitz was about as trustworthy as a drunken Walarian, and Mandell made that look good. This was nothing, however, compared to his dismay as the Doctor marched imperiously over to Mandell.

'Just a moment,' the Time Lord began. 'Perhaps it isn't my place – at least not more than anywhere is my place – but if you're in some kind of difficulty, perhaps I could be of some small assistance?' Frobisher wasn't sure whether he was talking to Glitz or Mandell.

Mandell turned slowly, looking down his nose at the newcomer; not an easy task, considering that he was several inches shorter than the Doctor. 'Now… Glitz and Dibber I know I can use, but you two… Who are you?'

The Doctor indicated his short companion. 'This is Frobisher, and I am generally known as the Doctor. I am also, as it happens, the former President of Gallifrey, and a… loose acquaintance of Sabalom Glitz.'

'No. You're an anomaly, and that means I don't know where we stand.' Mandell looked up. 'Gallifrey? You're a Time Lord, then.'

Glitz broke in. 'We didn't ask him to join us. He just turned up in his TARDIS.'

'Talking of which,' said the Doctor, 'when do I get it back?'

'Your TARDIS?' Mandell thought quickly. 'It'll be removed. Glitz has a task, and I don't want him getting distracted by it.'

'Look,' Frobisher protested, 'I know a little about the law – have to in my line.' He handed over an identicard. 'And I know this can't be on the level.'

Mandell examined the identicard. 'Avan Tarklu. Native of the planet Xenon…' He looked up. 'Shapeshifter, eh? I wondered how a penguin could be so lippy.' He looked back at the identicard. 'Occupation: private investigator, licensed to operate in Rassm City and surrounding system.' Mandell tossed the plastic back to Frobisher, grinning smarmily. 'You do realise, I take it, that the profession of private investigator is illegal in the Vandor system, unless approved by the Security and Intelligence Division.' The grin widened. 'Which means me.'

'I'm on vacation,' Frobisher answered hurriedly. 'I haven't even been back to my office in a year.' Frobisher was somewhat surprised to hear his own real name again. It was impossible, of course, but it was almost as if he had forgotten it. In those days he had spent less time as Avan Tarklu than as a series of other beings or objects.

At least Frobisher was a constant. When he was Frobisher, he was Frobisher, and that was that. He suppressed an urge to shiver. There was something in that idea which he didn't want to examine too closely.

'Vacation?' Mandell asked exaggeratedly. 'Well, then. I find you in the company of a pair of known criminals, and yet you're not working? I suppose you could be their accomplices…'

'We are not Glitz and Dibber's accomplices!' the Doctor said hotly. 'We arrived here quite by accident, and I am quite generously offering you the services of my not inconsiderable abilities.'

'If they're half as notable as your ego, you might have a point there. But it seems strange that you should so suddenly offer help to a man you've never met.'

'Not really. I have a few questions of my own I want answered, and if you truly are head of this planet's Intelligence service, then you might be able to help with them. Now, just what exactly is it you are trying, in your own idiosyncratic little way, to ask Glitz to do?'

Mandell sighed; this Doctor wasn't stupid. Mandell was rather disappointed in that, since the stupid were much easier to manipulate. He looked the Doctor in the eye, trying to remember all the involuntary signs of lying so that he could avoid giving them. 'I'm reluctant to tell you this, because if the word got out, it could cause panic in the population. But I'm going to have to trust you. A group of freelance thieves stole a relic from the Veltrochni ten years ago, and Glitz sold it to the highest bidder.'

'Which was your government, I presume?'

'Exactly. We kept it under wraps, but no secrecy is perfect, and the Veltrochni recently discovered that we have it.'

'And naturally they want it back. And I can't say I blame them,' the Doctor added pointedly.

'They've been rattling their sabres for several weeks, demanding its return. If they don't get it back, they will try to take it by force. That can only mean disaster for Vandor's population.'

The Doctor gave Mandell a look, and spoke in the tone of voice one would use to a child too dense to see the obvious. 'Then why don't you just give it them back? That would seem to be the logical solution.'

'We can't. For one thing, the current administration doesn't know anything about it. If I openly hand it back, the government will be swamped with other claims for whatever else might – hypothetically speaking – have found its way here. No... I made private contact with the Veltrochni Council of Houses, and promised to deliver it quietly. The deadline is one week from today. Now, if you can help me, perhaps I can help you...'

The Doctor tilted his head, considering the story he'd just been told. 'My feathered friend and I were recently accosted by two rather unsavoury assassins. What's more, they had travelled through time, and their journey began on your planet.'

'And you want to know who sent them?' Mandell was fairly certain he hadn't sent any time-travelling assassins out. And he had never met this Doctor before, so had no reason to kill him yet. Now that he knew so much, it was a different matter.

'Exactly.'

'Then perhaps we can help each other… The sole temporal engineering permitted on Vandor Prime is also aboard the Thor Facility. If someone there has been indulging in extracurricular activities, I'd be very interested to know about it.' Mandell had a dislike of people operating without his sanction. There was definitely something wrong here.

'All right, Doctor. Incredible as it may seem, I believe you. You help me, and I'll see what I can dig up. I will, however, keep your TARDIS in protective custody.'

'Can you legally do that?' Frobisher demanded.

'No.'

'Then can we have it back?'

'No. I'm doing you a favour, aren't I? If someone is messing around with time travel on this planet, I'm sure the last thing you'll want is for them to get their hands on your TARDIS.'

'They'll find that difficult,' the Doctor said coldly.

'They certainly will,' Mandell agreed. 'Especially once it's under guard. It's not that I don't trust you, but… Well, actually it *is* that I don't trust you.' He grinned nastily. 'You won't need it for a week or so anyway.'

'You don't believe all that guff, surely?' Frobisher asked. The whole thing stank like a month-old mackerel as far as he was concerned. Mandell was being very free with his trust if any of it was true, and Frobisher couldn't believe that for a moment. It was some kind of trap, he was sure, but he didn't know what kind. Most of the schemers he had dealt with back in his gumshoe days couldn't even pronounce half the words Mandell spouted, so Frobisher suspected he'd be out of his depth here.

The Doctor squinted at the departing Mandell and his lackeys. 'I suspect it was true, actually. The first rule of intelligence work is that what you *don't* know is more important than what you do, so he certainly wasn't telling us everything. But I fear it is true about the risks of the Veltrochni attacking. They're an honourable people, not one of your thuggish galactic conquerors. If they are threatening violence, then they're very sure that they've got good reason to do so.'

Frobisher could see where this was going. Once the Doctor got a bee in his bonnet about something, there was no stopping him until he satisfied his curiosity. 'Between those two goons in the TARDIS, and this business here, we're going to be around here for a while, aren't we?'

The Doctor looked almost pained, as if driven by some force he couldn't control. 'I have to. Besides, you heard what he said about the Veltrochni. Now, one of those two assassins who came after us was a Veltrochni. What does that suggest to you, eh?'

'Unless you're a conspiracy theorist, it suggests a coincidence.'

The Doctor recoiled from the very idea. 'Coincidence? When it comes to time travel, there's no such thing as coincidence. I'm sure there must be a link between what's happening here, and what happened to us in the TARDIS.'

'Then let's investigate on our own. This guy's setting us up to be patsies.'

'I know.' The Doctor set his jaw grimly. 'But he's right about two things – lives *are* at stake here, and Glitz does need watching. I can't just let them play their little games and get innocent people hurt.' Frobisher knew that the Doctor's curiosity was a force to be reckoned with. Once allied with a passion for life and justice, it was something that drove him. 'Let me put it this way, Frobisher: who is more likely to be able to track down unlicensed time experimenters? Two small-time criminals, or a planet's Intelligence service?'

Chapter Five

The *Thornton* drifted slowly, her engines and running lights dead. The communications array was gone, leaving just a burned patch of metal. Luckily for the crew of the frigate *Cobb*, the main airlock was still intact, if a little scraped.

Taking up position alongside the smaller ship, the frigate extended a docking tube and locked on.

The *Thornton*'s outer airlock doors cracked open, allowing the beams from helmet-mounted lights to probe the room through the jagged hole where the inner doors used to be. Six figures in spacesuits entered, weapons held ready. 'Life support's off-line,' one man with a scanning device said gruffly. 'But there's still an atmosphere.'

'Keep your suits tight all the same,' the boarding party's leader, Lambert, warned. 'The temperature would strip the lining of your lungs the second you breathe in.' She directed her light around the main bay. It was totally empty, though a few patches of frozen blood gleamed on the walls and floor. There were no bodies; just those eerie shadows that were the only residue left behind by vaporised bodies.

'Any lifeform readings?'

'None.'

Lambert nodded, and shouldered her weapon. 'We'll sweep the ship. I want to know who did this.'

Brokhal chewed on a dried bark-crawler as she watched the longer and more graceful Vandorian ship dock with the drifting one. 'Do our sensors detect any sign of what attacked the Vandor ship?'

'Indeterminate signs of external weapons fire,' Trelokh said. 'They may have allowed their attackers to board willingly.'

'Another Vandor ship?' Humans were a strange species, always fighting among themselves. In many ways Brokhal supposed they were like the Veltrochni, with their various different clans. Except that there hadn't been a clan war among the Veltrochni in over a thousand years. Brokhal was never sure whether to despise humans or admire them, for their devotion to internecine warfare.

'It is possible, but why?'

'The human Pack who occupy this world have a duelling tradition. Perhaps there was a blood feud…' Even as she spoke the words, she couldn't really believe them. A duel between individuals shouldn't lead to the death of the whole crew. Or if it was a duel between whole crews, then why not simply engage in ship-to-ship combat?

'In many ways,' she said, 'it does not matter who did this. The President and his underlings will almost certainly seek to blame us.'

Trelokh's youthfully white spines flattened. 'Then we must issue a denial of responsibility immediately.'

'They will take that as a sign that we wish to hide something,' Brokhal said dismissively. 'No… Let them think we did this.'

'Mother?'

Her son was young for such a position as Flight Director, and not well-versed in politics. Brokhal used a claw to crack the shell of another bark-crawler. 'It will make the humans fear us more. They will be more likely to return our property to prevent further… misunderstandings.' She hoped so anyway. She wondered what her ancestor, Brokhyth, would have done in this case. She was a Pack-Mother who had truly earned the respect of the humans…

Somehow, Brokhal couldn't see her esteemed predecessor feeling quite as unsure of herself as Brokhal did.

Niccolo Mandell's private shuttle curved in towards Vandor Prime's atmosphere. In a comfortable armchair in the luxurious passenger section, Mandell sipped a cup of his favourite coffee. It had been specially imported from Earth, since the local beans produced a vile brew which, even when freshly ground, tasted like something out of a drinks machine. Mandell thought it was probably something to do with the exact spectral composition of the light from Gamma Delphinus. It must react badly with the cells in coffee plants, he thought.

Wei, his deputy director, came through from the cockpit. Of oriental stock, Wei was tall, lean and angular, with a long and glossy black ponytail. 'Mandell *Io*, we'll be arriving in five minutes. Where do you want the Doctor's capsule?'

'Take it to the Foreign Technologies tether.' He was certainly not going to be fool enough to store it in the very place he wanted the Doctor to visit, though that would have been a more fitting place for it.

'A permanent addition to the collection?'

'Until after the heist. Then we can move it to the Thor Facility.' It wasn't as if the Doctor would ever be needing it again, and the chance to get hold of a working time machine was too good to pass up.

Dibber relaxed in the pilot's seat of the *Nosferatu*, while the Doctor, Frobisher and Glitz discussed the datapad Mandell had given them. Dibber could have contributed to the discussion, and knew that the Doctor and Frobisher would listen to even his input. Glitz wouldn't, but that was just his way.

71

Dibber didn't mind that Glitz looked on him as something of a burden. He learned more from the sidelines than he would from the middle of things, so he was content to let Glitz keep him there. To be honest, planning jobs wasn't very interesting to Dibber. He would much rather be out in the field, meeting interesting people, grabbing loot... A bit of fresh air and excitement was what life was all about. He'd learned that lesson long ago, back on Salostophus, before he'd even met Sabalom Glitz.

'This place is a fortress,' Frobisher was saying. 'We'd never get past the front door.'

'Nonsense, Frobie,' Glitz said. 'We just have to use our noggins, don't we? This calls for stealth and strategy, eh, Doctor?'

'This calls for Raffles himself.' The Doctor grimaced. 'Fortunately I can turn my hand to just about anything with equal grace.'

'You could help persuade the rest of them. Everybody knows you Time Lords can put the 'fluence on people.'

'Why on Earth would I want to do that?'

Glitz looked surprised. 'Doctor, these people we're dealing with are not as altruistic as young Dibber and myself. They're going to need a good reason to join in this little tickle.'

'You mean a profit,' the Doctor suggested archly.

'Well, yes. Not that it's just greed, mind you,' Glitz added hastily, 'but these people are professionals who expect to earn a decent living from their trade.'

'And do you have an idea of how to get round this?'

'Of course! We do a runner.'

The Doctor fixed him with a glare. 'You might be able to, but my TARDIS is in Mandell's hands.'

'And you're as mad as your tailor if you think he's going to return it. I know his sort, Doctor, and they're not on the level.'

72

'I know, but the logical place for them to take the TARDIS is this Thor Facility.' The Doctor was no slouch, Dibber noted. He might be honest, but he could stand up for himself.

'That's a thought,' Glitz agreed.

'Besides. Whatever else this Mandell person may or may not be up to, there are certainly lives at stake. Everyone on this planet for a start.'

'So? We can get offworld.'

Dibber didn't see a problem with Glitz's attitude there either.

'No we can't, Glitz,' the Doctor said with finality. 'Or I can't, anyway. Besides, Mandell has thought of that.'

'Yeah,' Frobisher chipped in. 'If you try to fly the coop, there's probably a microscopic bomb in your neck that'll go off. Mandell looked like the sort of guy who'd do that.'

Glitz fingered his neck gently. 'Rubbish... He never even touched me.'

'He didn't have to. Look at this.' The Doctor held out the datapad so that Glitz and Dibber could see the last line. 'Kerlanogen on the surface of this datapad. Enough to kill in ten days, without the antidote. Antidote to be exchanged for the cylinder.'

Glitz paled, and Dibber was relieved that he'd stayed away from the pad. 'You mean we...?'

'Not *we*, Glitz. Just you. Kerlanogen doesn't affect Time Lords, mesomorphs like Frobisher don't have stable DNA for it to latch on to, and Dibber never touched the pad.'

Glitz looked like he'd seen a ghost - probably his own. 'You're a doctor - you could whip up an antidote in no time, right?'

The Doctor smiled disarmingly. 'Easily.' Glitz perked up. 'In

73

the TARDIS' lab. I rather think you're stuck with us, Glitz.'

Dibber tried not to laugh. He was concerned, of course, but he knew the Doctor was too honest to let Glitz die. If it had been anyone else, Dibber would have a gun at his head already, but the Doctor had earned some leniency back on Ravolox. He wasn't that bad for an honest bloke.

The man with the thinning white hair and lined, pugnacious face went into the taxi garage through the main bay. Kala Mandell rested her chin on the heels of her hands, and tried to look inconspicuous as she watched him enter. He looked pretty fit for a man who must be at least seventy. Probably a spectrox user, she noted. That in itself wasn't a crime, but spectrox was now so rare that a taxi mechanic being able to afford a dose was definitely grounds for suspicion.

Most of the women in Vandor Prime's police force had their hair cut short, but Kala simply tied her locks in a bun at the back of her head while on duty. That took her to the edge of looking severe and matronly, but she was just young and pretty enough not to cross over that line. Sitting at this street-corner breakfast stand fifty levels above the ground, she'd already had to arrest two marks who thought she would turn tricks for them. Maybe her looks were on the wrong side of the line after all, she reflected.

The man had disappeared inside, and Kala thought about getting a warrant for search and seizure. In the case of anyone else who was displaying more wealth than they could account for, she wouldn't hesitate. Now, however, she definitely didn't want to tip her hand too early. Monty Kast had been a big fish a few years back, and Kala had never believed that such people ever truly reformed or retired.

If he was indeed back in the criminal business, then it was

likely to be a wide-ranging scheme, and when she took him down, she wanted to take the whole thing down. That way she'd make Captain for sure. Nic would be proud, too.

The other cops on her shift tended to live with people with exciting lives – other cops, paramedics, pilots... Kala didn't mind that her man was a civil servant, because at least it meant that most days he was there when she got home. He never complained about the odd hours she worked. He had always said that he didn't mind her job, since her exploits would give them some stories to tell the kids one day. Now she'd learnt she was pregnant at last, that old joke actually meant something.

Kala wasn't sure all her stories would be suitable for a toddler's bedtime. How was she supposed to tell her young daughter (Kala was convinced the baby would be a girl, though the pregnancy was only three weeks along – too early to tell) that her mother had killed several people, or been mistaken for a prostitute while staking out certain areas of the city? That was worst down in Methuselah Town, where any woman under sixty was assumed to be available in some form, but it could happen anywhere. Of course, the fact that she used to pose as one on the Vice detail did make those mistakes more likely.

No, she thought to her unborn baby, I'll tell you the stories like this one. The stories of patient waiting and watching, using my brain. And no doubt you'd be bored stupid and want to hear about shoot-outs and flier chases in exciting detail. She couldn't help but smile, in the process getting a funny look from a customer opposite. He probably thought she was on vrax or something, she realised, and that made her want to laugh. She managed to suppress the impulse.

Think about Monty, she reminded herself, think about the

job. Most especially, think about the promotion you're going to get when you wrap up the case.

'I feel faint,' Glitz complained as the *Nosferatu* descended towards Methuselah Town. 'Are you sure that poison takes a week?'

'Absolutely positive,' the Doctor reassured him. 'We'll get you seen to in plenty of time.'

'Yer... right,' Glitz said uncertainly. 'I'll just go and wash my hands, eh? Maybe help slow the progress?'

'Anything's possible,' the Doctor agreed solemnly. Glitz hurried out of the crew room towards a washroom. Given how nervous he looked, Frobisher doubted he'd just be washing up.

'So, Doc,' Frobisher said, 'when are you going to tell him?'

'Tell him what?'

'That you slipped the antidote into his drink when he wasn't looking.'

'Didn't I mention that?' the Doctor asked with wildly exaggerated innocence. He tutted. 'It must be my age. Memory's the first thing to go, isn't that what they say?'

Frobisher was hardly complaining. He'd only just met Glitz, but could tell at once that he was the sort of person who was going to grate on him. Or vice versa, which might be more fun. All things considered, Frobisher would rather be back in his room listening to Benny Goodman.

'What about you, Dibber?' asked the Doctor. 'Are you going to take the weight off our friend's mind?'

Dibber grinned. He'd guessed right – the Doctor wouldn't let Glitz die.

'Reckon not, Doc – not yet, anyway. Makes a change for him to sweat a bit.'

Glitz returned a few moments later, looking a little

healthier. 'There you are, Doctor, I feel better already.'

'Good thinking, that, Glitz,' the Doctor said approvingly. 'Exactly what I would have done.'

Glitz perked up at that, reassured by the Doctor's confidence. Frobisher had to admire the Doctor's strategy here; it kept Glitz from running, but wouldn't hurt him. Likewise, his mate Dibber was in on the trick so wouldn't be hustling the Doctor. Frobisher liked that arrangement.

'Now, why exactly are we landing here instead of the spaceport?'

'You said it yourself, Doctor,' Glitz answered. 'That Mandell's about as trustworthy as a tabloid editor. I'll feel a lot safer if we aren't where he's expecting us to be.'

The Doctor rose. 'You know, my appreciation for your talents grows, Glitz.'

Glitz shook his head with blatantly false modesty. 'I have to be careful, don't I? In my line of work if you don't watch your step, you're for the high jump, aren't you?' That, Frobisher had to agree, was certainly true.

'Then perhaps a career change…?' the Doctor interrupted. Frobisher was glad, already tired of the self-promotion. 'But first, we ought to get in touch with these confederates of yours as soon as possible. I imagine you know where we can find them.'

The *Thornton*'s bridge had proved to be ruined, the consoles and inspection panels smashed – some from the inside, others by vandalism from without. By the time Lambert and her team reached the engineering hall, they had started to find a few bodies.

They were all frozen into grotesque sculptures by the absolute cold, but that was not what had killed them. They were beaten, or shot, some others asphyxiated by the halon system. There were no fallen attackers, however.

It was downright creepy, Lambert thought. Man had been telling tales of ghost ships since the first reed raft was put in the water, and they had taken those tales with them to the stars. None of the people welded to the walls and floor of the chamber would ever move again, but the lights from the team's helmets animated them just enough to make Lambert want to run back to the *Cobb*.

It was the ice in their eyes, she knew deep down. It was reflecting the light as little pinpoints that followed them around the room. She tried to ignore it, knowing that it was impossible – humankind had a predilection to let itself be unnerved by the presence of its own dead.

She cast her beam around engineering, noticing that there was damage to the control systems, and all the lockers had been emptied of tools and protective clothing. That was odd, she thought, then turned to the reactor core. She stopped in her tracks.

The reactor core, which should have made the engineering section uncomfortably warm, was just a dark hole in the blackness. Forcing herself to remember why she came aboard, she nudged the helmet's microphone switch with her chin. 'Lambert to *Cobb*.'

'Go ahead,' Captain Franke's voice returned.

'We've reached the engineering section. The crew are all dead or missing. I saw some heat-flash shadows, so I expect the missing ones have been vaped. This was definitely no accident, sir. The reactor core is gone.'

'What? Totally destroyed?'

'No, sir, I mean it's *gone*.' She took a deep breath, knowing how silly this was going to sound. 'Somebody has stolen it.'

Chapter Six

They called it Methuselah Town partly because it hadn't changed a bit in living memory, and partly because the vast majority of its populace seemed to be grimy drifters on the far side of middle age.

Being young, Dibber didn't like it much. True, it was just the sort of place where someone with a loose attitude to the law could best get along undisturbed, but that didn't mean he had to like it. Every city on every planet had a similar area. Dibber had left Salostophus with Glitz to see the galaxy and make a bit of profit on the side. If he'd wanted to spend his life in rancid slums, he could have stayed at home.

Glitz, on the other hand, was in his element here. He was like a zoo animal returned to the wild.

The *Nosferatu* had set down in a disused factory, whose roof had long since collapsed, and Glitz was rubbing his hands with anticipation as he followed the others out of the ship. He seemed to have cheered up a bit, Dibber noticed. It was probably the prospect of trying to win round their old mates.

'Excellent work, lad,' Glitz said of the landing. 'If memory serves, Monty lives not a million miles from this friendly lay-by.'

'Just over there, I think, Mr Glitz,' Dibber agreed, pointing to a clump of buildings about a mile away. The buildings were orbiting a central tower block at a barely perceptible rate.

'Good, good,' the Doctor said cheerily. 'He'll suffice for our first recruit.'

'You and he should get on like a house on fire, Doctor,' Glitz said. 'Monty's well into sorting out the latest equipment, and all that sort of fiddly business. On the way, you can think of how you're going to persuade him to be charitable.'

The Thor Orbital Facility was something of a misnomer, as it was not actually in orbit around Vandor Prime. The designation was merely part of the secrecy surrounding the Security and Intelligence Division's research and development complex. Powerful gravitational repulsor fields allowed it to descend far enough to spend most of its time in the upper atmosphere. They also enabled it to move around, so as to avoid being definitively pinpointed by anyone who might wish harm upon it.

Theoretically, something as large as a five-mile-wide asteroid should be easily detectable by any sensor on the planet, but the theory didn't allow for such an object being slightly out of phase with the local space–time continuum. It was visible to the naked eye when sub-orbital, of course, but avoided such inconvenience by largely adopting holding patterns over uninhabited areas of the planet.

It currently hovered over a temperate area of the great northern ocean, sitting in the calm eye of a dark grey storm created by the force of the repulsors. They also pressured the air underneath, and forced a shallow depression into the surface of the ocean itself. Had Vandor Prime still retained a natural weather system, all the equatorial butterflies in the world would do as well to pack in the wing-beating business and head home, totally outclassed.

Even in a crisp white lab coat, Cronan somehow managed to look seedy and greasy. Lank, thinning hair, beady eyes and a receding chin surrounded a prominent nose, making him look rather rodent-like. He didn't care about that, because he knew he was superior to everyone else here. He didn't need any IQ tests to tell him that; he thought so, therefore he was. It was a neat little paradigm.

He brushed aside a guard's greeting with a curt phrase ending in 'off' as he passed through the central core. There were as many guards as staff in the asteroid, a testament to the level of security in which the place was shrouded. Most other people would have been worried about so many law-enforcement types being around, especially since many barely legal, quasi-legal, and downright illegal programmes were being operated.

In this case, however, the security was an advantage. Everybody scrupulously avoided observing each other's pet projects, and even the illicit ones were protected by the assumption that they must have tacit government approval to be here at all.

Cronan loved it. Here he could do what he liked without fear of getting caught by those who didn't like it. Unfortunately, business being business, he still had to deal with other people. The asteroid didn't fund itself.

He slipped though a metal door and into a small visiting room. It was dull compared to the shiny metal stairways of the main core, and gave visitors the uncomfortable impression of being in a prison cell. This was reinforced by the presence of armed guards outside the door. Visits were by approved appointment only, at least if the visitor wanted to leave alive. Cronan invited his guest to sit down in one of the two uncomfortable chairs.

The visitor was Barrand, the pilot of a vetted supply shuttle. At least that was his profession for the purposes of

81

visiting the Thor Facility. 'So,' he said, breezily, 'what have you got for us this week?'

Cronan bridled at this presumptuous familiarity, but wasn't quite stupid enough to press the issue where business was concerned.

'Your usual order – Rush, spectrox… but there's a couple of specials on offer. We've messed around with the PCM formula to come up with little individual hits. That's pretty common, though, so it's only four-fifty per unit wholesale. But…' He grinned. 'I got a real deal for you.' He palmed a small vial of white dust and passed it across. 'Introductory price, seven-fifty a unit.' He tried to conceal his increasing excitement as he waited for Barrand's reaction, seeking approval for this new piece of art.

Barrand sniffed at it, and touched a speck of the powder to his wristband. The sensors inside spat out a stream of figures, and a slow smile crossed his face. 'The PCM's still good, OK,' Cronan went on, feeling the need to explain things to Barrand as if he was a child. Cronan felt that way about everybody. 'But this… trust me, you won't make a loss on this one.'

'I know what I'm looking for,' Barrand said sharply. 'Mr Zimmerman only hires professionals.'

Cronan shrugged. 'Whatever. I'm not just saying stuff, right. People who want the best synthesis and refinement get products from Thor, it's that simple. If you can find vraxoin purer than that anywhere in GalSec space, we'll refund triple your money.' He knew he would never have to make good on that particular promise, so it was an easy one to make. There *was* no purer source of vraxoin. 'In the Delphinus group it's a seller's market. You could get a bargain price out in Andromeda, but you'd be getting fifty per cent purity at best.'

'We'll take a thousand units today. If Mr Zimmerman is happy, we'll talk about a standing order.'

'I'll get things sorted out,' Cronan said. Barrand was so predictable. Of course he was going to take the deal; who wouldn't? And the best thing about it was that all the law-enforcement types who filled the station would help out without saying a word against him. Their inferiority was a blessing.

Monty Kast ran a hand across his thinning white hair, and straightened up from under the shuttlepod. Every time he had to do a servicing on the underside of one of these things, it seemed to get more difficult to sit back up afterwards. Those inspection hatches weren't designed for good posture. Mind you, they weren't designed for humans at all. The shuttlepods had been built at a time when a sixty per cent unemployment rate had been a small price to pay for accurate robot maintenance.

Monty preferred it when there were service bots doing these jobs – he might have been poor, but at least his back hadn't hurt. And, of course, service bots could always be reprogrammed by someone with a little imagination and a hefty gambling habit. Humans, sadly, could not.

He was getting too old for this, he reflected. Not that the age reached his eyes: they were still clear and sparkling. That was more than could be said for the garage, which was old and stained with a lifetime of fuel and coolant vapour.

'It's probably the lateral compensators,' a voice said from behind him. 'They're usually the first to go in these vehicles.' Probably some civilian looking to charter a pod, he thought, turning. They got that a lot.

Instead, he found himself facing two bearded ruffians in

bohemian spacer garb, a man in a patchwork coat, and… a penguin? He wondered if maybe the coolant was leaking from the shuttlepod, and causing him to hallucinate. All the same, there was something awfully familiar about the first two… Before he could gather his wits, the one with the curly blond hair and multicoloured coat had stuck his head into the inspection hatch.

'Yes… I thought as much. Very nasty. You'll need to replace the whole unit.'

'I can see that,' Monty said. 'Who are you?'

'A friend of mine,' said Glitz, stepping forward. 'And now a friend of yours, Monty my old mate.'

'What?' Who were they? Maybe they'd been sent by one of his creditors. He'd lost a lot on that last race… It took Monty an anxious moment to place that bearded face. 'Glitz? Sabalom Glitz?'

'In the flesh, as it were,' Glitz confirmed cheerily. He clapped an arm round Monty's shoulder. Monty mostly felt relieved that it wasn't one of his gambling creditors round to collect. 'You remember my young friend Dibber?'

'Of course.' That was the more youthful ruffian. Monty nodded at the third visitor, who was even bigger than Glitz. 'Who's the dilly in the test pattern?'

The Doctor smiled and thrust out a hand to shake. 'If you mean me, I am known as the Doctor. And this is Frobisher.' He indicated the penguin, who inclined his head.

Monty nodded back, trying to let his mind catch up with his ears.

Glitz broke in. 'Now, Monty, I reckon you and I have some business. Is there somewhere we can talk?'

Monty nodded again, and led them into the shuttlepod itself. Sabalom Glitz after all these years… He wasn't sure about that "we can talk" bit, though. That usually presaged either a risky job offer or a begging session. Glitz wasn't above either, if Monty's memory served him.

'Stay on watch, Frobisher,' the Doctor told the penguin.

'Right you are, Doc.'

This was something Monty *could* take in his stride. He'd been around a lot longer than Glitz or Dibber, and seen enough not to be fazed by a mere sentient penguin.

The interior of the shuttlepod was cramped but clean. Two rows of seats faced each other, and Monty sat opposite Glitz and Dibber. The Doctor sat next to him. 'I'm sorry I can't offer you boys a drink,' Monty began. 'If you'd come round after hours…'

'Not to worry,' the Doctor told him. 'We're on duty, so to speak.'

'On duty?' What the hell did he mean by that?

Glitz looked suitably embarrassed. 'Well, we've brought you an offer, haven't we?'

Monty had expected as much. It was flattering, if a little rude, to be so direct, but Monty doubted he was quite up to it these days. 'I have a straight job now,' he replied, trying to instil his voice with a pride he didn't feel. 'It doesn't pay much, but it's a steady living, and people tend not to shoot at you too much.'

'I assure you, Monty,' the Doctor interrupted, 'that shooting is the very last thing I want here. In fact it's precisely to avert violence that we need your help.' He sounded sincere, but, of course, all the best con men did. Most importantly, Monty didn't know this man; that made his words less convincing.

'I repair shuttlepods and taxi cabs, I'm not a GalSec ambassador.'

'But you do look at the news, don't you?'

'Sometimes. I'm not all that good at reality.'

'And what about this situation with the Veltrochni?'

Monty shrugged. 'Klein says they're manufacturing the crisis to make themselves look big. I don't believe a word of it, but it doesn't matter, does it?'

'Oh, it matters, Monty. You didn't always repair cabs, did you?'

Monty went on the defensive immediately. What was Glitz trying to do by bringing this guy here? 'My business is my business.'

'As a matter of fact,' the Doctor continued, 'ten years ago you helped to steal a cylindrical relic from Veltroch, and Glitz fenced it.' Monty wished he had a gun, and the reflexes to use it. This guy must be a cop, and Glitz had betrayed him. 'We need your help to steal it again.' This was – Monty's thoughts stopped cold.

'Say that again?'

'We need your help – and the help of the others – to steal the Veltrochni's cylinder again.'

Monty was stunned. 'But why?'

The Doctor leaned forward. 'Because the Veltrochni want it back, and could well destroy this planet if they don't get it.'

'You work for them?'

'No. I'm just looking for the best solution all round. I can't promise any profit, Monty, but the Veltrochni may well put up a reward. The important thing is that you'll be helping to save millions of lives, starting with the population of this planet.'

Monty leaned back in his seat. This was just too bizarre. Steal something he helped steal years ago? Return it to its rightful owners? It was a stupid waste of effort... But anything might be better than working here. 'What would be in it for me?'

'The lives of yourself and anyone else on this planet that you care about. And I think I know someone who might be persuaded to pay a legitimate wage, with the proper encouragement.' The Doctor allowed himself a half smile. 'If nothing else you'd have my eternal gratitude.'

Monty barked out a short laugh. 'Is one person's gratitude more valuable?'

'If he's the former President of the High Council of the Time Lords, yes.'

That impressed Monty. You didn't bump into Time Lords that often, but it was certainly wise to keep in with them, especially if you wanted your past to stay in a reasonably chronological order. And an ex-President? Must've fallen on hard times if he was hanging around with a penguin and the likes of Glitz and Dibber. The whole thing was about as believable as a lawyer's tax return, but he was damned if there wasn't something about this Doctor that made Monty want to trust him...

'*You* trust him?' he asked Glitz, nodding at the Doctor.

Glitz hesitated. People like them never really trusted anybody. 'Well, sort of. He's not a bad bloke, really. Honest, of course, but he doesn't let it handicap him too much...' Monty doubted that the Doctor would ever realise how high this praise was by Glitz's standards.

'You'll never get Jack to do it. Not for no gain.' Jack Chance might be a thrill-seeker but he wasn't exactly desperate for a way out of his lifestyle like Monty was. Nor was he, Monty supposed, as stupid.

'Don't you worry,' Glitz said. 'The Doctor will persuade him. He could talk an ayatollah into opening an off-licence.'

'That I have to see.' Monty sighed. One last wild chance, or back to work for less than the legal minimum wage: what a choice. 'All right, Glitz, I'll go along for now. But if I see anything I don't like, I'm out.'

'Well said, Monty,' Glitz said appreciatively. 'You know it makes sense…'

'Not really, but if the cops are going to hound me anyway, I might as well be hung for a sheep as for a lamb. If it comes off, maybe I'll get my retirement out of it, and not have to work in this damn garage any more.' He shook his head sadly. 'The galaxy's changed around us, Glitz. It's getting so's you can't make a dishonest living any more.'

Brokhal stared impassively out of the hologram field as Klein greeted her. Mandell watched with interest, noting that it was trickier to read her body language through the transmission. 'Can I help you, Mr President?' she asked.

'In a way I hope not,' Klein said. 'We've just received word that one of our patrol vessels, the *Thornton*, has been attacked and boarded. Their last message spoke of contact with a Veltrochni Dragon, and we wonder if your countrymen witnessed anything that may help in our investigation.' A diplomatic way of hiding the accusation, which Mandell knew wouldn't fool Brokhal for a moment.

Mandell was right. Brokhal growled softly. 'You mean, I think, did we do it? The answer is no, Mr President. This attempt to divert us from the true matter at hand will not succeed.'

The President maintained his neutral expression, despite the strong urge to show some sign of derision. 'Pack-Mother, what am I intended to think? Our patrol craft reports being shadowed by a camouflaged Dragon, and immediately thereafter is attacked and stripped, the crew murdered.'

This was the game governments played, of course. The President must know as well as Mandell and the Pack Mother that the Veltrochni hadn't done this. They would have no need to rifle the ship, and would simply have erased it from space. But the game had rules, especially in those rounds when it threatened to spread into a wider conflagration.

'You may think what you like. We did not do it. But if one of my ships was in the vicinity, perhaps they have information that could assist you, as you say. I will ask my commanders.' She vanished suddenly, the link terminated at her end.

Klein shut off the hologram link, and looked questioningly at Mandell. 'Could the Veltrochni have done it?'

'Certainly. But why would they want to?'

'To look at our latest engine designs, of course!' Mandell didn't like his tone at all. It was too patronising.

'They could do that by monitoring communications at the shipyards – which I'm sure they do, incidentally. Anyway, the Veltrochni drives are far more sophisticated than our own. Why should they go to all this effort to steal an inferior engine?'

Klein frowned, desperate to prove that this was an enemy he could use to his own advantage. 'To test whether they could take one of our ships.' A hostile force always boosted the election turnout, Mandell had noticed. A good interplanetary crisis always took the heat off if there was any local scandal, and he resolved to check up on who the President was sleeping with these days; perhaps some bubble was about to burst, and Klein's bodyguards were about to receive a duelling challenge on his behalf. That could be why Klein was so keen to find a decent enemy.

'Not their style,' Mandell said placidly, knowing that it would annoy Klein.

The President's face went red. 'Not their style? Whose side are you on anyway?'

'The side of the truth,' Mandell lied. He smiled appeasingly.

While it was always useful to have an enemy to direct other people's attention towards, right now he couldn't risk making the Veltrochni that enemy. Otherwise it wouldn't look good when he went to meet them at Elchur. 'The Veltrochni aren't that roundabout. They're like a rubber band – you can stretch them so far, and then suddenly they snap back and give you a sore face without warning. And if it had been them, they could simply have transmatted aboard. But the most likely thing a Veltrochni Dragon would do is reduce the ship to a few wisps of plasma which we would never even have found.'

'So you think they didn't do it.'

The penny was dropping at last. 'That is what I said. Unless, of course,' he added nastily, 'that's what we're *supposed* to think.' Klein's eyes almost crossed as he tried to wrap his head around that one. Mandell never ceased to be amazed at the stupidity of the electorate.

'Then who? Pirates?' Klein scoffed. Despite the stories, space piracy was extremely rare. The simple fact was that it just wasn't profitable. Carrying anything through space was so expensive that the simple evasion of taxes and excise duty offered more than enough profit to make any criminal happy. The only occasional pirates who did operate were those who did it purely for the thrill.

Mandell shook his head. 'Not pirates in the way you mean.' Actually the answer was quite simple, if irritatingly vague. 'It was done by someone who needed engineering parts, and couldn't get them any other way.'

'That's a great help,' Klein muttered sarcastically.

'Glad to be of service, sir,' Mandell replied blandly. 'Now that that's cleared up, I have some things to attend to…'

Chapter Seven

The Foreign Technologies tether was a wide squat dome outside the fringes of Vandor Prime's atmosphere. It was linked to the ground by a forty-mile vertical magnetic levitation cord, up and down which carriages made the hour-long trip.

The Coriolis effect put plenty of stresses on the construction of every tether, but sufficient safeguards were built into the environmental control fields to compensate for that, and keep the tether steady.

Rather than labs, the tether had wide-open hangars and dry-dock facilities, since it was built to handle spacecraft. It was here that the salvage from battles, or the rare ship brought in by a defector, were first brought for examination. Once they had been fully deconstructed and analysed here, they would be sent on to the Thor Facility, or a military shipyard, or wherever else they could best be put to new use.

The Doctor's TARDIS had been brought to a small dry dock near the tether's hub. The dock had smooth walls with plenty of room to bring in equipment, while a long channel led to a launch port on the outer surface of the dome. SID Deputy Director Wei was overseeing attempts to enter the TARDIS, and had rounded up a posse of off-duty engineers who weren't engaged in studying other ships.

He had then gone home for the night, leaving the TARDIS in the tender care of supervisor Colman. Colman had once reverse-engineered a Dalek time controller, so Wei felt that he would be best able to discover the secrets of the Doctor's machine.

Wei returned in the morning, to find Colman's team scattered around the small plain-walled dock, glaring at the TARDIS. If he hadn't known that the whole lot of them were zero-rated for psi abilities, he would have thought they were trying psychokinesis on it.

'You haven't even opened it yet?' he asked. He wouldn't have minded so much if they were baffled by the interior workings, since it was the product of a far more advanced technology, but he had certainly expected them to be able to open the doors.

'It's quite odd.' Colman shook his head. 'It's almost as if we aren't actually touching the thing itself. There isn't a mark left on it.'

Wei looked at the TARDIS. It was wood; he could see that it was wood. Wood couldn't resist that sort of punishment, so how come it wouldn't open? 'Have you tried blasting it?'

'Blasting it?' the scientist echoed, annoyed. 'We've blasted it, burned it, drilled it, cut it... We've tried diamond and borazon drills, thermic lances, sonic lances, laser cutters, all of them useless. Right now I'm just waiting for the plasmic lance to come up from the main dock. If that doesn't open it, nothing will.'

Sha'ol looked up at the maglev tether which tapered away into the sky above. They would be going in essentially blind, and Sha'ol did not approve of such a tactic. It was in clear violation of the second Precept which R'Shal passed down into Tzun law millennia ago.

'We should have brought pulse lasers,' Karthakh growled.

'How many opponents are there?'

Karthakh peered at the hand-held scanner. 'Fifteen hundred lifeforms.'

'Many will be technicians and scientists. Unarmed civilian workers.'

'But there will be armed guards.'

'Ten per cent of installation staff is the standard human procedure,' Sha'ol recalled. That didn't sound much, but they would be heavily armed, and no doubt there would be automated defences as well. The humans were less advanced, but they were not fools.

'Seventy-five to one,' Karthakh muttered. 'That will be a challenge, unless we can seal off the area we want.'

The warrior who knows himself but not his enemy will suffer as many defeats as victories, went the second line of that Precept as Sha'ol recalled it. 'It would have been prudent to bring the pulse lasers.'

Two swords clashed, hard enough to strike sparks. They weren't laserblades or chainswords either, Glitz noticed, but old-fashioned steel.

The combatants, both orientals, wore gaudily coloured satin uniforms with wide sleeves, tied and belted with colourful silk. Some cymbals and gongs clattered distantly behind them as they flew through the air like leaping salmon and duelled across the tables. Diners and drinkers maintained an admirable calm – or petrified gaze – as the fighters moved among them.

The female fighter lost her sword, which was batted cleanly through the audience by her opponent's swing. It contrived to slice the tops off some carefully placed pineapples on a buffet table. In retaliation, she bounded forward into a high somersault, snatching his sword from his hand with her feet, and sending it sailing off to slice open the coconuts next to the pineapples.

Glitz watched, mouth agape, as the pair continued their act. 'Friends of yours?' the Doctor asked. Glitz nodded dumbly. He'd forgotten how well Chat and Liang could move, and was astonished to find that rather than slowing down with age, they seemed to be more agile than ever.

They were standing in the audience of the Delphic Circus, where patrons could wine and dine while watching acrobats and creative cooking. Chefs at hotplates were surrounded by admiring onlookers as they juggled both ingredients and utensils. The air was filled with spice and smoke, and everyone seemed to be enjoying themselves immensely.

The Doctor pointed to a shadowy alcove at the rear. 'If I'm not very much mistaken, they'll be in there when they're finished.' He started off towards the backstage area, ignoring the signs that insisted it was for employees only. Glitz followed the Doctor's lead, and the pair threaded their way between the diners and dancers.

They had left Dibber, Frobisher and Monty to study the datapad with Mandell's instructions now that the Doctor had assured them it was cleansed of poison. Glitz didn't feel particularly cleansed, but the Doctor had assured him that all was well and, after all, he did have the right qualifications.

The two acrobats were just coming out of the ring when the Doctor and Glitz reached the backstage area. For a moment, they hesitated opposite each other, then the woman grinned. 'Sabalom Glitz!' She grabbed him in a bear-hug. For all her slightness, he felt as if she was crushing him to death. 'I've missed you, believe it or not.'

'How long has it been?' Glitz managed to say when he caught a breath. 'Ten years?'

'Seems like yesterday. Still hanging around with Dibber?'

''Fraid so,' Glitz admitted. 'He's not exactly the most

sparkling of company, but there's no finer fetcher and carrier in all the system.'

'I'll never know why he takes all that crap from you.'

Neither would he, Glitz suspected. 'Isn't that what apprentices are for?'

Wei watched closely as Colman manoeuvred the plasmic lance into position. It looked like any other tripod-mounted cannon, except that the business end tapered off to a point. The rest of the technicians had taken shelter behind a force screen just in case, but Colman stayed to make final adjustments.

'We're ready any time you are,' he told Wei.

'Start cutting.'

Colman flicked a switch, and a beam of pure power stabbed at the TARDIS. The wooden surface hissed, and the paint on it started to bubble. It was working, Wei thought exultantly. The TARDIS was proving more resistant than even dwarf star alloy, but it was breaking up all the same. In a few minutes they'd be inside.

His smile froze as a loud trumpeting noise emanated from the TARDIS, and it faded from sight. Colman hurriedly switched off the lance, then stepped into the space where the TARDIS had been. Luckily the lance had been pointed out of the launch port. 'What the..?'

Wei blinked. The TARDIS must have had some sort of defence mechanism that took it away from imminent danger. There had been no way to predict that, but he knew Mandell would criticise him for it anyway.

'Search the tether just in case it's only made a local jump to evade the lance, and track down Glitz's ship in case it returned there.' If it had gone any further than that, they might never find it. 'And pray that –'

A web of energy arced across the dock, and two figures materialised on either side of the plasmic lance. Wei realised with a shock that the larger one was a Veltrochni.

Alarms blared as security robots descended from overhead conduits almost immediately. The Veltrochni switched the magazine in his KEM rifle to explosive-tipped darts, and opened fire one-handed. A flurry of darts slammed into the security robots, punching through their armour before detonating. Wei and the others leapt for cover behind monitor consoles and portable generators.

Shards of robot casing and circuitry scattered across the floor as the robots sparked and burst. Explosions blasted craters in the far wall, and reduced lab benches to fragments.

The other intruder, smaller and grey, meanwhile leapt nimbly around the burning wreckage, picking off technicians with well-placed disruptor shots.

Wei had never been so terrified in his life. He had no idea who these intruders were, and didn't really care. All he wanted was to get out in one piece. And change his underwear. Driven by the instinct to escape from danger, Wei shoved Colman aside and bolted for the door.

The door was already closing, but Wei flung himself headlong across the floor.

The door slammed shut an inch from his foot.

Wei lay on the floor for several long moments, his legs too rubbery to stand upright. He knew he had to get security down here, but first he had to stop shaking long enough to stand.

Karthakh punched through the wall panel beside the door, ripping out a handful of wires. With a quick short-circuit, the emergency pressure seal clamped over the door, as it would if the dock had been depressurised.

Sha'ol was efficiently herding the remaining four humans into the little control room to one side of the dock, and Karthakh joined him. The humans were all pale with shock and fear. Karthakh thought that was a good thing, as it would make them more amenable to co-operation.

'Who is the superior officer?' Sha'ol asked.

'Me,' a scrawny human with grey hair answered. 'I... I'm Colman. Chief of –'

'There is no need for fear. We wish only to know where the Doctor is.'

Colman's mouth moved silently, fear muting the words. Karthakh was disgusted at this show of weakness.

The supervisor managed to gasp, 'I don't know.'

Sha'ol leaned forward, and attached a small crystalline disc to the side of Colman's head, just behind the ear. 'You may speak without fear.' Colman took on a vaguely muddled look. 'His TARDIS was here. He should be with it.'

'TARDIS?' Colman's face cleared. 'It's gone. We were trying to cut it open, and it just took off.' Sha'ol and Karthakh exchanged glances. This was not good. 'We think it was a defence mechanism.'

Karthakh was already checking the portable scanner. 'Artron energy readings,' he said aloud. 'Two hundred yards in that direction.' He pointed to one side and upwards. 'What is that place?'

'Gunboat launch bay,' Colman answered.

'Was the Doctor inside the TARDIS?'

'No. It is being held to persuade him to work for us. He and his associates have been given a ship, the *Nosferatu*. They are to steal a cylinder, a Veltrochni relic, from the Thor Orbital Facility, and take it to Elchur.'

* * *

97

Glitz had introduced the Doctor to Chat and her brother, Liang. 'The best cat-burglars in the Delphinus group,' he said. They had then retired to the pair's dressing room to talk more privately. Divested of their ceremonial make-up and wigs, Chat proved to be a heart-faced woman with shoulder-length hair, while her brother was leaner of face, with a mop of black hair.

'An exquisite display,' the Doctor said encouragingly. 'You certainly know your stuff.'

'Two dozen years' practice makes fairly perfect,' Chat said. Liang had yet to utter a word. He didn't speak much in general, since Chat spoke so much more effectively than he did. He had always been the listener of the pair. 'Are you a fan?'

'Not exactly,' the Doctor admitted, a little theatrically. 'As a matter of fact I am simply a traveller. But at this precise moment, I'm a traveller who happens to be looking for the members of a team who stole something from Veltroch ten years ago.' Liang started to rise, but the Doctor made a placating motion. 'Don't worry. I'm not with the police, and I'm certainly not here to arrest anyone. Quite the opposite, in fact,' he added rather uncomfortably.

'The opposite?' Chat didn't bother to deny anything, seeing as they were in the company of equals. 'Let me guess, you and Glitz have got a job on to steal something else, and you want our help?'

'Actually, not something else. The same thing,' the Doctor said solemnly. 'Not that stealing it would be my first choice, and in any case I intend to return it to its rightful owners.' Liang couldn't believe his ears. They had been willing to listen, because Glitz was an old acquaintance, but this was a fantasy.

Chat shook her head. 'What did you plan to do with it? Sell it to the Veltrochni? They won't give you a reward for it.'

'A reward isn't quite what we had in mind,' the Doctor said grimly. 'I am not a thief by nature. My interest in this is to return the Veltrochni's property to its rightful owners before they devastate this planet to take it back themselves. I imagine you do know about their ships that have been visiting this system?'

'We try to get away from the newscasts, but unfortunately they're difficult to avoid.' Chat smiled, her whole face lighting up. 'We're in.' The Doctor started in surprise, and Glitz was positively stunned. She laughed aloud. 'Didn't expect that?'

'Not exactly, no,' the Doctor admitted.

Chat grinned. 'Let's just say I have my reasons. I may even tell you them some day.'

Gorrak stood on the factory floor that ran through the heart of the *Speculator*, looking at a spiderweb of enormous chains and ropes as thick as tree trunks. The factory was a huge arena intended for mining asteroids for raw materials, but now it was filled with dozens of sweaty Ogrons hauling on the lines. 'How does this help us?' he asked his chief engineer. Borrk used to carry heavy things in a sapper regiment, so he was uniquely qualified to maintain the ship.

Borrk indicated the stolen reactor core, which had been crudely welded into place at the heart of the *Speculator*'s engines. Ogrons might not actually understand much of quantum mechanics, but they were good with their hands, and could copy what they saw others doing. Borrk had seen Men installing engine cores, so he was able to copy what they did. 'It overdrive, Boss.'

'Overdrive?'

'Yeah. Make ship go faster than faster,' Borrk said, with the eagerness of all second-hand vehicle salesmen across the galaxy.

Gorrak wasn't too sure about this. He was no expert, but he was fairly certain that it was bigger engines that made ships go faster, not smaller ones; no matter how many chains you added. 'How does it work?'

'This newer engine. It add extra boost to old engines.'

Ogrons had never actually developed space travel for themselves, but had been taught to fly some kinds of vessels by other races. Other ships they had learned to fly by simply copying what they saw the crew do. Gorrak knew that other races called his people stupid and empty-headed, and it was true to some extent. An empty mind, however, had enough room to be filled with the ideas of others.

This tended to make Ogrons indebted to their ships' owners, and so for the most part they became a race of mercenaries, working for anyone who was willing to supply board and lodgings. It also often meant slavery. What people considered unimportant – like Ogron lives – they tended not to value or defend. Gorrak had seen this for himself, working for Men and Draconians.

Now that he had his own ship, big enough to accommodate his whole Nest, Gorrak discovered the joys of self-employment. The primary joy being that the Nest was allowed to keep all the booty from their raids, instead of handing over the majority to others. It also meant that his nestlings had no one to fear other than him. Not Men, not Draconians, and most especially not the Metal Gods.

It had been the Metal Gods who first discovered the Ogrons, and sent them to stars, but only to be exploited under the threat of death. When the races of Men had defeated the Metal Gods, many had wanted to destroy the Ogrons too, but here their fear had proved to be their saviour. Men realised that the Ogrons were afraid of the Metal Gods, not willing helpers, and so decided to spare them.

Ogrons then became useful to Men and, unlike the Metal Gods, Men allowed them to keep a payment for their services. Apart from that, nothing had truly changed. Ogrons were still hired muscle in the service of those who couldn't even tell the difference between a good rock, a bad rock, and a mere stone. All the same, Gorrak thanked the spirits of the mountains that he had never been employed by the Metal Gods. Men and Draconians were bad enough.

Wei had conveniently overlooked his own cowardice when explaining things to the squad of security guards who had joined him in the corridor outside. He tightened the straps on a riot vest, and hefted a reassuringly large energy rifle. 'They're armed and extremely dangerous,' he was saying. 'Shoot to kill, you understand?'

'Yes, s–'

There was a distant explosion, which sounded as if it came from farther along the corridor. 'What the hell?' By the time they cut the door open, all they found was a group of dead or unconscious engineers, and a gaping hole in the far wall.

'What's through there?' Wei demanded of the nearest guard.

'If they keep going, the gunboat launch bay. That blue box of yours is there.'

'Damn!'

* * *

The security officers who were guarding the launch bay opened fire with their laser pistols as Karthakh marched along the corridor towards them. His armour, however, was designed to absorb directed energy to recharge its holographic projector. As a result, the laser shots didn't even break Karthakh's stride.

Reaching a suitable point before the barricade, Karthakh loosed a couple of explosive darts at the ceiling above the guards. The ceiling exploded, depositing chunks of rock and broken pipes on the guards' heads. Though it didn't do too much damage, it did cause the guards to start panicking, and try to get out of the way. This gave Sha'ol clearer shots at them with his disruptor.

As several guards fell twitching to the ground, Karthakh now took aim at the centre of the barricade, and fired. The explosive darts blew a gaping hole in the makeshift barricade, and sent guards flying headlong across the corridor.

Karthakh smashed the buckled door aside. Beyond it was a pair of large delta-winged gunboats, large enough to carry several people. There was no sign of the TARDIS until Sha'ol peered inside the gunboats' entry hatches. The TARDIS had materialised inside the far one. Sha'ol was pleased; for this, the Doctor would come to them.

They could hear movement outside, so while Sha'ol started up the gunboat's engines, Karthakh blew a couple of holes in the other boat. It wouldn't do to let the humans follow them out.

Seconds later, as Wei and his riot squad burst in, the gunboat lifted off the floor and shot forward, rapidly vanishing into the blackness outside.

Chapter Eight

Frobisher was beginning to forget what a good fish tasted like. There wasn't even a river within miles as far as he could see, so a relaxing swim in a decent stretch of water was out of the question too. When the Doctor got back, he thought he'd probably shift into something with better wings, and go for a long flight. If he could find some good thermals, there was plenty of meditation to be had while being a circling condor.

The *Nosferatu*'s hatch opened, and the Doctor and Glitz entered, followed by two Asiatic humans in loose clothes. Monty grinned like a maniac. 'Chat! Liang!' He did his best to take both of them in his arms with one hug. 'I haven't seen you two in… what?'

'Six years,' Chat supplied.

'Too long,' Liang murmured.

Monty nodded, eyes moist. 'Far too long.' He half-laughed. 'To be honest, I never expected that a life of crime could lead to tears like these.'

'Any life with friendships can do that,' Chat told him. 'Criminal or otherwise.' She turned to Dibber. 'You still hanging around with Glitz?'

'Looks like it, Chat.' Dibber didn't seem to be much of a one for heartfelt conversation, Frobisher noted. After spending an hour with Glitz, that was a definite improvement.

'And this,' the Doctor told the new arrivals, 'is my chum Frobisher.' Liang and Chat both bowed from the neck.

'It seems we are to be conspirators,' Chat said. 'So I'm pleased to meet you.'

'Me too,' Frobisher agreed. 'I reckon we're going to need all the help we can get.'

A draught of displaced air preceded the transit carriage's arrival at the top of the forty-mile-long tether. Four members of the SID riot squad, in full body armour, stepped out. They swept the area with cold eyes and gun muzzles before Mandell emerged into the smoke-stained entrance bay.

Wei and the assembled staff shuffled nervously. 'Welcome aboard, *sifu*,' Wei began.

Mandell raised a hand to cut him off. 'Formalities can be attended to later, Wei. I trust we aren't about to be interrupted by yet more armed intruders?'

'No, Mandell *Io*. I've had security tripled.'

'Good,' Mandell said mildly. 'One open day per year is quite enough. How did they get in?'

'We're not certain,' Wei admitted. 'It looks like an open-ended transmat beam, but we can't figure out how they could transmat through the deflection barrier. It was operating at full strength.' Mandell looked into Wei's eyes, trying to judge how worried he was. It looked to him as if Wei wondered whether he would still be breathing in an hour's time. Wei was sensible in that regard.

'Well, then, your tactics were correct, if about as useful as copper insulation. How did they leave?'

'They took a gunboat from the roof bay.'

A straight and simple answer; Mandell was impressed. 'Did you track them?'

'They were on a heading to enter parking orbit, but then the signal stopped. They must have disabled the transponder. I have two more gunboats on patrol, trying to identify them by visual contact.'

'If you find them, I want them taken alive.' If they had indeed been able to transmat through a shield specifically designed to prevent such action, he would much rather find out how it was done than just kill them out of hand. He was a professional, after all.

Glitz had gone through to the cockpit, and was surprised when Chat followed him in. 'I don't know why you agreed,' he admitted to Chat, 'but I'm glad you did.'

'Why?' She looked down. 'Did you ever ask yourself what was most important to you? To me, it used to be the thrill and the challenge. But now I've got that with my art. I don't need the larceny to make me happy any more.' She sat beside him, and hesitated a moment before speaking again. 'For once, just once in my life, I'd like to do something good. Something that isn't just to make myself feel good.' She shook her head gently. 'You see, that's just about the only thing I haven't tried yet, that *might* make me feel good. I don't know if that's making the least bit sense.'

Glitz considered this. Fool people into thinking you're nice and generous, and they'll give you more than you can take otherwise. It had worked before. 'I think I do, yeah.'

Chat laughed. 'I'm glad you came to me for help. You're my friend, Sabalom Glitz. I cried for a week when you and Dibber left with your shares of the money, and I don't want to lose you a second time.'

Glitz wasn't exactly sure how to take that. If he was boasting to Dibber, he might have said it sounded like she fancied him. Here on his own, though, he doubted that was the case. Women like men who could give them a good life, not old lags like him. He thought he ought to give her some sort of answer. 'I don't want to lose me either.'

* * *

Frobisher caught sight of the Chinese girl's eyes as she returned from the cockpit, and was surprised. There was something in them that reminded him of himself when he was younger. He had once spent fourteen years of his life as a supermarket till in Walthamstow to be near the girl who worked there. In Chat's eyes, he saw something of what he had felt back then.

It was odd, seeing something of yourself in someone else. He wondered if that was because it was like stepping outside one's own identity, or whether it was just because the look of love always looked weird to outsiders.

Though he'd never say it to her, he didn't think much of her taste. Still, as the Doctor said, it took all sorts.

Mandell had sat down in the Administrator's chair in the Foreign Technologies tether. A semicircle of monitors arrayed in front of the seat repeated displays from all the main terminals in the control centre around them. 'Now,' Mandell said, a little more languidly.'What else should I know about, while I'm here?'

Wei relaxed somewhat, now that his life wasn't in imminent danger.'There is something…' He stopped himself. It was so unlikely to be important that he was reluctant to risk the scorn he knew it would bring. Then again, seemingly unimportant or unlikely events often turned out later to shape the fate of people, governments and even worlds. And where this vision was concerned, nothing could be taken for granted… 'One of them was a Veltrochni,' he stated bluntly.

'A Veltrochni?' Mandell looked panicked at the thought. 'Those two-timing bastards… they could at least have the common decency to let us get our double-cross in first.'

Wei activated one of the monitors. He keyed in the time

and location code that he recalled from their search of the security recordings earlier. A recording of the events in the dock appeared on the screen, starting with the activation of the TARDIS' safety device. Then the Veltrochni and his unidentified associate arrived, and all hell broke loose. Wei was glad the camera angle didn't show his hasty exit from the area. Mandell wouldn't take too kindly to seeing that.

Mandell merely pursed his lips as the scene played out. 'Whoever he is, he's from Pack Lorkhal; not one of Brokhal's entourage. Stop it there!' Wei hastily froze the playback of the security logs. Mandell tilted his head, as if listening to the memory of a distant voice. He tapped the screen, over the shorter grey figure. 'Enhance this image.'

Wei did so, and the figure swam into focus. Its skin was mushroom grey, and it had spindly limbs. Large jet-black eyes were set into its oversized head. 'I don't believe it... It's a Tzun.'

'Impossible!' Wei exclaimed. 'They all died out millennia ago.' He grunted. 'Except Sha'ol, of course, but he –' Wei's throat went dry.

Mandell nodded solemnly. 'Exactly. Sha'ol and Karthakh. The Doctor said they were fleeing two attackers, and now we know who.' He grimaced. 'That's all I need, isn't it? This pair after the man I need to save my bacon.'

'The Doctor has proved resourceful so far, Mandell *lo*,' Wei said, hoping to cheer his boss up. If the boss was cheery, he'd be less likely to take out his stress on Wei. 'He might finish the job first.'

'What? With that pair after him? There's more chance of Sabalom Glitz being elected President than Sha'ol and Karthakh failing to fulfil a contract.' Mandell drummed his fingers on the desktop. 'Have you any coffee?'

'I think so.'

'Get some. I need it.'

Wei gestured to an aide, who hurried off. '*Sifu*, perhaps we could make a deal with the bounty hunters. Offer them more.'

Mandell shook his head. 'They're the worst kind of professionals there are, Wei: ones who have integrity. Once they've accepted the contract, that's that. No, we'll just have to kill them, if we ca–' He broke off, wondering how he could have been so stupid. It must be lack of caffeine, he told himself. 'Hang on a minute... We won't be needing the Doctor after he's been to Elchur. So long as their contract doesn't have a time limit on it, they might accept a side deal to wait until after the Doctor has done his part...'

'Brilliant, *sifu*,' Wei responded eagerly.

'Yes,' Mandell agreed. 'Put out a general hail to the ship they took.'

The *Speculator*'s engines might be aged, but their churning still made the floors vibrate with a mechanical heartbeat. Like the rest of his Nest, Gorrak found it vaguely comforting. It was like being in the womb of some passive mountain goddess, and so definitely reassuring. It wasn't like being in one of the little ships that most masters provided for their Ogron troops. There it felt like being in a ration tin.

Gorrak looked at the scanner screen in the *Speculator*'s main control room. There were no holotanks here; just clunky consoles with good solid dials and switches, and two-dimensional monitor screens. There were lots of differently coloured blips moving to and from a nearby planet. Gorrak didn't know what each specific colour referred to, but he did know that every blip was a spacecraft.

There were rich pickings here, he saw. He cracked massive knuckles, and grinned to himself. With so many ships, there must be some that would bring the Nest riches and food, and they could keep all of it to themselves.

There was a mad cackle from what used to be the briefing room. The Nest's matriarch had set up home there, in defiance of Gorrak's leadership. So far Gorrak had been unable to think of a way to get rid of her that wouldn't lead his nest-mate to kill him. The matriarch was her mother, after all. As far as Gorrak was concerned, she was a pest.

'What you look at?' he grumbled.

'My daughter's mate drooling.'

'These ships good targets. Make Nest rich. Feed us for long time.'

'You have no rock in your head,' the matriarch snapped back. 'This place not good.' She had probably seen omens again, Gorrak reflected. She did that a lot, being a Shaman. She wasn't a very good one, in his opinion; a good Shaman should be able to win them favour with the gods. 'Bad omens here,' she went on. Gorrak wondered what she'd taste like minced. 'Two baby cousins ate another today.'

Gorrak laughed. Childhood was a fun thing, he remembered. Utterly terrifying, but fun all the same. 'Hah! They good lads. Grow up like me.' All Ogron children who survived must have eaten some of their siblings at some point. Food was scarce enough on Braah to mean starvation for undernourished offspring. In order to supplement that, the survivors didn't dare let a good corpse go to waste.

'Hah?' the matriarch exclaimed. 'This cousin not dead yet.'

Gorrak's face wrinkled into revulsion. 'This mean we have to capture more ships,' he said finally. 'Then there is food for all. This good omen, not bad.' Pleased with this display of his superior intellect, Gorrak turned back to the main control room. If he could just find out which ship was nearest...

As he had promised himself, Frobisher took a long flight, soaring on the thermals that formed a three-dimensional road system above the city. It was quite conducive to meditation, and he thought it was a shame the Doctor could never try it. Just stretch out the wings, and slide through the air...

He didn't register it at first, but the flier that was parked on the roof of a distant building looked very out of place. It was quite a distance from the deserted factory, but on a direct line of sight.

Frobisher might have been on vacation with the Doctor for a long time, but he still had a detective's instincts, and they led him to overfly that roof. Two men in dark suits were watching the factory through some sort of telescope. That couldn't be a coincidence. He hurried back to the factory, changing back to his more comfortable penguin shape behind the *Nosferatu*.

'Doc,' he called out as he entered the crew room. 'We're being watched.'

The Doctor nodded. 'I wondered when you'd realise that,' he said proudly. 'Mandell was bound to keep an eye on us. He's taking an awful risk by relying on us to do his dirty work for him. The slightest slip by us could leave him in serious trouble.'

'Why don't we, then?'

The Doctor motioned with the datapad. 'Because at the moment it would leave this planet in even worse trouble. Whatever Mandell and his cronies may be up to, there are millions of people here who are totally innocent, but would

110

suffer the consequences. I, for one, cannot let that happen.'

Frobisher agreed with him. Having so many lives depending on oneself was incomprehensibly stressful, and Frobisher wished he could just change shape and walk away from all this. How the Doctor kept sane, Frobisher had no idea. Surely it was impossible to become used to bearing the responsibility for whole planets on your shoulders?

Even if that was possible, Frobisher was pretty sure he never wanted to get used to it. He was just a private eye. A middle-aged being with endless curiosity and a love of jazz. He wasn't a superhero; superheroes could do everything without the slightest doubt or fear. Frobisher couldn't.

The Doctor smiled at him. 'I'm glad you're back, though,' he said. 'I think we might require your skills now.'

'Something wrong?'

'It's Oskar, the other member of the gang. None of the others know where he is.'

'If he was a member of this gang,' Frobisher mused, 'he must have a rap sheet as long as a Wagnerian opera. The cops will have more up to date information on him.'

'Exactly. Which is why I want you to go and pay them a visit.'

An hour later, Frobisher was skimming through the records, searching on the key phrase 'Oskar Goetz'. It was taking the computer a while, since it was checking not only the planetary police records, but those for the entirety of GalSec space. If Oskar had so much as let as a library book go overdue anywhere on any human-occupied planet, a record of it should come up. Eventually.

'Kala?' someone asked from behind him. Frobisher turned, recalling that this was the name of the cop in the picture

Monty had given him. Apparently she'd been watching Monty for a while.

'Er, yes?'

It was a short man with a shaved head and olive skin. 'I heard from Pell last night. Says he's coming to town at the weekend and we should meet up.'

'So?' Frobisher hoped he wasn't going to ask for advice, but could see that he was.

'So should I say yes?'

'It's your life. D'you want to say yes?'

'Well, sort of, but he does live on Teal Beta.'

'So?'

'I might not see him again for ages.'

'Never pass up a good thing,' Frobisher said. 'Something special may not come again, so you should take the chances that arise.'

'Right… Well, I –' a communications monitor buzzed in another room. 'Damn, that's me. I'll catch up with you in a minute, OK?'

'Yeah, sure,' Frobisher agreed, fervently hoping otherwise. As luck would have it, the terminal he was working at beeped, and he saw that the information he wanted was there. He printed out a hard copy quickly, then reset the machine, and left.

Once out of the police headquarters, Frobisher relaxed, and shifted into a more nondescript form. This time he became a short humanoid in a trenchcoat and fedora. Round-rimmed glasses somehow stayed over the two round eyes in his otherwise featureless head. It was several moments, in fact, before he realised that he had unconsciously returned to his true form.

It was a form he hadn't adopted in several months, and he

wondered why his instincts had chosen it. To remind him that it was there, perhaps? That it had been just as long since he had actively taken part in a detective investigation? Whatever, the Doctor would have to know his latest discovery. Their quest had hit a hurdle.

Kala passed the nondescript faceless alien in the trenchcoat as she turned into the station house. She knew Monty of old, of course, and had seen Glitz before, but there had been a new face at the garage. Kala was both irritated at the extra complication, and intrigued by the newcomer. He certainly wasn't as down-market as Monty or Glitz and Dibber, and she thought he might be one of Jack Chance's friends. He certainly dressed like a reject from the Cafe Terrestriale.

It would be best to check up on him before barging in with questions. Like any good cop, Kala knew that it was best to only ask those questions to which you were already pretty sure of the answers. That way you either corroborated your data, or caught someone out in a lie.

She stopped to bundle her coat into her locker, then went through into the main office. She called home and left Nic word that she might be late again. Then she went on into the records office, and found a terminal.

'G'night, Kala,' Jemson said, passing her on his way out. 'Oh, and thanks. You were right; I will.'

'What?' She must have missed something there, but he was already gone. 'What was he gibbering about?' she muttered to herself. It must be the strain, she decided.

Chapter Nine

Karthakh switched off the communications monitor. Having previous knowledge of his people's communication frequencies and scrambler codes proved quite useful when he and his colleague visited an area where the Veltrochni were engaged in any kind of operations. This star system was no exception, and Karthakh had spent several productive hours eavesdropping on the communications network of a number of Dragons in the Delphinus star group.

The mention of a cylinder in the communications sparked something in his mind. He didn't have the genetically enhanced memory that Sha'ol was gifted – or cursed – with, but he paid enough attention to recall the human at the hangar mentioning such an object. If the cylinder was the relic from the Council of Houses, then it was unique; it must be the same one that the Doctor had been sent to recover.

'The same relic?' Sha'ol asked.

'The stolen object is unique,' Karthakh admitted. 'I do not imagine it could be anything else. The Doctor must be after the same thing.'

'Excellent,' Sha'ol said. 'Then we know where the Doctor will be going. First, the Thor Orbital Facility, then Elchur.'

Karthakh wasn't so sure. 'He is a Time Lord, not a thief. Even if he has agreed to help out, there is no reason to assume he will do anything more than plan their activities.'

'My people have a knowledge of the Doctor,' Sha'ol said quietly, gazing into the distance in a manner Karthakh recognised. He was experiencing old memories that were as clear to him as the present. Karthakh repressed the urge to let his spines flatten at this display of something so unnatural. He had thought he might get used to it after so many years, but this had never yet proved the case. 'As a Time Lord his mannerisms alter slightly with each regeneration, but monitoring through several incarnations has shown his psychological profile to remain largely constant. It suggests that he enjoys the challenge of operating in the field. It is most likely that he will lead by example.'

Sha'ol returned to the pilot's seat. 'We know who some of his associates are. They will be known to the criminal fraternity on Vandor Prime. It should not be difficult to trace them. Do you concur?'

'Yes.' He not only concurred; he was positively looking forward to it. He sometimes wished that Sha'ol could adopt a more conversational tone in keeping with most species. Karthakh felt sorry for him at times. Like the rest of the S'Raph Tzun, Sha'ol had been genetically engineered: programmed to think and act in a certain way. He had no real family, except for Karthakh.

Sha'ol turned back to the flight console, and began operating it fluidly, as if he had been born to it.

It had been a difficult choice for Karthakh when he had first met Sha'ol. On the one hand, the Veltrochni had declared holy war on the Tzun after they had wiped out a whole generation of Veltrochni hatchlings. However, it was also a matter of honour that a Veltrochni must allow no harm to come to a guest, no matter what the provocation.

Karthakh admitted freely to himself that if he had known that the ship which asked for sanctuary in his family's plantation so long ago contained a Tzun, he would have refused and blown it out of the sky. But he didn't know, and by the time he found out, the Tzun was already protected by that ancient law. Hiding him had been simple enough, since the other members of Karthakh's family had died long before. A lightning strike in a storm had started a fire, and taken them all, along with half the plantation. Karthakh had been serving aboard a Dragon at the time, and returned to an empty and gutted home.

At first Karthakh had longed only for Sha'ol to recover from his injuries and leave. He had even contemplated accepting the dishonour and killing his guest. Eventually, though, he had realised that Sha'ol did not deserve such treatment. He had not chosen to be born into such a hated species. Even the characteristics of that race had been genetically engineered into him. In many ways, Karthakh wondered if letting him live might actually be more of a punishment, for he was the last of his people. There were a few scattered Ph'Sor Tzun colonies across the galaxy, but the Ph'Sor were half-breeds with other species, not true Tzun. When the Confederacy was destroyed, their worlds all became independent.

It must a terrible weight to bear, and Karthakh was glad that it wasn't him who had to live with being unique or so alone. Sometimes he wondered if that was why he grew to accept the Tzun's company so readily; even his company was infinitely preferable to remaining alone. Veltrochni were meant to be surrounded by family, not wander the galaxy in solitude. All either of them had left was each other.

'Gunboat 424,' a voice crackled over the intercom. 'This is Vandor Prime calling gunboat 424.' Sha'ol and Karthakh looked at each other. Karthakh doubted they should answer, but that itself might be suspicious. 'This is Vandor Prime calling Sha'ol and Karthakh,' the voice went on. 'I know you can hear me, and wish to discuss a business arrangement.'

Karthakh doubted that, but was intrigued all the same. Sha'ol switched on the communications system fully, and Karthakh assumed that must be wise. He had never known Sha'ol to be wrong about tactical decisions. 'This is Sha'ol.'

A hologram of a bearded human materialised in the centre of the gunboat's flight deck. 'Good evening. I am –'

'Mandell, Niccolo,' Sha'ol rapped out without missing a beat. 'Director of Vandor Prime's Security and Intelligence Division. You may speak.'

Mandell hesitated, to Karthakh's amusement. 'I understand you are in the process of fulfilling a contract on the Time Lord known as the Doctor?' The human now tried to look relaxed and superior, without success.

'That is correct. Do not attempt to interfere. When our contract is fulfilled, we will return your ship.'

Mandell shook his head. 'I didn't quite have interfering in mind. Quite the opposite in fact. Can you tell me if your employer specified a time by which the Doctor must be delivered?'

'No,' Karthakh admitted. 'However, we have personal standards to uphold. If you know who we are, then you must know that.'

'I understand that,' Mandell said. 'It's just that, at the moment, I need the Doctor's... assistance. Now, I could simply spend a lot of time and effort trying to keep you away from him, but I'd rather not. Instead I'd like to propose a new arrangement. If you can tolerate waiting until the end of the week, when the Doctor has fulfilled his obligations, I will deliver him to you, along with a suitable bonus for your co-operation. I don't believe that such an arrangement would in any way infringe your current contract?'

Karthakh considered the merits of the scheme. There was

no shame in it, especially since they already knew from the Veltrochni communications net what the Doctor would be doing. In essence, Mandell was offering them a bonus for nothing. Karthakh looked at Sha'ol.

'We agree,' Sha'ol said simply.

'How did you get on at the station house?' the Doctor asked Frobisher. Even though they were still sitting in a disused factory in a run-down area of the city, the *Nosferatu*'s furnishings were perfectly comfortable for a gathering of fugitives. 'Did they indeed have records on this... Oskar?'

'Well, they did,' Frobisher said, neatly using one flipper to unwrap a chocolate pilchard. 'It turns out he's dead.'

'Dead?' Monty echoed. He sat down heavily in one of the crew quarters' chairs. 'Dead...' Monty looked out the ship's viewport at the decaying rooftop, in the hope that the others wouldn't see his tears. He hadn't actually been particularly close to Oskar, but every old colleague who died took a little piece of Monty's past with him. That was what the aging engineer grieved for. He could foresee a day when everyone who knew him of old would be gone. After that, who would there be to remember him when he died?

'How did they catch him? He was a master of disguise.'

'Mistaken identity,' Frobisher said. 'Apparently a local crime syndicate thought he was a politician they wanted rid of.'

Monty nodded sadly. 'Mistaken identity... He'd have wanted it that way, I suppose.'

'Still a shame,' Chat said. 'He was a bit distant, but he was still one of us, you know?'

The Doctor looked at Monty for a moment, then nodded. 'I understand, but there will be a time for grief later. For now, we ought to move straight on to the last member of your band.'

'Just like that? Grieve later?' Monty was surprised that he didn't seem to be bothered by the loss of Oskar. What happened to other people had never really made much impression on the likes of Glitz, but he'd expected better of the Doctor. Monty was as much jealous of that sanguine air as he was chilled by it.

'Later,' the Doctor repeated stubbornly. 'We do have a schedule to keep to, otherwise there may not *be* a later. Not for this planet, anyway.'

'Jack won't go for it,' Chat warned. Liang, Monty and Dibber all nodded in agreement. 'I think we should just go for it as we are. The Doctor's smarter than Jack, and Frobisher's a perfect replacement for Oskar's talents.'

The Doctor shook his head. 'Knowledge is the key,' he lectured them. 'Our best hope of success will be to know everything we can about this cylinder and how you stole it before. Besides, I may be far more knowledgeable than your Jack Chance, of course, but I don't have the previous experience with the cylinder that you and he do. I presume one of you knows where we can find him?'

The five thieves looked at him askance. 'I'd have thought even the Time Lords would have heard of Jack's Cafe Terrestriale,' Glitz said.

The holographic sign that floated above the roof read 'Jack's Cafe Terrestriale'. Through the ingenuity of the designers who had installed it, the words faced any observer in perfect clarity from whatever angle he or she looked at them.

'Cafe' was perhaps too small a word for the building's nature. It was a modest-sized galleria mall, with bars, eateries and amusement areas encircling a wide indoor park on the ground level. That was all overlooked from above by several holo-theatres, and a true amphitheatre for live performances. Above that, with access strictly monitored, were a variety of casinos and entertainment palaces of the less family-oriented kind.

Every concession in the Cafe Terrestriale had Ancient Earth as its theme. A copy of the 1920s era Maxims restaurant snuggled in between a western saloon and a wine bar. Neon and glass bulbs meticulously recreated from images of Las Vegas lit the area from the casinos above.

It was a spectacularly perverse mix of styles unseen for millennia. It was also, of course, supremely tasteless, though no one alive in the eras which had been recreated was still around to explain this fact to the masses who frequented the place.

The owner watched these masses from what could be considered a sunken office in the roof, which was ringed by a circular window that gave an unobstructed view all around the Cafe Terrestriale. The glass was one way, since he had been known to use the office for bedtime escapades with whoever took his fancy. There was no shortage of willing volunteers. Well, they were only human, he thought egotistically.

Jack Chance was pushing sixty now, but took just enough rejuvenation treatment to look twenty years younger. In terms of fitness, it made him a good thirty years younger. He kept the faint touches of grey in his coiffured mane, though; he felt it gave a respectable air that attracted the girls. Youthfulness and maturity in one package, and not a downside in sight.

He activated his personal assistant with a snap of his fingers. 'What's up, sweetheart?'

In past centuries, people had interfaced with their

computer equipment through keyboards, or voice commands, or wetware. Throughout history, though, people had always felt most comfortable interacting with other people. This had allowed a fashion for humanoid computer interfaces to develop. The holograms could be visually indistinguishable from real people, or as bizarre and unreal as the customer wanted. It would then be a more user-friendly – literally – interface than a keyboard, mike, speakers, screen, skull jack and all the rest of it rolled into one.

The holographic image of Jack's ex-wife joined him at the bar. He hadn't picked that form so much for its looks as so he could enjoy hearing her speak only when spoken to. Most people had their PAs set to full opacity, making them indistinguishable from real people, at least to the naked eye, but Chance preferred his to be faintly translucent. He liked to keep a distinct difference between the real and the unreal.

'The usual things,' she answered with a sigh. 'The President is returning from Mars today. The shares index has dropped ten points, and forecasts are for the Terran market to open down twelve to fifteen points. More dull political stuff, if you want.'

'Forget it. Political news is always the same anyway.'

'Just the names that change, huh, Jack?' She blinked, as if just remembering something. 'Oh, weather control will be off-line in the capital this afternoon for essential maintenance.'

'Which means what? Rain? Blizzards? Scorching sun?'

'Your guess is as good as mine.'

'Off.' Jack felt a twinge of guilty pleasure as his ex vanished into thin air. He wondered if it was legally possible to marry one of those holograms. He decided against it; she might be more co-operative, but you couldn't really have sex with a hologram. Not that it stopped some fetishists who chartered his rooms, but Jack liked his partner at the very least to have a pulse.

According to the antiquated scanners in the *Speculator*'s main control room, a bulk freighter was passing quite close by, carrying foodstuffs to space stations. That was a good omen, Gorrak thought. That would show the matriarch what was what.

Borrk had assured him that the *Speculator*'s tractor beam was working perfectly. Instead of going out in the shuttle, they could drag ships in. The tractor beam had originally been installed for asteroid mining, of course, but Gorrak couldn't care less about that.

It was with a surge of pride that he watched the swollen freighter being dragged towards the nose of his ship.

Gorrak looked back at his troops. 'Check your weapons.' The surrounding Ogrons laboriously squinted at the controls on their plasma rifles. A blue-white flash spat out in the middle of the room, and an Ogron in the front row popped in a shower of blood and twitching limbs.

An Ogron in the centre rank shrugged, looking at his smoking rifle. 'Mine loaded,' he deduced cheerfully. Gorrak laughed approvingly with the rest of the squad.

This didn't stop him from looking through the thick transparisteel windows in the airlock doors. Already the hapless freighter's hatch was falling towards the outer door as it was swallowed up by the *Speculator*.

Jack Chance toured his property every day, greeting the

regular customers, smiling at families, and propositioning anybody who looked attractive enough. He had just stopped to help himself to a drink at one of the bars, when he became aware of someone approaching.

It was a middle-aged man with drab clothes and a drab face. He had 'accountant' written all over him. Something similar anyway, Jack thought. 'Can I get you something?'

'The word on the streets is that you can get me out of here.'

Chance repressed a smile. There were enough words on streets to fill several dictionaries, few of them reliable. 'I'm just a businessman. I run this place, import some foodstuffs and holograms… I'm not quite in the league you're looking for.'

The man slid a credit chip across the bar. Chance picked it up. 'Hang on a minute.' He slid the chip into the reader under the till. It was one he had modified himself to read fingerprints on the chip, rather than its veracity. According to the prints, checked against a database hacked from the Justice Division offices, the guy was a government clerk. More importantly, he didn't match any records of police or security men.

Jack stepped back to the man. 'Well,' he admitted slowly, 'there is this Kaldanian freighter setting off for the Rassm system tomorrow. Their captain bitches to the bartender here all the time, and right now he's short of a galley assistant… You'd be scrubbing dishes the whole trip, but –'

'That doesn't matter,' the man said urgently. 'Just name your price to make sure I get aboard.'

'For two thousand, and a few rounds of drinks for the captain tonight, I'm sure we could swing it.' The man hesitated, then wiped his brow in relief, and dug a credit chip out of his pocket. Jack stopped him. 'Ah, you know how it is… On a war footing and all, credit doesn't go that far. I prefer cash.' It was less traceable for a start.

The man visibly repressed an urge to speak – a curse most likely, Jack thought – and nodded. 'All right, cash it is. I'll be back in an hour.'

'I ain't goin' nowhere,' Jack advised him cheerily. 'The captain should be in tonight. I'll introduce you when you come back… If you've got the cash.'

'I'll have it.'

'Good.' Jack watched him go, and then helped himself to a Rush tab. Purified adrenalin and endorphins grown from his own cells flooded his brain, bringing a chemical-free buzz. Someday it'd occur to the government to make it illegal, but not today. Reinvigorated, Jack switched on the communicator screen under the bar. 'Kallas?'

'Yes, Chance?' an older well-groomed man in a private spacer uniform replied after a few moments.

'I think I got you your new galley assistant. How much is he worth to you?'

'A thousand?'

Jack thought about this. 'Make it two.'

'Two?' Kallas echoed. 'Is he worth two?'

'No,' Jack admitted, 'but he's going to be working for free. You can pay me two grand for services rendered, or pay him four as a wage – the choice is yours.' Jack liked the idea of making a total of four thousand off this deal. It was symmetrical somehow; he arranged a new worker, but collected the full wage himself. The guy was a civil servant after all, so it would serve him right.

Kallas nodded. 'OK, two it is.'

'Glad to hear it. Bring your cash round tonight, and I'll

introduce you.'

'I'll be there.' The screen went dead. Jack grinned cockily, not caring that nobody saw it. It wasn't as if he needed the money, but it was fun to put one over on somebody. He liked that sort of challenge.

A few buildings had moved around during the afternoon, jostling for the best weather. Smooth crystal walls encased the assorted themed sections of Jack's Cafe Terrestriale. Residents of numerous planets thronged the main piazza. Most of them were humans from various GalSec planets, though the occasional alien could be seen as well. It was an eclectic mixture to say the least.

'It's a bit on the garish side,' the Doctor opined. 'Definitely not very tasteful. Now, if they were to redecorate with something a little more stolid and imposing, this complex could be a real architec-'

The others exchanged glances, and Glitz wondered if he was starting to develop hearing problems; surely the Doctor hadn't just said what he thought he'd just said? 'You feeling OK, Doc?' Frobisher asked in a low voice. 'Not feeling giddy or anything?'

The Doctor stopped. 'What do you mean by that?'

Frobisher coughed. 'Er, nothing, Doc. Just… Just thought you looked a bit peaky there.'

'Peaky?' The Doctor frowned at him, then tapped his chest. 'Perfect health, Frobisher. I have *never* felt "peaky". Now, where are we likely to find this friend of yours?' he asked Glitz.

Glitz pointed up at an inverted dome suspended from the roof. 'He'll probably be in there.'

'He always liked his comfort, Mr Glitz,' Dibber agreed.

'Don't we all, lad,' Glitz agreed, with what sounded to Frobisher like a wistful tone. Frobisher certainly couldn't disagree with him there. He still wasn't sure exactly whether Glitz was on the side of the angels or not, but either way, it was nice to meet someone who just wanted to be comfortably-off rather than run the universe.

There was a polite 'Ahem' from behind them, and the group turned to find the Cafe's Maître d' waiting with an infernal air of polite superiority. Frobisher thought he looked awfully like David Niven. In fact, he realised slowly, it *was* David Niven. Or at least some kind of replica. A clone or android perhaps.

The Doctor looked the Maître d' up and down. 'Haven't we met somewhere before?'

'I don't think so, sir, and I'm sure I would have remembered.'

'Ah.' The Doctor smiled. 'Remember all your customers, do you?'

'Every one, sir, with perfect clarity. Now, how many in your party?'

'We're not here to eat, I'm afraid. One meal a day is quite sufficient for most humanoid lifeforms.' There was a faint groan from Dibber. 'Actually we'd rather like to see the owner of this establishment. A Mr Chance?' the Doctor finished hopefully.

The Maître d' nodded understandingly. 'Mr Chance is very busy, I'm afraid. But if you'd like to make an appointment for tomorrow…'

Frobisher nudged the Doctor. 'Is that who I think it is?'

'Not exactly. Did you notice how his skin and clothes blend together just inside the cuffs? He's some kind of computer-generated projection. I imagine that when he said he remembers all the customers, he means that the program which runs him maintains a constant database.' The Doctor stopped, facing the hologram bullishly. 'And I personally am not going to take no for an answer from a mere collection of photons and personality algorithms.'

The Maître d' also halted. 'Sir, this is hardly the proper –'

'All you have to do, hologram, is summon the owner of this establishment. Until you do, we are going to do our best to attract his attention ourselves.'

Liang grinned suddenly, and flicked his wrist. A silver dart with a cord attached speared an orange on a neighbouring table. To the astonishment of the middle-income family sitting there, Liang brought the orange into his own hand with a twitch.

'What are you doing?' Chat demanded, looking almost as shocked as the family.

'Getting Chance's attention.' He lashed out with another dart, sending a new fruit sailing towards her. She caught it neatly.

'This is childish.'

Glitz and Dibber grinned and rose. 'Excuse me, madam,' Glitz said to the mother of the neighbouring family. 'The service here is a little slow, so my friend here and I would like to share your meal.' He picked up a piece of meat and flicked gravy back on the plate. 'In fact, we might even pay our share too,' he added generously.

The father rose. 'What the hell do you think you're doing?'

'Eating,' Dibber told him bluntly. Frobisher wondered if it would be worth shifting into something inconspicuous and leaving.

'This is a restaurant, after all,' Glitz said, 'what else would we be doing?'

'We could be robbing them,' Dibber responded.

Glitz silenced him with a look. 'But this is our lunch hour, Dibber. That makes us simple diners, just like these good people here.'

'Oh, yeah.'

The Doctor turned away from their antics. 'Well?' he asked the Maître d'.

Jemson handed the viewer to Kala. 'Makes you think, doesn't it?' They were both sitting in a police flier parked on a roof overlooking Jack Chance's office.

She looked through, finding the Doctor's distinctive coat easily. 'I knew it,' she muttered with relish. 'I knew he must be one of Chance's friends.'

'So you said. And said. And said.'

Kala looked at him. 'Have I been that overboard about it?'

'It does tend to feature fairly regularly in your conversation,' Jemson admitted. He shrugged. 'It's OK, though.'

'No, it isn't.' Kala hated the idea of harping on too much about the same thing. That tended to annoy people. 'If I've been going too far with it...'

'Not yet.' Jemson shrugged. 'We all have our little drives, right? Anyway, seeing as how you're right, I don't think you have to worry about it. At least, you're right about this bunch all meeting up. As for what they're actually doing together...'

Kala shook her head. 'We've got Glitz, Dibber, Chance, Monty, Chat and Liang. Just about the whole gang. I can't believe they're only having a drink for old times' sake, can you?'

'Not really, no.' Jemson scratched his cheek. 'There's still Oskar, but he's dead... You reckon the Doctor's his replacement?'

Kala thought about this. The Doctor was a bit too conspicuous to be their disguise expert, but several vastly different faces had shown up in the records last night when she searched for him. 'Maybe. I don't know, though. There's something about him that doesn't fit with the rest of them.'

'Apart from the others at least having some fashion sense?'

'That goes without saying.'

Jemson nodded slowly. 'So, what d'you want to do next?'

To be honest, Kala wanted to go home and let Nic give her a back rub, but work had to come first. 'We should bring them in. Even if we can't hold them on anything, we might at least scare up something on what they're doing. If nothing else it'll throw a spanner in whatever they're planning.' She started tying up her hair even tighter, not wanting to leave any of it loose enough to be grabbed by a fugitive. 'Call Tac and have them send along a team.' Jemson looked doubtful; such manpower requisitions usually took some time. 'I put in a request for possible support yesterday,' she added. 'Just in case.'

Chapter Ten

Ingrid Bergman materialised beside Jack, much to the distress of the girls he was with. 'What?!' he demanded irritably, over their protestations. He wanted to stop to tell the pair that this was a projection, but if it had self-activated, then something important must be going on.

'I said that there's a disturbance in the main suite.'

Jack grimaced, as he heard his companions bolt out the door. Not that this would make much difference to his reputation. 'Disturbance? What, a dissatisfied diner? A riot? What?'

'You'd best look for yourself, Jack,' the hologram responded.

Sighing, Jack stepped over to the one-way glass, where the hologram indicated. It took him a moment, but then he picked out the source of the trouble. Below, at one of the sumptuous tables, two people were tossing not just food, but cutlery, to each other. Somehow they were slicing up fruits in mid air and not missing a beat. Meanwhile, a pair of disreputable ruffians – who looked vaguely familiar – were talking to a horrified-looking family at the next table. A man in a Technicolor coat was talking to an older man, using cutlery and pieces of other people's dinners to build some sort of model, and the Maître d' was arguing with a penguin.

This sight somehow managed to sidle around Jack's higher brain functions. He was seeing it, but the information wasn't registering yet because it was impossible. He couldn't be seeing something impossible, because the impossible couldn't happen; that was why they *called* it impossible.

'Tell me that's not Glitz. Tell me that's not Sabalom Glitz…'
Dibber would be with him. And the two acrobats would be
Chat and Liang; the older man Monty… but who were the
big guy in the coat and the penguin?

Jack felt the blood drain from his body, leaving only a sense
of empty horror. He was perfectly happy with his
girl-attracting, wallet-stuffing lifestyle as it was
thankyouverymuch, and the last thing he wanted was his
past to catch up with him.

The slab-sided freighter had now been drawn fully inside the
Speculator, where it hung in a zero-gravity area over the
factory floor. Chains and automated asteroid mining
equipment laced it, pulling chunks apart.

Gorrak almost wished he could take the ship back outside
and fly off in it, away from the stresses of leading the clan.
But he was their headman, and was responsible for them. He
still sometimes wished he had more rock in his heart.

Some of his clan were busy dismantling the freighter,
cutting it apart so that the hull plating could be used to
patch holes in their own adopted home. Borrk was
supervising, occasionally using a kick to drum up some
speed from a lowlier Ogron. 'Borrk?'

'Boss?'

'Keep working. I go to flight deck.'

'Yes, Boss.' Borrk never questioned anything. Gorrak was in
a good mood as he went up to the flight deck in one of the
little Man-sized carts that were used to travel through such a
huge ship.

Before doing anything else, he tossed a crate of meat pies
on to the deck in front of the matriarch. 'Good food,' he
grinned. 'Men always have good food in their ships.'

The matriarch merely grunted, and Gorrak wondered why he bothered trying to prove his worth. She was his mate's mother – it was her place to despise him, that was the way of things.

'Boss,' another Ogron called, seeing him. It was the scar-faced Urggat. Gorrak grunted. 'The ship sent message before we killed the crew. Radio in here pick it up.'

Gorrak grimaced. That meant armed ships would be coming here; ones they were not equipped to fight off.

'Start overdrive. Take us away from this place.'

'All right, what the fipe do you think you're doing?'

'Jack Chance, I presume,' the Doctor beamed. 'I'm so glad to finally meet you and congratulate you on this fine establishment –'

Chance pushed the Doctor back a few paces. 'Am I going to have you thrown off this building before or after you tell me why you're causing trouble in here?' The Maître d' and a couple of waiters were hastily escorting the neighbouring family to another table on the far side of the complex.

Glitz interrupted them. 'You're an old mate, and we thought we'd drop in and say hello.'

Jack nodded. 'Hello, goodbye, now sod off.'

Glitz forced a show of injured pride, while privately thinking that he'd get the bastard for this attitude. 'Jack, Jack… Is that any way to greet your old mate? Especially when he's bringing you some good news?'

Jack looked at him sceptically. 'My lottery numbers came up?'

'Not exactly,' the Doctor said. 'My, er, associates and I have a proposition for you.' He handed Jack the small datapad. 'I'm sure you recognise this artefact, Mr Chance.'

'You cops?'

Glitz was offended at that suggestion. Did nobody trust him these days?

The Doctor shook his head. 'No. I am known as the Doctor, and this is my associate Frobisher. The others I believe you know.'

Jack nodded again. 'Of old. And this thing –' he tossed the pad back to the Doctor '– is also old news.'

'Not any more. We need your help, Chance. To steal this artefact from its current owners.'

For a moment, Glitz thought Jack was going to explode, but then he burst out laughing instead. 'Yeah, right! Give up my place to go back to thieving? No way. I don't need that any more. The money just ain't good enough.'

'This isn't about money,' the Doctor said severely. 'It's about avoiding a war.'

'The Veltrochni? They're just stirring it; sabre-rattling. Nothing'll come of it except that some of us will make a profit.'

The Doctor fixed him with an icy glare. 'I know the Veltrochni of old, Chance, and if this artefact is so important to them, they will be more than willing to attack and destroy this entire planet. But if we can return it to them before that –'

'The answer's still no, fun though it might be. I got better things to do than get killed attacking the Thor Facility. Have you looked at the list of defences in your pad there?'

Glitz was puzzling over the difference between the Jack Chance he remembered, and the one who now stood in front of him. 'Half a millisecond. I thought you laughed at death.' Some part of Glitz was vaguely cheered that Jack was proved to be bluffing after all. It made him feel a little less inferior.

Jack nodded. 'And I still do. It's just that now the skinny bastard can pay to come see me, like everybody else.' He leaned his chin on one fist, and eyed the Doctor. 'Normally I charge for services rendered, but if you want your tailor spaced, it's on the house as an act of charity.'

The Doctor smiled. 'Are you this hospitable to all your patrons?'

'Only the ones who invite me to give up this comfortable life for a shot at a conviction. I have to wonder why a total stranger would walk into my place and ask that.'

'You're saying you don't know who I am?' The Doctor glared at Chance.

'That's right,' Chance said.

The Doctor sat back, eyes wide. 'You think you're some kind of "made guy" and you don't know who *I* am?' The Doctor sounded offended, and his voice rose. 'I've been causing trouble in this galaxy since before humanity left its miserable little planet. You may have heard of me: the Bringer of Darkness? The Oncoming Storm?' Chance began to wonder about this man. He had a look of fervour and passion in his eyes that one usually only saw in religious fundamentalists the instant before they detonated a suicide bomb. And he had heard of the Oncoming Storm... Some Draconian nickname, wasn't it? 'I've been tried more times than I can count by humans, and twice by the Time Lords. The Droge of Gabrielides once offered a whole star system for *my* head; can you match that?'

Jack swallowed nervously, and Glitz couldn't blame him. What did someone have to do to get that sort of price on his head? 'So, what were you up for?'

The Doctor waved the question away. 'Oh, just the usual sort of things... Inciting civil war, Presidential assassination,

piracy, interfering with the course of history, genocide…
Nothing special, really.'

'How?' Jack coughed, and started again, less squeakily. 'How
did you get off with that?'

'Hmm?' The Doctor gave him a long look. 'I killed the
prosecutor.'

Glitz was suddenly disappointed. The Doc might be a Time
Lord, and pretty resourceful, but he didn't know that much
about the criminal fraternity. You didn't get off that way;
they'd just draft in another prosecutor. Still, he had to admire
the Doctor's style. Jack laughed. 'Nice try, Doc. You know, for
a minute there, you almost had me thinking you were a
decent normal person like me.' The Doctor's eyebrows
raised at this extravagant compliment. 'But the answer's still
no. I got a nice thing going here; I got girls, boys, more money
than I could make from thieving, and all for less effort too.
It's a lifestyle I find a damn sight more comfortable than –'

There were several simultaneous crashes from the various
doorways, and a chorus of alarmed yells from the customers
throughout the Cafe Terrestriale. Everyone at the Doctor's
table looked around, to see armed police officers in full body
armour pouring in. 'Nobody move! This is a raid!'

'Bastards!' Jack snarled, pulling a gun on Glitz. 'You set me
up!' Glitz was equally surprised, and hurt by the accusation.
With a fluid scissors kick, Liang kicked the gun out of Jack's
hand, and that broke the spell that had held the small group
frozen.

'Run,' Glitz suggested, and bolted for the kitchens, followed
by Dibber. People flung themselves under the tables and into
the 20th-century-style buildings as the police opened fire
with stun lasers.

Glitz had no idea what the others were doing, and didn't

much care. The important thing was for him to get away safely. He and Dibber burst into the kitchens, and leapt across worktops. Dibber took the opportunity to scatter hot oil across the floor and set it alight. The cops who followed them through were forced back by the sudden wall of flame.

Chat and Liang used their darts and cords to tug the stun lasers from two officers, and started returning fire. Even though they were wearing body armour that would resist the stun charge, the police presence all took cover. It was a natural human instinct to duck away from being shot at.

Chat didn't know how the cops had got on to them, but wasn't entirely surprised that they had. The whole group had criminal records a mile long, and most likely some or all of them had been under surveillance the whole time.

She pushed the Doctor towards the Vegas casino. 'Come on, we can get out through here!'

'But Frobisher –'

'Made it to the fire stairs. Let's go!'

Frobisher had found more policemen at the foot of the stairs, and hurriedly started going back up, looking for a way out into a police-free area. He cheated a bit, lengthening his penguin legs to take the stairs more quickly, and soon reached the top of the stairwell. If there was even a few millimetres of a gap under the door, he could slide under it... It was hermetically sealed, though the window beside him seemed like ordinary glass. He turned back to check on the progress of the cops who were following him, and saw that they were almost on him. Thinking quickly, Frobisher shifted one arm into a crowbar even as he swung at the window pane. It smashed easily and he wriggled through.

Now he was out on the roof of the first storey of the Cafe Terrestriale. Unfortunately, even this first storey was atop a five-hundred-foot cluster of buildings that was currently following a slow flight plan across the city's green belt. He started hurrying along the crystal awning anyway, knowing that the first order of business was to get the hell away from the cops.

'There's the penguin!' a voice called from the window, and a pair of riot police pulled themselves through the shattered glass. They started shooting as their comrades tried to follow them, and Frobisher leapt forward in the hope of dodging their fire.

Unfortunately the rain had made the crystal surface a lot slicker than it looked, and he soon found himself hurtling face-first down the awning. He tried not to think about the stun bolts following his tail downslope. Abruptly he realised that there was something else he'd rather not think about – the edge of the awning was approaching a hell of a lot faster than he would have liked.

With a squawk of horror, he hit the edge with his chest and arced off into the air. Even for a shapeshifter, there is something deeply disturbing about suddenly finding oneself hundreds of feet above the pavement, and feeling the inescapable tug of gravity. For an instant, that fear paralysed Frobisher, and he started to plummet.

Adrenalin kicked his brain back into gear, however, and he hastily grew two pairs of coiled springs, like legs.

He slammed into the pavement, and the springs bounced him back into the air, giving him time to grow a longer pair of wings, bringing his body in until he had taken the form of a duck. Gasping for breath, and hoping that anyone on the street below had an umbrella, Frobisher recovered himself, and banked off towards Methuselah Town.

Jack took a flying leap over the bartop, and opened the trapdoor that was set into the floor. It led directly to his private garage, from whence he could take a flier out of the building.

Damned cops. They couldn't leave him alone even though he'd gone straight. Well, straight apart from the occasional bit of smuggling or black-marketeering, but those weren't *real* crimes, like burglary and armed robbery.

Someone, he promised himself, was going to pay for this.

Raising the hinged filter mask from the front of her helmet, Kala strode into the main dining suite, and felt a sense of satisfaction as she saw the forensics team already tending to the table at which their quarry had been gathered.

She passed through the room, and into the manager's small office. This was where the important information – if any – would be, in encrypted files. She had, of course, made sure to have the proper warrants made out. There was something about being married to a civil servant that had made the paperwork of her job become a little more comprehensible. She supposed some of Nic's professional ethos must be rubbing off on her, though she didn't envy him his office job.

'Any casualties?' she asked Jemson.

'No. Even the fugitives stuck to the stun settings on the weapons. We've a few shocked diners, but no real injuries.' Kala grimaced. No doubt the department would be on the receiving end of some more litigation after this. The only way to make sure it didn't bring her down was to prove herself right. 'Find Chance – now!'

* * *

Glitz stepped back into the *Nosferatu*, trying to remind himself that Jack Chance and the others were accomplices, not competition. It would help if they would act that way; acting like competition was a sure and certain way to get on Glitz's bad side.

He had always hated competition, ever since reform school. It was a truism that when two hunters chased the same prey, they usually ended up catching each other. Much better to get rid of the rivals first.

Monty had made it back first, and was dozing on a bunk. 'Check the booze, Dibber,' he suggested. 'I feel a long night coming on.'

The pair hadn't been waiting long when the ship's main lock opened again. Glitz and Dibber reached for their guns, fearing the cops had found them. It was, however, only Chat, Liang and the Doctor.

Glitz raised his glass to the Doctor. 'Here,' he said in admiration, 'that was some story you spun Jack, Doctor. You almost had me believing it.' Bragging about past exploits was as much a part of the job as evading the law, as far as Glitz was concerned. It wouldn't be much fun if you couldn't tell a few stories to admiring petty crooks in the bar.

The Doctor paused. 'Probably because those things were are all true.'

'What?' Glitz blanched. 'You can't be serious.'

'I'm perfectly serious. Well...' He let a twinkle show in his eye, and Glitz was inexplicably relieved. 'I have been falsely tried. I just told your friend my story in such a way as to make him fill in the gaps in the way I wanted him to.'

'Clever, that. I like it.'

The Doctor sighed. 'Don't like it too much, Glitz. That is, after all, what Mandell is trying to do to us.'

'Yeah, he's a real sneak is your pal Mandell,' Frobisher agreed, coming in with the stiff gait of the very tired.

The Doctor visibly relaxed. 'I was beginning to worry about you. How did you get away?'

Frobisher gave a penguin shrug that saw his head almost disappear between his shoulders. 'Nothing fancy. I just used the four-sprung duck technique.'

From outside there was the whine of a flier coming in to land. The group exchanged glances.

'Cops?' Chat asked.

'Probably.' Glitz agreed. 'They don't seem able to take a hint, do they?' He nodded to Dibber, who hefted one of the large multi-blasters, which was easily capable of blowing a flier to shreds with one shot. 'Well, then? Have a look!'

Dibber sighed, and peered round the edge of the hatch, only to have a hand shove a blaster muzzle into his cheek. Dibber backed into the ship slowly, and Glitz decided that if push came to shove, he would take a chance at shooting past Dibber.

His finger tightened on the trigger, as first an arm, then a figure, followed the hand with the blaster into the ship after Dibber.

'So, this is what you're calling home these days, is it?'

It was Jack Chance, now wearing calf-length fancy boots and a knee-length leather jacket that almost concealed the shortened plasma rifle strapped to his thigh. He lowered the blaster pistol, and looked around at the furry seat covers and chromed bar fittings in the crew area. 'What is it? A flying pimpmobile?'

'Call it more a mobile headquarters,' the Doctor answered. 'Now, are you here to finish the conversation about setting people up, or...?'

'To be continued, Doctor. Right now I came to join your little party.'

'I knew you'd see reason,' Glitz said proudly. 'You know what makes sense.' He gave Chance a cheery grin.

'Think again, Glitz – I ain't coming along for loyalty or the money, OK? I'm coming because I owe somebody a beating.'

'Er, yeah…' Glitz agreed nervously. He had nothing against violence *per se*, just so long as he wasn't on the receiving end. 'Not me, I hope?'

'I haven't decided yet,' Chance deadpanned. 'When I do, you'll be the first to know.'

Chapter Eleven

Pack-Leader Hyskanth looked at the blackness in the viewing cube attached to his command couch. 'The distress signal came from here?'

The *Thazrakh*'s lead prospector gestured an affirmative. 'The signal was weak; a freighter reporting that another vessel was colliding with it.'

Hyskanth glanced at the reading that threaded along the edges of the display. No sign of wreckage. 'Are there any vessels in detector range?'

'Two Vandorian patrol vessels, a frigate and corvette. They are undoubtedly responding to the distress signal. We are scanning for residual weapons signatures; no result so far.'

Hyskanth started sharpening his foreclaws on a small whetstone. 'Continue the search, and let me know when it is complete.'

The two new ships slowed as they entered the area, the stretched bar-bell form of the *Cobb* coming alongside the small angular corvette *Mead*.

Aboard the *Cobb*, the lanky and unshaven Captain Franke was surprised to see an unshrouded Veltrochni Dragon show up on the navigational sensors. It seemed to be quartering the area, conducting a search of some kind. They must have picked up the same transmission that his own ship had, he realised.

The Captain of the *Mead* also saw the Dragon in her main display tank, but came to a quite different conclusion.

'Hail the Veltrochni. Tell them to stand down and prepare for boarding.'

The communications officer obeyed, and in a few moments, a Veltrochni face appeared on a small monitor. 'This is Pack-Leader Hyskanth. We are responding to a distress signal.'

A likely story. 'Pack-Leader, I receive a distress signal in time of crisis from a Vandorian freighter, and arrive to find a Veltrochni warship and no freighter. What am I supposed to think?'

'You are supposed to think that we are searching for your missing ship,' Hyskanth growled. 'Since you seem incapable of doing so.'

So, the Captain thought, they were admitting already that their story was a bluff... 'Pack-Leader, I must insist that you stand down and prepare for boarding. I do not wish to fire upon your ship, but I will if I have to.'

'What the fipe is she doing?' Franke breathed. Her first command, and she was going to screw it up. She probably believed all that guff the newscasts put out, criticising the Veltrochni and going on about how warlike and expansionist they were supposed to be. Hell, he'd be pretty warlike himself if he thought someone had stolen his property. 'Get me an open line to Hyskanth.'

'I'm trying, but they're not responding.'

'This is free space, Captain,' Hyskanth rumbled ominously. 'Do not attempt to disrupt our operations.'

The Captain of the *Mead* then made a very small, predictable and foolish mistake. 'Starboard weapons array: ten per cent burst across their forward shields. Let them know we mean business.'

* * *

Aboard the *Cobb*, Franke saw the flash out of the corner of his eye, and cursed. '*Mead*, take evasive action!' He gestured to his own communications officer. 'Hail the Veltrochni, and tell them –'

A stroke of green lightning swept through the *Mead* as easily as if it wasn't even there. The Vandorian ship was reduced to a few pieces of scorched metal even before the flash imprinted its purple afterimage on Franke's retinas.

'Tell them it's a mistake,' he finished in a whisper. Almost a hundred people had simply been removed from life, their very molecules stripped away from each other. Only their computer records and the tears of their friends and families would be left to show that they ever existed.

'Captain,' Lambert asked, 'do we return fire?'

In many ways he should, of course. The Veltrochni had just destroyed a Vandorian ship in free space while on a rescue mission. He was not stupid, though. It was the *Mead*'s Captain who had killed her crew by firing first without cause. 'No. Hail them.'

Liang had lain awake for some time, but given up attempting to sleep. It felt vaguely as if this city block was also sliding on a journey to somewhere. He told himself it was just nervousness, or perhaps the result of some of Glitz's gut-rot. As far as he was aware, this block was an older one, simply built on to the ground.

Or maybe it was his subconscious telling him that this whole set-up was something he should have backed out on. Glitz and the Doctor had admitted that the government was involved, so even if they towed the line, how long would it be before the police were banging on the door?

Liang wasn't so worried about himself, but Chat was his

responsibility, wasn't she? She may be his older sister, but he still had to look out for her, much as he assumed she felt she had to look out for him.

He knew he had to sleep, though. If he was to be alert to look after her properly, he had to sleep tonight.

Jack Chance poured drinks for the Doctor and himself. When the Doctor waved away the offer, Chance poured the contents of that glass into his own with a satisfied smile. They were sitting in the *Nosferatu*'s cockpit, and Chance had turned the pilot's and co-pilot's seats around to face each other. 'So, Glitz tells me you got some sort of bounty hunter trouble?'

'A very odd pair of bounty hunters,' the Doctor agreed. 'A S'Raph Tzun and Veltrochni warrior, working together.'

Chance's features briefly quivered. 'It sounds like Sha'ol and Karthakh.' Jack glared at the Doctor. 'They've never failed in a hunt. Sooner or later they'll find you. And that means they find us.' Dammit, he thought; just when he thought this couldn't get any worse, now it turns out those two are prowling around. What gods had he lost any bets with recently?

'OK, let's start it this way – who could have hired them? Who wants you dead badly enough that they'd fork out enough mazumas to buy their services?'

The Doctor pursed his lips. 'I'm afraid there would be rather a long list. In spite of my obvious charm, there are those maladjusted types who seem to think that the universe would be better off without me.'

'I bet. I've only known you for a day, and I could think of worse things than tossing you off the roof of this building. No offence, by the way.'

'None taken,' the Doctor said, with heavy irony.

'Are you sure they're only after you? I mean, you said they wanted "the Time Lord known as the Doctor…" Could somebody be trying to take down a bunch of Time Lords? I mean, you guys do have enemies, right? Everybody has enemies.'

'"Guys"?' The Doctor echoed. 'The Time Lords are not just "guys"! Ten million years of time travel isn't common.' He shook his head, then hesitated. 'There are… those who consider themselves champions of reality. Groups who despise time travellers for polluting the very essence of causality… I suppose some of them might have tried something like this. It would certainly be a lot easier for them to kill travelling Time Lords such as myself than it would be to attempt any assassinations on Gallifrey.'

'Ordinarily my advice would be to find them first. You know what they say, "Do unto others as they would do unto you, but do it first."'

'That is more or less why I'm here. Someone on this planet knows what's going on, and it must be someone very rich and very powerful.'

'Unfortunately we all seem to be a little busy right now…' Jack tossed the Doctor the blaster pistol he had been carrying. 'This might help if they show up again.'

The Doctor gave it back. 'It might, but I doubt it. I imagine that's exactly the sort of defence that they're used to, and plan for. Sha'ol is a S'Raph Tzun, Chance; they are to planning what beavers are to dam-building.'

'So what are you going to do when they come to give you a plasma sandwich? Offering them more money to let you go will just piss them off, if that's what you had in mind.'

'I'm a Time Lord, Chance. I've faced down entire Dalek armies, so I think I'm perfectly capable of handling those two individuals. They're not the most violent entities I've met, you know.'

'Why am I not surprised?' He shook his head, and tapped the datapad. 'The next question is, how we case the joint. I don't trust this data of Mandell's for a moment. I ain't going in on this job unless I know what's really in there.'

'On that we most definitely agree,' the Doctor said heartily. 'Somehow I have to get into this "Thor Facility" and scout the place out.'

'You don't exactly look like a black-project scientist, Doc.'

'I may not have to. Not for a scouting mission, at least. You know, I think your insubstantial friend David Niven has provided the answer to one of our dilemmas.'

'Like what?'

'These holograms like your Maître d' – are they common on this planet?'

'Yeah. You can assign a holo to interface with any computer-based task. All mine are old Earth figures; I got Ingrid Bergman, David Niven –'

The Doctor held up his hands. 'I get the idea. Would other buildings have the same type of system? Government buildings, perhaps?'

Chance nodded slowly. 'Well, they probably wouldn't be old Earth movie stars, maybe not even humanoid, but they'll have holograms as interfaces, yes.'

'Then if we knew what the Thor Facility's holograms looked like…' He opened the cockpit door, and grinned at Frobisher.

'Hey, what are you looking at me for?'

Chance nodded slowly. 'Who's going to question a hologram? It can pop up anywhere unchallenged…'

The Doctor indicated the datapad. 'And here we have a

schedule of authorised shuttle visits for this month. Quite handy that, wouldn't you say?'

Jack grinned. 'I reckon it's time to hit the shuttle port then! We'll snatch a flight crew, hijack one of their shuttles, and be –'

'No!' The Doctor calmed down. 'That would just alert the asteroid's security force. No, somehow we have to get there legitimately.' He took the pad back from Chance. 'I wonder what visitors are due to go in on those shuttles…'

Chance sipped his drink. 'Visitors none of the staff have met before?'

'Exactly,' the Doctor sounded pleased that he'd made that deduction, and Chance felt vaguely proud without knowing why.

Security control in the asteroid was a sprawling mass of polished consoles and winking indicator lights that were cultivated throughout a smooth-walled cavern. Armed guards were stationed at every door. In the centre of the room, a large hologram of the asteroid hung, with tiny thumbnail holograms of the security monitor's input scattered wherever there was a scanner.

Occasionally a security officer would touch one of the thumbnail images, and it would expand to give a good three-dimensional view of whatever that particular security monitor was showing.

SID Deputy Director Wei was watching the docking permissions with a careful eye. 'Hold for identification, please,' he heard someone say. Since most identifications were prearranged and automatic, this was enough to interest Wei. He went over to Kapra, who was supervising operations.

'What is it, Kapra?'

'This visitor, sir,' Kapra said. 'The shuttle pilot claims to have Professor Hoffman from the Academia Solaris on board, but the identity signal they're transmitting doesn't match the records of the Professor's appearance that were sent by the Academy.'

'Let me see.' Wei consulted the two images: the Academy record of a very professorial-looking man with a white beard, and the shuttle's transmission of the Doctor's image attached to some forged documentation. 'It's all right,' Wei told Kapra. 'The Academy transmission was in error. Let them dock.'

While they were doing so, Wei would notify Mandell that the Doctor was making a move.

The Thor Facility's main docking bay was kept thoroughly separate from the smaller bays which handled the delivery and removal of chemical or biological samples. To Monty, it didn't look much different from any of the municipal hangars he visited in his taxi, except that it was far cleaner. Every step and rail on every gantry and catwalk was chromed to an impossible brightness, and he could have eaten his dinner off the floor.

He brought the shuttle in gently, and touched down as near to the interior doors as possible. If the Doctor had to leave in a hurry, it would be best not to have to run across too much open floor first.

Monty had lived on the wrong side of the law for a whole working lifespan, and knew when something was amiss. The ease with which they had got into the facility was downright suspicious. 'This smells like a set-up to me, Doctor. Are you sure you want to go through with it?'

'That's why we're not all coming right now. I should've thought that was obvious. Now, there's no sense in both of us endangering our lives. You stay in the shuttle, and get out of here at the first sign of trouble.'

It was traditional to protest at these sort of instructions, or, more rarely, agree too readily. Monty was too experienced for either of those. 'I know the drill.'

Mandell groaned when the comm unit chirped. 'What is it, Wei?'

'It's the Doctor, Mandell *lo*. He's boarding the asteroid now.'

Mandell was immediately alert. 'Excellent! Is this him making his move?'

'I don't think so, *sifu*. More likely a reconnaissance trip.'

'Oh. Still, it's progress… Make sure he sees what he wants to see, but don't be linked to him.'

'Understood.'

'Professor Hoffman,' the Doctor said brightly, shaking Kapra's hand furiously. 'I do believe you're expecting me.'

Kapra smiled nervously. This walking mass of exuberance wasn't quite what he had expected from a professor at the leading GalSec educational system. 'Indeed, your reputation precedes you.'

'I'm sure it does,' the Doctor said agreeably. 'There can't be too many human "experts" in temporal mechanics.'

'It's been a very exclusive research field,' Kapra agreed. 'Which is why we asked you to examine it. Our own temporal engineers are competent and keep it safe, but when we heard you were in-system, it seemed a good idea to have you look it over.'

'Mmm,' the Doctor said in an affable tone. 'And right you

were, too. I'm quite curious to see this set-up of yours.'

Glitz, Dibber and Chat ignored the muffled thumps from the wardrobe in the Captain's cabin of the *Nosferatu*, which could be heard all the way down in the crew room. 'Why don't we just kill him?' Dibber asked. Though it wasn't her style, Chat was tempted to agree with him; the Professor's struggles were beginning to give her a migraine.

'That would be killing the golden goose, Dibber,' said Glitz patiently.

'What?'

'The one what laid the golden eggs,' Glitz explained. 'These scientific types aren't like ordinary nerks, are they? They're the ones who invent all the stuff that's worth anything.'

Dibber paused. 'Nobody invented diamonds, or machonite, or –'

'What I am saying, Dibber,' Glitz went on with exaggerated patience, 'is that people like the Prof in there have to invent stuff before we can nick it. Besides, you heard what the Doctor said: if we kill him, he'll walk out and Mandell will kill us.'

'Not if we fight back.'

'Be serious, Dibber. We've got a pair of multi-blasters and a couple of Ensen rifles, while Mandell has gunships, space cruisers and hundreds of specially trained troops. So the Prof stays put for the duration and gets out in one piece. Which reminds me: it's about time you fed him.'

'Me?' Dibber protested. 'Why do I have to do it?'

'Because you're in my employ,' Glitz said expansively. 'That means I'm the boss.'

'All right,' Dibber muttered. 'I'm going.' He pulled a few prepackaged snacks from the food unit, and disappeared through the door into the short passageway.

Glitz shook his head. 'I sometimes worry about him, you know. He just hasn't got my best interests at heart.'

Chat closed her eyes. 'Why should he have? Neither have you.'

'Me?'

'You take too many risks, Sabalom. I think sometimes you want to get caught.' She didn't have to see him to know his expression was becoming one of over-dramatic outrage. 'It's part of the criminal image, isn't it? You have to have done some time to be a real crook, right? So you can say you survived it.'

'You've never been inside, have you?'

'No,' she admitted, 'but that's because I don't get caught. Didn't,' she corrected herself. She was going straight now, she reminded herself, and the fear of getting caught was over. 'Anyway, you know I didn't mean it that way.'

'Eh?' Glitz was evidently baffled.

Chat opened her eyes again, and looked at him. 'Sometimes I worry about you too.' She wondered if he'd notice the difference between his supposed worry for Dibber and hers for him. Somehow she doubted it.

Kapra had taken the Doctor on a brief guided tour of the facility, which mostly consisted of sparklingly clean corridors bordered by frosted windows that didn't let anyone see much in or out.

Finally they had come to a mid-level area. Rather than a single room, it was more of an inhabited corridor that completely ringed the heart of the asteroid. Enormous corrugated machines filed along the centre of the floor all the way around. They hummed constantly, and pulsed with a strange dark light. 'What are those things?' Frobisher's voice whispered in the Doctor's ear.

'Some kind of time dams,' the Doctor answered softly, as if talking to himself.

'You mean the asteroid can travel in time?'

'No, these could only set up a static time field. Most likely these are responsible for keeping the place slightly out of phase with reality. But there's too much equipment for that here... they must be doing something else with it.'

'Another time field?'

'Probably. To set up a time field within a time field, the energy expenditure required increases exponentially.'

'Fascinating isn't it,' Kapra said proudly. Frobisher could tell from his voice that he must have a hand in building or designing all of this. He had a happy tone that was almost fatherly. 'They keep both time fields fully functional. Expensive, but very effective. This installation is exceptionally secure. One might even say uniquely.' Frobisher managed not to laugh, for that would betray his presence.

'It's very impressive,' the Doctor agreed, and Frobisher could tell he was being truthful about that. He went over to a console that was attached to the nearest time dam. The display showed a one-hour time field set up around the entire facility. There was a smaller patch at the heart of the asteroid as well, however. 'What exactly are these time dams for?'

Kapra smiled. 'The most secure vault is out of phase not just with reality but with the rest of the asteroid as well. I can show you the direct effects if you'd like, but it's a little warm.'

'So long as there's somewhere I can hang my coat,' the Doctor replied, 'I'd be happy to have a look.'

Kapra nodded understandingly. 'There's an office just round here.' He led the Doctor to a room that was more a cubbyhole than a real office, with barely space for a few workstations and a seat. The Doctor hung his coat on a wall hook, and left. 'You're not locking it?'

Kapra shook his head. 'Everyone here is strictly vetted. They're not going to steal a coat.'

Their voices faded into the distance. Once the room was unoccupied, the colours on the Doctor's coat began to run, flowing downwards like melting wax. The first part to reach the floor pooled out, forming webbed orange feet. The rest of it faded to black and white, coalescing as if poured into a penguin-shaped mould. In a few instants, Frobisher was no longer an extra layer on the Doctor's coat. It was a blessed relief to be back in a simpler form too; the stress of generating so many pigments had left him dizzy. He felt like a chameleon that had got drunk and woken up on a Jackson Pollock painting.

He wouldn't dream of telling the Doc how painful that coat was to a shapeshifter, though, not when it was for a reasonably good cause. No pain, no gain, as the saying went. Frobisher went to the door and poked his beak out. This was actually quite refreshing now that he thought about it, just like his old days as a gumshoe back in Rassm City. Hopefully this would be even easier, since surely the latest office building was a more civilised environment than the alleys and bars of a decaying metropolis.

All the same, the penguin form was a bit too conspicuous. Regretfully, he'd have to change it to something less noticeable. Straightening his shoulders, Frobisher flowed into the shape of Kapra, and stepped out into the corridor.

Chapter Twelve

The Doctor and Kapra continued their tour around the rotunda. The Doctor frequently left Kapra in his wake as he marched off to examine this or that piece of equipment more closely. 'This is fascinating stuff,' he said absently. 'Who designed all this?'

'It was before I joined the staff. I understand the work was contracted out to an offworld combine. They certainly seem to have done a good job. It's never failed us yet.'

'Ah.' The Doctor put a companionable arm round Kapra's shoulder. 'And you wouldn't happen to know the name of this combine, would you? Professional interest, you understand.'

Kapra's long features took on a frown. 'Chronodyne Industries, I think. Their head office is on Dronid, I believe.'

The Doctor looked at him intently. 'Dronid? Are you quite sure of that?'

'Well, as I said it's before I joined the staff, but –'

'Supervisor Kapra report to the Director's office,' a tannoy voice demanded. 'Supervisor Kapra report to the Director's office.'

Kapra looked apologetically at the Doctor. 'I'm afraid I'll have to go. If you'll follow me, there's a refectory on the way. I can leave you there for some refreshments if you like.'

'A capital idea,' the Doctor agreed encouragingly, after a moment's thought. 'I've seen enough here to be sure that you know what you're doing.'

'Thank you, Professor,' Kapra said happily. Likewise, he had also seen enough of his visitor's expertise to know that he too was even more knowledgeable than his reputation suggested. Pausing only to collect the Doctor's coat, they returned to the more populated area of the facility. Kapra pointed to a set of doors. 'You can get something to eat in there.'

'Thank you very much,' the Doctor told him. 'It's been a most educational visit.'

Kapra nodded. 'For both of us. I'll be back in an hour.' He left. The Doctor made a show of heading for the refectory doors until Kapra was out of sight. Then he strode purposefully off in completely the opposite direction.

Any sort of electronic recording device would undoubtedly register on the asteroid's internal sensors, so Frobisher was glad that his memory was as good as it was. He was carefully memorising the location of every guard post, every lab, every storeroom...

'Supervisor!' He didn't realise the voice was calling him at first, until a guard's hand tapped his shoulder. 'Supervisor,' the man said. 'You've been paged to report to the Director's office. Didn't you hear?'

'What? Oh, er, right. Thanks,' Frobisher said uncertainly.

The guard shook his head. Scientists...

Frobisher didn't mind; he was pretty certain that he'd got all the important data, so now he just had to return to the shuttle. As soon as he was in the lift that ran through the central axis of the asteroid, he shifted to the shape of the guard who had stopped him. Presumably it was less likely that the guard would be paged.

The Doctor had also been stopped a couple of times, but his forged documents of clearance allowed him to pass unhindered. He was quite proud of the work he had put into them.

There were a lot of things going on on this asteroid that could benefit the planet, but plenty more that should be stopped. Still, humans had a history of devising ingenious ways to harm themselves and he certainly couldn't stop them.

Right now he was most curious about the lab with the frosted windows. He wondered what was in there. Anything hidden was generally worth seeing, he had found.

Despite what Kapra had told him earlier, the door was locked. Whoever designed the lock wasn't very good at it, however, and the Doctor was able to force it with a laser probe.

Inside, glass dividing walls separated the main room into little airtight cubicles. From the equipment and the hermetic seals, the Doctor could see that this was some kind of pharmacology lab. It couldn't hold dangerous specimens, though, as there was no airlock.

Curious, the Doctor moved to the nearest piece of equipment. It was some kind of molecular separator, with a number of phials of white powder still in it. The Doctor tipped one out into his hand, and brushed the powder lightly with his fingers. 'It can't be…' he looked around for a scanner, and picked one up off a nearby desk. He scanned the powder sample. 'Vraxoin… But no organic molecules, so they can't be breaking it down from Mandrels.' His eyes narrowed.

Kapra's meeting with the Director hadn't lasted as long as he had expected, and had merely covered everyday formalities. He was surprised that Professor Hoffman wasn't in the refectory, however, and set off to look for him.

Cronan was, as usual, rejoicing in his sense of personal superiority when he came down from his quarters.

He took the open door to his lab as an insult. How dare

anyone intrude in his domain? He took a small blaster from his pocket. Weapons were naturally forbidden in the facility, but rules made by others had never meant much to Cronan. Only the ones that he made himself mattered, and chief among them was 'Thou shall not mess with my stuff.'

The Doctor heard the door open, and dropped to the floor as someone entered. Whatever else was going on here, if someone was manufacturing vraxoin, they wouldn't want that information spread around. Whether it was the government, or some scientist working on his own, they would want him silenced.

Keeping the desks and equipment units between him and the newcomer, the Doctor managed to work his way round to the door while the new arrival worked his way deeper into the lab.

The Doctor disappeared round the corner towards the time dams just as Kapra came into the corridor from the other direction.

Kapra saw the open lab door, and wondered if his guest might have gone in there. It was against protocol for a member of staff to enter another department's lab, but it happened occasionally.

Kapra stepped into the pharmacology lab, where he saw Cronan looking angrily around with a gun. 'Is something wrong?'

Cronan virtually exploded. 'What the fipe are you doing in here? This is my lab, dammit! Get out, you worm.'

Kapra flinched from the unexpected vitriol. 'I was just looking for Profes-' He stopped as his eyes fell upon the scanner left lying amidst some white powder on the desk nearby. It was vraxoin. 'Oh no...' He looked up at Cronan, and saw the rat-faced man glance down at the desk.

Cronan raised his gun. 'Serves you right,' he snarled. Kapra backed out of the lab into the corridor, and bolted back towards the lift. Cronan leapt over a bench to follow him out and shot Kapra in the back.

Alarms blared immediately, set off by the unauthorised energy discharge. A pair of uniformed guards charged in, and Cronan ran for it.

Wei himself eventually found the Doctor in the rotunda with the time dams. 'Dropped my pen,' the Doctor explained. 'Had to come back for it.' His face grew grimmer. 'Tell Mandell I want a meeting,' the Doctor muttered into Wei's ear. 'The furniture factory in Methuselah Town, at eight.'

Then the Time Lord was gone, and Wei was very glad that Mandell hadn't engaged someone with less regard for life to do his dirty work.

Cronan made it to his personal flier and was out of the Thor Facility just in time. By now the guards would have found his stock of vrax in the lab. This was his mysterious intruder's fault, and that person would regret it, he promised himself.

There were security monitors all through the asteroid, but Cronan had bypassed the ones in his lab, so that they recorded directly on to data crystals and sent innocent pictures to security control. He slotted the latest crystal into his flier's monitor, and ran the image forward until he found what he was looking for: a man with curly blond hair and a multicoloured coat over striped yellow trousers...

Frobisher didn't like the sound of what the Doctor had told

him at all. 'Vraxoin?'

The Doctor nodded as they walked back into the *Nosferatu*. 'Somehow one of the scientists is synthesising it artificially.'

'You think it's one of the government's black ops, or just a few rogues who work there?'

'There was no way to tell. We'll see what Mandell has to say. I've demanded a meeting tonight.'

Frobisher nodded absently. 'But what about our other problem, Doc?'

'I'm more certain than ever that the Thor Facility has something to do with that.'

'How can you tell?'

'One thing at a time, Frobisher. We must gather our evidence before we start making accusations.'

With its repulsorlift field repelling even the dust from the floor, a flier settled into its cradle on one of the middle levels of a floating housing block. The man inside, obscured by the tinted canopy, made no move to get out of the vehicle. He simply sat and took note of his surroundings, appearing neither nervous nor relaxed.

A second flier drew up outside the docking cradle. One of the rear doors slid open, and Cronan emerged. Without looking back, Cronan marched unflinchingly over to the first flier.

The flier's canopy opened as he approached, and he reached it to find a tall and slim but slightly seedy-looking man with close-cropped dark hair looking up at him. 'You're very punctual, Reno,' Cronan said, 'I like that. It shows respect.' Respect was good for business.

'You get what you pay for,' the scruffy-looking Reno

agreed, relaxing slightly. Cronan noticed that one of his hands was out of sight. Holding a weapon, no doubt. He didn't take that personally; these days everyone had to look out for themselves. Besides, there was a bomb in his coat pocket, linked to a heart monitor. If Reno killed him, he and his flier would accompany Cronan straight to hell. 'What can I do you for?'

Cronan proffered a hand-held computer link. 'You can spread the word of the Lord.'

'Still on that godhood kick, Cronan?' Reno grunted. 'Everyone should have a hobby.' He glanced at the computer link. 'You want me to spread the word about this guy?'

'That's right. Free of charge. I've made a deposit in your account to cover the effort. I want anybody who might be interested to know that there's ten million GalSec credit bars on offer to anyone who kills this man.'

'A tidy sum,' Reno murmured. 'Everyone on VP who owns a blaster will be out looking for him.' And most likely killing each other, as was usually the case when rivals went hunting.

Cronan nodded patiently at his inferior's denseness. 'That is kind of the idea, Reno.'

Wei hurried into Mandell's office, looking stressed. That immediately made Mandell worry, since nothing ever stressed Wei.

'*Sifu*,' Wei began, 'We have a problem.'

'What?'

'I was going through the post-action reports, and found this, from Reno.' He handed Mandell a datapad. Mandell scanned it.

'Theft,' Mandell murmured aloud. 'Intruders on the Rock… alarms… street bounty placed by Cronan… Bounty?'

Mandell gritted his teeth, and maintained a straight face. He really ought to cut down on his caffeine intake, he thought. 'Why is it that the path of my life must be littered with landmines as well as pet turds?' Whom the gods would destroy, he reflected, they first assigned employees from the local government end of the gene pool.

'Wei, people think it's easy being a diabolical mastermind,' he grumbled. 'You see it in the newscasts every night: the self-opinionated moaning about corruption, just because they can't get any, and they're jealous of it…'

'Yes, Mandell *Io*.'

'Somebody should tell them that it also means you never get a good night's sleep, and your blood pressure gives your doctor nightmares.' He rubbed his eyes to try to get some life back into his head. 'All right… Pull Cronan in for debriefing. And Wei, do *not* let the police talk to him under any circumstances.'

He sure as hell didn't want Kala finding out what he was doing as part of his job. Nobody on the Thor Facility knew about the vraxoin… but Mandell did. He had always assumed the knowledge would be useful should he ever need Cronan to do anything for him. The security work Kala would understand, but there were some associations he'd had to make which she would take exception to. He'd much rather kill Cronan than risk losing her, and that sort of revelation about him would hurt her so much… Mandell wasn't bothered about hurting people generally, but his wife and their unborn child were the sole exceptions. He wouldn't let anything hurt them.

'There's one other thing. The Doctor wants a meet. The old furniture factory in Methuselah Town at eight.'

Mandell blinked, but then shrugged. He'd expected something like this, and it wouldn't hurt to reaffirm his terms and conditions. 'All right, have my flier ready for me then.'

Jack was curious to meet this Mandell; he sounded like a right bastard, and Jack kind of liked that. Not much, but enough to take some satisfaction from besting him. They might even be kindred spirits; Jack had always had a thing for villainy. He always wanted to be a lovable scoundrel. Failing that, he'd settle for being a rich one.

Liang, Glitz and Dibber were watching with Ensen rifles from a hidden spot, while Frobisher had concealed himself somewhere in the crew room. Nobody else knew where. By this time the Doctor had thought their fellow conspirators should be aware that Frobisher wasn't a full-time aquatic avian. Somehow, they hadn't been too surprised.

The Doctor had also told Glitz that he had been cured of the poison all along. Frobisher had been against that, while Glitz was armed, but the Doctor hadn't wanted to risk Niccolo unnerving Glitz further by referring to it if they should meet.

Monty sat in the ship's flight deck, ready to take off at a moment's notice. Only the Doctor, Jack and Chat would deal directly with Mandell. Jack wasn't sure why, but felt reasonably confident anyway.

A smooth black flier touched down outside the ship. Mandell, Wei, and several immaculately dressed bodyguards emerged.

The trio met him at the airlock. 'I'd prefer to speak alone,' the Doctor said.

Mandell canted his head. 'There are three of you. Wei and one guard should come in with me.'

The Doctor nodded, and led them inside. They all took

seats in the comfortable crew room. 'Drink?' Chat offered, handing Mandell a glass. Mandell took it, and winced. The glass was chipped, and scored his hand. 'Dammit!'

'Sorry,' Chat apologised. 'This ship isn't exactly new...' She handed him another glass.

'Doesn't matter,' Mandell said dismissively. 'What did you want to see me for?'

'Firstly to pull the police back,' the Doctor told him. 'You seem to have a problem with the right hand not knowing what the left is doing.'

'I'll see what can be done, but you must understand that our part in this is strictly unofficial.'

Jack grinned sourly; he could guess what that meant.

'I also want to know how aware you were that certain members of your Thor Facility's staff are synthesising vraxoin.'

'None of us knew that,' Mandell answered, a little too quickly for Jack's liking. He was enough of a good liar to recognise the ability in others. This Niccolo Mandell was a smooth piece of work, and no mistake. 'The scientist in question is currently being hunted by both SID and the local police force. The stock of vraxoin has been destroyed, of course.'

The Doctor nodded slowly. 'As you say... Then I only have one last question: exactly where on Elchur do we take this cylinder once we have it? You'll excuse me if I'm too cynical to hand it to you.'

Mandell shook his head, smiling. 'Perfectly understandable. We're setting up a meeting with the Veltrochni on Elchur near the old town. You can check that with them, if you have the means. If you prefer to hand the cylinder directly to their Ambassador, that's fine by me.'

'That is exactly what I intend to do,' the Doctor promised. 'That's all my concerns. We'll let you know when we're on our way.'

'The frequency on which to contact us is in the datapad.'

'Indeed. I wish I could say it's been a pleasure, but...'

'But it's been business,' Mandell said understandingly. 'Don't worry, I'm not offended.'

The Doctor showed the three SID men out.

Frobisher hadn't been impressed by Mandell's answers either. He shifted from being a floor panel back into penguin form, as the Doctor and the others came back in. Jack stuck his head through into the flight deck. 'Monty, get us out of here. Take us back to the Cafe Terrestriale. It should be safe once Mandell pulls the cops off our backs.'

'Just a minute.' The Doctor approached Frobisher.

'I want you to follow Mandell, and keep an eye on him. I think it'd be best if you did some of your shapeshifting jiggery-pokery.'

Shapeshifting could get tiring, and if there was an easier way to do something, Frobisher would rather be counted in to that. 'Aw, do I have to?'

'There aren't too many penguins on this planet, and we don't want to be conspicuous. Unless you have a nostalgic attraction to hanging around police stations.'

'Inconspicuous?' Frobisher eyed the Doctor's garb beadily. He brightened. 'What if I wore a rubber glove on my head? Nobody would recognise me.'

The Doctor paused in thought, but then shook his head. 'All the marigolds I've got are still in the TARDIS, and that's out of our reach. Shapeshifting it is. And, Frobisher, do try to think of something inconspicuous,' he implored.

* * *

Cronan got home understandably late. The cops had already been, leaving warning tape around his apartment door. Cronan was glad for that small mercy – if they'd already been, he wouldn't have to worry about them showing up later.

Someone tutted from a chair in the midst of his wrecked living room. Clothes and belongings had been strewn everywhere by searchers, and Barrand was sitting in the middle of it all.

'You nearly gave me a coronary,' Cronan moaned. 'I thought you were a cop.'

'You may wish I was. Mr Zimmerman is not pleased that you got yourself caught. He doesn't like the idea that you might rat on us. He wants to talk to you.'

Losing made Cronan sulky and rebellious, like many people who never really grew up. 'Maybe I don't want to talk to him.'

Barrand produced a gun, aimed loosely but imperturbably at Cronan's torso. 'As I said, Mr Zimmerman wishes to speak with you.'

Cronan swallowed, both fearful and angry. He'd show them somehow, he was determined, but first he had to stay in one piece, and show respect. 'All right, all right, put him on.'

Barrand touched a control on his wristband, and held it out to Cronan. 'Take this.'

The gun suggested to Cronan that this was an order, not an offer. Reluctantly, he took the wristband, and the room immediately faded around him. Cronan nearly yelped, as he found himself suddenly alone. He couldn't feel the floor under his feet, and had no idea whether he was standing, lying or floating. He couldn't see either; there was neither brightness or darkness, just blindness.

Someone was with him, though; he could hear them

moving around. 'Mr Cronan,' the cultured voice said icily. 'I am so glad you have deigned to join us.'

Cronan tried to turn to face the direction of the voice, but wasn't sure whether he actually moved or not. 'Who are you?'

'I am a business partner, Mr Cronan. One who does not like it when little men interfere with ongoing business.'

'Hey, I'm the one who was interfered with!'

'Yes, your stupidity did rather get in the way. I am talking about your bounty.'

'The bounty? What? On that bastard who –'

'Yes,' Zimmerman snapped. 'I have already invested a great deal in seeing to him. I will notify my people that you will also be paying them. If you interfere again, I will have you removed. From now on you will follow Barrand's instructions to collect the body.'

Frobisher adjusted the set of his tuxedo as he stepped from the cab, and paused to pay the driver. He had kept the penguin colour scheme, as it was something he was proud of; he wore it like a badge of office. This time, though, it was stretched out into a six-foot frame in a suit and tie, with white shirt. He adopted a rather dashing clean-cut face, with blue-grey eyes under straight brows, and let some of his new trimmed hair fall in a little comma over his right eye. That seemed appropriate somehow.

A sardonic expression was placed neatly on his tanned face. Once the cab had disappeared into the night, Frobisher slipped quietly behind a parked flier, out of sight of the security cameras. There, he compressed himself into the shape of a small bat, and fluttered up the outside of the SID building, looking for Niccolo Mandell.

Mandell's office was on the top floor, naturally, and the

windows were sealed so tightly that it was impossible to hear through them. This was frustrating, as Mandell was talking to someone over a communications link. Finding no way to squeeze through and eavesdrop, Frobisher transformed back into a bat for the trip to find the Doctor. He'd try the Cafe Terrestriale first.

Glitz had found the most comfortable seat in Jack's Cafe. Actually, it was just one of many seats around the room that doubled as a club from the Victorian era of Ancient England, but it felt sufficiently comfortable to him. It even smelled of real leather. It had been a long day, and his feet hurt. It was never very easy being the sort of person who was alternately either sneaking around or on the run.

The others had all gone off on their allotted tasks, sent out to pick up bits and pieces that the Doctor wanted, while he had locked himself in the *Nosferatu* to plan something or other. Glitz wasn't so sure about that; a right bunch of schemers the Time Lords were, and usually nothing good came of it.

He settled for wondering what Chat had meant by the remark that she worried about him. She obviously didn't think he was a screed like Dibber... The alternative seemed to so fantastical as to be impossible. Could it be that she was actually attracted to him? Half of Glitz was afraid to think that, lest it prove untrue and let him down. The other half was more open-minded. Stranger things had happened, he reminded himself. After all, had he not got notorious charm when it came to females of a certain age?

Chat wasn't of that age, though, and his charm for the rest of the gender was rather less notorious. He was supposed to chase them, not the other way around. He didn't even know how to *be* an object of affection.

* * *

In low orbit, Sha'ol and Karthakh's gunship was still circling Vandor Prime. If anyone could have tracked it, they would have found that it was keeping pace with the Thor asteroid, but far further out in orbit.

Inside, Karthakh was sleeping in one of the two small cabins. The Doctor's TARDIS was in the other. Sha'ol sat in the helm alcove of the gunship, trusting the automatics to handle the current flight. Disengaged from immediate action, his thoughts could travel along well-worn paths.

He had heard tales from many cultures, of orphaned offspring raised in the wild by other creatures, as if they were members of that other species. The orphans were more fortunate than him, he thought. They would never know what they were missing from their lives. Sha'ol had no such blissful ignorance. His eyes could turn inward, recalling the memories of generations past as if they were his own.

On these long journeys, he could relive the lives and times of ancestors he had never met. He hadn't lived through those times in which the galaxy had changed, but remembered having done so. Though he doubted Karthakh realised it, Sha'ol had perfectly clear memories of the destruction of his people.

Vibrant energy slicing deeply into planetary crusts and triggering massive quakes and volcanic eruptions. Searing heat shaving off long slivers of terullian from the hulls of Stormblades. Damaged Tzun ships collapsing in upon themselves as their graviton generators went critical. Wavefronts of plasma racing across cityscapes, causing buildings to explode into dust, and citizens to vanish like shadows.

If he ever slept, these would be what humans called nightmares, but he was engineered not to sleep; that particular necessity had been designed out of his branch of the Tzun, to make them better pilots.

Sha'ol responded to the buzz from the communications system.

'Yes?'

'Sha'ol?'

'Reno,' the Tzun replied, recognising the voice. He remembered everyone he met, of course. Another feature that had been programmed into him.

'You still looking for that penguin?'

'Yes.' Sha'ol touched a control to sound a wake-up signal in the cabin. 'You have him?'

'He's at the Cafe Terrestriale now.'

'Excellent.' They could now track him, and safeguard their ability to follow the Doctor in case Mandell double-crossed them.

'There's something else. Another bounty on the Doctor. Ten million credit-bars. Every gunslinger on VP will be on their way here.'

Sha'ol considered. This was a nuisance. He could hear Karthakh emerge from the cabin. 'Is the Doctor at the same location?'

'Not that I know of,' Reno's voice answered.

A human might have nodded slowly, but Sha'ol was perfectly still. 'For your usual fee, we would prefer you to pass on the word that he is there.'

'If you say so,' Reno agreed. 'The usual fee.' The channel went dead.

'Is that wise?' Karthakh asked.

'If there are many other hunters, it would be to our advantage to thin their ranks. Prepare yourself.' Sha'ol turned back to the flight console. 'The others may need some encouragement to leave the Doctor to us.'

Slowly, the gunship began to fall out of orbit, heading for the Jewelled City.

Chapter Thirteen

Heera the Drahvin dismounted from her skybike on the roof of the Cafe Terrestriale, and checked her laser rifle and chainsword. This was where the prey was, according to Reno. She had no idea who the male in question really was, but for ten million she didn't care. All that mattered was that his death would make her rich.

She found a broken window, and slipped into the complex.

Braunschweiger, one of the few Taran androids to have won their freedom, walked around the mezzanine level overlooking the main dining piazza. Any other being might have hoped that nobody would notice the combined automatic shotgun and microgrenade launcher under his leather jacket, but this thought never occurred to him. Anybody who got in his way was dead, and that was the end of it.

Emotionlessly, he scanned the piazza for any sign of the humanoid physiognomy he had memorised from Reno's information. There were several different buildings for him to check, which might take some time, but Braunschweiger was nothing if not thorough, and he was hardly likely to get tired.

He did get occasional physical malfunctions, and required periodic upgrades, though. That was one disadvantage to freedom – it was necessary to pay for repairs and upgrades. Now he was a servant to economics rather than a living master.

He didn't feel any anger about that, but he didn't feel anything about anything. It was simply the way things were.

Sha'ol consulted the charts that were logged in the gunship's navigational computer. A complete guide to Vandor Prime's surface was included with the data banks, since this vessel belonged to a security force that might be needed anywhere in the system.

He had programmed the autopilot to take the ship to the Cafe Terrestriale. Normally Sha'ol had no truck with such devices as autopilots, but in this instance it was proving quite useful.

There was a landing area on the complex's roof, and Sha'ol saw a skybike there, which could hardly belong legitimately. Evidently at least one hunter had taken the bait.

As the gunship landed on the roof, Karthakh picked up his KEM rifle, and tossed the disruptor to Sha'ol. 'It is time.'

Sha'ol nodded, and input a last few commands into the autopilot. Then he removed a small panel from the console, and lifted the disruptor.

Saldan, a local human bounty hunter, was scouting the Cafe Terrestriale more subtly. He had stuck a cheroot in the corner of his mouth, and sat in on a card game in the casino. From his seat, his permanently narrowed eyes had a good view of the main piazza outside.

It didn't take the dusty human too long to notice that he was not alone in the Cafe. Of course, there were plenty of diners, tourists and sundry others, but he was the first to notice another bounty hunter: specifically, Marlock the Keratian. The dapper black-clad rival was in a seat on the far side, watching everything hawkishly.

So what was he going to do? Offer Marlock a deal to split the reward? Or blow away his rival before the latter knew that he wasn't the only hunter on the trail?

It was the screams of startled patrons that first alerted Heera to the situation. People were running out of the casino, and there was a series of gunshots. She wondered what was happening, and then noticed Saldan walk back out, trying to look inconspicuous.

'What the hell was that?' Frobisher yelled.

'Nothing good,' Glitz answered. 'That was blaster fire.' He wasn't exactly keen on going to investigate, but if there was danger heading their way, Glitz wanted to know about it in time to escape. He dashed out of the Victorian club, and along the short alleyway that emerged between the casino and the western saloon. People were screaming and milling around in confusion. Glitz was pretty confused too.

There was something familiar about the woman who was approaching. She was statuesque, blonde, with a sensor over one eye. Heera? he thought. She was a bounty hunter...

Braunschweiger caught movement on the far side of the piazza; his database identified the woman as Heera, a rival bounty hunter. Logic suggested that to ensure he alone won the reward, it would be necessary to stop her finding the target first.

Abandoning any attempt at concealment, Braunschweiger cocked the microgrenade launcher and aimed one-handed.

Glitz dived for cover as the air in the Cafe Terrestriale's mezzanine exploded into Technicolor blaster fire and quadrophonic screaming. It was difficult to tell what was the terrified yelling and what was the noise of energy weapons and stun grenades going off. Glitz knew it was a sign that, in the words of the 20th-century philosopher, everything was going straight to hell.

An explosion blew Heera off her feet, and Glitz wondered where the shot had come from. She scrambled for cover, firing up at the mezzanine opposite.

Glitz decided that discretion was definitely the better part of valour, and looked for a way out. Any way out would do; even a cell in the local rehab centre would be better than being caught in a full-scale battle.

Frobisher emerged from the alley just in time to see a ruffian with a blaster taking aim at his head. He barely had time to form a hole in his chest for the shot to go safely through. While the ruffian tried to figure out how his shot had hit the wall, Frobisher floored him with a double-sized boxing glove that had suddenly grown from one flipper.

'Glitz!'

'Over here!' Glitz waved him over from behind a juke box, and Frobisher took a flying leap towards it, narrowly avoiding a stream of gunfire from somewhere in the crowd.

Sha'ol scanned the mêlée quickly, looking for any of the Doctor's group. The avian was the easiest to find, though a one-eyed Drahvin was about take a chainsword to him from behind. Sha'ol gunned her down with a pinpoint disruptor shot. In the time it took for the surprised avian to turn to see the fallen body, Sha'ol switched the disruptor to a stun setting and shot him too.

The avian staggered but didn't fall, which was most

unusual. Noting the lesser effect of the disruptor on this species, Sha'ol fired again. This time the avian *did* fall.

The other bounty hunters then ignored the creature, assuming it was dead.

Glitz saw Frobisher fall, and heard the distinctive whine of an ultrasonic disruptor.

The automatic shotgun and microgrenade launcher were still firing from the mezzanine, and a bulky male figure was trying to make his way downstairs while blazing away at anyone who even looked like they might get in his way.

Without warning, a polycarbide dart impaled the gunman, but this didn't seem to impede him much. There was a blurring, as if something made of glass or water was moving by, and a second dart speared the android. This dart was explosive-tipped, and the shooter's torso exploded into smoking fragments.

Glitz could always try to rescue Frobisher, but he looked dead anyway, and it wouldn't do anyone any good if they both got killed. He ran for the door instead, his momentary guilt having passed quite efficiently. There was no sense in rescuing a corpse, let alone getting himself killed attempting to do so.

It was not mere cowardice. Glitz had had few friends, but he'd been loyal to those few, as much as was practical. He'd get even with Frobie's killers, but couldn't do that if he too was dead.

Everyone threw themselves to the floor as the crystal roof exploded inward. A security gunship lowered itself into the piazza, automated turrets picking off anyone who was armed. Then a whine took away Glitz's consciousness.

Karthakh surveyed the damage with interest as he lifted the

unconscious Glitz and carried him over to the gunship. Sha'ol had brought it down by remote control, and was now giving a speech into one of the security cameras.

By the time Karthakh had secured the prisoners in the ship, Sha'ol was finished, and joined him aboard.

Pleased with the way things had gone, Karthakh sat back to enjoy the flight as Sha'ol took the ship back out into space.

Jack shook his head slowly, trying to work out what had happened to his beautiful monument to getting rich quick. All he could manage in terms of speech was a little squeak in the back of his throat, but Chat imagined he felt much the same as she did about Glitz's absence.

He was gone, but not among the dead. She hadn't had to worry long about what had happened to him, for as soon as the Doctor returned he'd found that the security system had recorded everything. She had expected to see a police raid, or something of the sort, but it was quite a surprise when the culprits announced themselves.

It was a S'Raph Tzun who stood looking up at the monitor. 'The security system of this complex remains functional, and should allow you to view what has occurred here. It is reasonable to assume that the Time Lord known as the Doctor will have the opportunity to view this recording. That being the case, he should know that we have taken custody of his avian companion and his associate. They will not be released until the Doctor turns himself over to us when his mission is completed.'

The image faded. Chat looked over at the Doctor; swap him for Glitz... And surely Dibber must feel the same way. 'Well, Doctor. What now?'

The Doctor frowned. 'They have Frobisher and Glitz. I

180

should have dealt with them before… I'll have to turn myself over,' he decided. 'All we have to do is –'

'No way,' Jack said suddenly. He looked up, eyes burning. 'They didn't threaten to kill Glitz or Frobisher. I say we do the job first, either way.'

Chat supposed that was reasonable. These bounty hunters obviously knew about the arrangement with Mandell, so perhaps they had a stake in it. One them was a Veltrochni, after all… 'All right. How? Without Frobisher –'

'Frobisher's skills would be a bonus,' the Doctor said, 'but not actually essential. I imagine you didn't have a Whifferdill handy when you stole the cylinder originally.'

'Hardly,' Liang answered. 'Oskar was a master of disguise. The best. And, of course, we had a couple of Veltrochni holosuits.'

The Doctor looked at him. 'Do you still have them?'

'One of them's still working,' Monty answered. 'It's back at the garage.'

'Then we can do this without Frobisher,' the Doctor reassured them. 'It's lucky for Mandell that I turned up,' the Doctor said rather grandly. 'The defences guarding this cylinder are mostly concerned with time.'

Monty frowned. 'You mean time-locks? Things that don't operate until a specific hour? That's not a problem –'

'If only it were so easy.' The Doctor let out a long breath, and Chat got the impression that he was quite impressed by the problems he had uncovered. Admiring of them, even. 'The entire asteroid is phase-shifted one hour into the future for a start.'

'So?'

The Doctor gave him a look. 'So, it's rather difficult to break into a place that isn't there yet!'

'But you got in to case the joint,' Jack pointed out.

'Yes, through the fortified main entrance. Storming it's out of the question, and although we can slip in that way, we'd never get the, er, loot, out. Worse still, the vault is phase-shifted as well. One day into the past.'

'So you can't get in, because it's been and gone?' Chat ventured, getting the hang of this temporal malarkey.

'Precisely,' the Doctor agreed. 'But it also means that even if you can steal the thing, then the guards will be waiting for you at the gate, to get you for what they already know you're going to do yesterday!'

'That's stupid,' Jack protested.

'That's temporal mechanics,' the Doctor corrected him severely. He thrust his hands into his pockets, and thought for a moment. 'Stupid it may be,' he admitted, 'but it's also very effective.'

'But you're a Time Lord,' Jack said pointedly. 'Isn't this sort of thing exactly your bag?'

The Doctor winced at this sort of colloquialism. 'My "bag," as you put it, is saving lives.'

'That's OK, then,' Jack agreed. 'Since if you don't sort out these time barriers we're all dead.'

'Your logic has its point,' the Doctor admitted. 'Which is why I've done a few calculations, and – being something of an expert in these matters – come up with something we can use…'

Karthakh checked on the prisoners. They would be comatose for hours. 'What now?' he asked his partner.

'Now we make for Elchur. That is where Mandell is to meet with the Doctor and deliver him to us. The journey will be short –' The Tzun fell silent as a beeping emanated from the console. 'Strange… we are being approached by another vessel.'

'Evade them,' Karthakh said irritably. He was in no mood to have their plans disturbed so quickly. This hunt would make them so rich he need never track beings for money again. It would be good to stop.

'Naturally. I am attempting to do so, but there is a tractor beam locked on to us.'

Karthakh growled, as the forward gantries of an enormous ship passed around the gunship. 'They are docking.'

Karthakh consulted the gunship's onboard sensors. 'I'm reading several lifeforms in their airlock…' He let out a gasp of surprise. 'They are Ogrons.'

'Ogrons?' Sha'ol echoed. He hesitated. 'Interesting. They would not normally operate without the consent of an employer…'

Karthakh was less impressed by the Ogrons' enterprise; they were a hostile force to be repulsed. 'These primitive creatures are an obstruction.' He picked up his KEM rifle. 'I'll go and kill them, and be right back.'

'Stop,' Sha'ol commanded. Karthakh didn't take well to orders, but Sha'ol usually knew what he was talking about. 'This turn of events may offer a minor strategic advantage. We know the Doctor has acquired the backing of an unknown number of associates. It would be prudent for us to have reinforcements also.'

'These Ogrons?' Karthakh growled deep in his chest. The Veltrochni looked after their own; they didn't run squealing for help from dirt-grubbing primitives.

'The Ogrons are a race of mercenaries,' Sha'ol said. 'They will be acquainted with such procedures.'

'You cannot trust a species which fights for anyone who

will feed them. They do not honour the contract as we would; if someone offers them more, they will change sides. They are no better than guard animals.'

Sha'ol thought for a moment. 'Not if they fear the consequences.'

Gorrak was trying to ignore the constant rumbling complaints of the matriarch. Not enough food, she moaned; the gravity was all wrong; the air tasted foul; there was no stone here… It never ended.

Perhaps, he thought hopefully, the new prisoners might appease her. It had been many years since she had killed an enemy, so maybe that was what was making her so sour.

They were an odd group, even by Gorrak's standards. The little grey one was a type of alien he didn't recognise, but the big one was a Veltrochni. They were very dangerous, he recalled from his time as a mercenary. There was also a human and a bird of some kind, who were both stunned.

'You are the leader?' the little grey prisoner asked.

Gorrak laughed at his insolence. 'I big boss.'

'I am Sha'ol of the Tzun Confederacy. This is my partner Karthakh. We have a proposition for you.'

Gorrak frowned. How come the prisoners were making him offers? Behind him, he could hear the matriarch laugh. 'A good prisoner this. Funny.' Gorrak ignored her and, stumbling over the word, said, 'Proposition?'

'You and we both work for hire. We are currently on a commissioned job, and will share the payment with you if you help us.'

'Help?' The thought of the reward was interesting, but Gorrak had vowed to keep his clan free.

'Allow us to travel on this ship, and use it as a base. We may require some of your... men, but there will be profit in it for you.'

'This one has ore,' the matriarch interrupted. 'You should not listen to him.'

'Silence!' Gorrak roared. That was the decider: if the matriarch didn't want the agreement, then he did. 'I agree.'

The matriarch snorted. 'You have no stone in your heart.'

Karthakh suddenly reached out and lifted Gorrak clear off the ground by his shoulders. His claws dug in to the Ogron skin. 'One thing, Ogron. Do not cross us.' He dropped Gorrak.

'I understand. Not cross partners.' Yet, Gorrak told himself. Not until after he got over the idea that anyone could lift him like that...

Monty had gone to get the holosuit, while the others relaxed in Jack's mercifully undamaged private apartments. Jack himself badly needed a dose of Rush to cheer himself up if he was to be any good to the others during the heist. He stiffened with an oddly pained grin, as the Rush took effect.

'See, Doc, this is my favourite part of these things.' He knew the Doctor would be surprised, and wasn't disappointed. 'It's the anticipation, you see. Most people get bored and impatient waiting around, but me... This is like smelling the cooking from the kitchen, and knowing there's something good on the way, but not quite what. Like Christmas Eve.'

'The difference being that you don't go risking your life opening Christmas presents or eating out.'

Chance shook his head. 'Nah, Doc. Once something's over, it's over. But before...? Ah, that's where the excitement is.' He searched his mind for a better example. 'Springtime, yeah? Springtime on old Earth. The air's filled with bees; the sun's heating up, the sap's flowing... But there isn't quite a new bloom yet. You're just looking for it, and encouraging it, and dying to see what soft colour it'll be. That's the best bit.'

'This isn't a game, Chance,' the Doctor snapped severely. 'Nor is it a pastoral scene. You will be risking your life out there. Aren't you just a little afraid?'

Chance barked a laugh. 'Afraid? Hah! Any fear comes near me, it gets a swift kick in the nuts.' He blinked a couple of times, remembering who he was talking with. 'Well yeah, I am in a way, but it's part of the fun.'

'Fun?' the Doctor echoed disbelievingly, eyes wide. 'Fun? Fear is a defence mechanism, not a sideshow.'

Chance shrugged. 'Yeah, but it's life. If you ain't afraid of dying, then how do you value living? At least if you're scared, you know that you're alive; you know your life means something. You know it has value. I mean, that's why people go to fright nights in the amusement blocks.'

'And why you commit crimes?'

'Well,' grinned Chance, 'the money comes in handy too.'

Glitz's head felt like it was about to burst. For some reason, he was also bumping around in mid-air, his stomach resting on some sort of uncomfortable rock. He opened his eyes slowly, trying not to throw up.

He found that he had been slung over the shoulder of someone very large who was dressed in a rough uniform and leather armour. His carrier dropped him to his feet once it became clear that Glitz was awake. Glitz looked up into the face of his towering captor, and was both surprised and vaguely insulted.

It was an Ogron. How the hell had *he* been captured by someone as thick as an Ogron? They were a species who made Dibber look like some kind of genius. 'All right,' he snapped. 'I can walk, you know.' He turned around, wondering whether he was still in the city.

It was obvious that he was not. From the constant engine noise, he seemed to be aboard a ship of some kind. It didn't look much like a ship – more like a cross between a bombed-out factory and a zoo. Semi-functional machinery was sprawled throughout the whole area, while some Ogron pups watched curiously from amidst them.

Several other Ogrons were escorting the captives; one of them had Frobisher in some sort of net. 'Look at this,' Frobisher called out to Glitz. 'These goons have got no regard for other people. I mean, do I look like a fish? No, but they put me in this net anyway.'

'No talk,' Frobisher's captor grunted, and slapped the penguin across the head.

'I'll peck your eye out in a minute,' Frobisher warned.

'Walk.' A hairy Ogron hand shoved Glitz forward. As the little group made their way along, Glitz saw that it was some kind of colony ship. A network of cryogenic chambers had been filled with lice-ridden bedding for an Ogron clan, and there was no sign of the original inhabitants. Sweaty Ogrons were busy at menial tasks in the workshops, mainly hammering out metal plates and suchlike, either for the ship or into pieces of armour.

Eventually they reached a set of disused officers' cabins. An Ogron unlocked one, and Glitz immediately pulled the door open. 'After you,' he offered cheerily. Blankly, the Ogrons marched inside, and Glitz slammed the door on them. Shaking his head at how stupid the big creatures were, he turned to leave, and walked straight into a figure that was – if anything – even larger.

This one grabbed his shirt in one massive clawed fist and

lifted him bodily off the ground until they were at eye level. 'You are their prisoner,' the Veltrochni hissed. 'Do not presume everyone on this ship is as primitive as these Ogrons.'

'Er, look,' Glitz began, 'maybe we can make a deal...' Every cell in his body was screaming at him to run, but he couldn't while his feet weren't even touching the floor.

'No deals. You will stay where we put you.' The Veltrochni opened the cabin door with his free hand, allowing the Ogrons out. Then he shoved Glitz inside. 'Do not interfere with our mission, and you may live to tell this tale.'

Chapter Fourteen

The Thor asteroid was now moving gently over arctic tundra. Monty supposed that Frobisher might have felt quite at home here.

'Now,' the Doctor asked from the shuttle's co-pilot seat beside him, 'is everybody absolutely sure of where they have to be and what they have to do?'

'We have done this sort of thing before, Doc,' Jack said drily.

'Don't worry,' Dibber said over the communications relay. 'I've got it all straight.'

'Good.'

Getting aboard the asteroid wasn't difficult. The security staff recognised the Doctor as Professor Hoffman, and had been expecting him to return. They hadn't expected him to return with Mandell, however.

'These are some of the Professor's assistants,' Mandell told the Director of the facility. He indicated Monty and Chat. 'They'll be helping him service the time dams.'

'Right, sir,' the Director agreed readily. This was unusual, but he wasn't going to question the director of SID, or pass up the chance to have his equipment checked over by a real expert in the field.

Mandell turned to the Doctor. 'You know the way, I believe?'

'I do indeed. With your permission, Director?'

'Go ahead, please.'

Mandell hesitated. 'Actually, this might be interesting... I don't believe I've seen the workings of a time dam before. I'll accompany you.' The Director's smile froze. Like most people on the facility, he had his own extracurricular hobbies which he'd rather his boss didn't find out about. True, it was nothing as bad as what Cronan had been doing, but all the same...

'Then I'll be getting back to work,' the Director said. 'If you'll excuse me?'

'Don't let me detain you,' Mandell agreed. The Doctor and Mandell led the two new assistants out of the docking bay.

'Nicely done,' Monty said admiringly. Even in a career as long as his, he rarely saw this type of sheer bravado.

'Thanks,' Liang said from inside the holographic image of Mandell. To be honest, Monty was surprised the holosuit still worked after all this time, especially after the tweaking it needed to keep the energy emissions low enough to not trigger the facility's alarms.

Jack hated paperwork. Whether it was the Cafe's accounts – and there was work of fiction second to none – or working out positions on a chart, like now. 'Dammit,' he muttered, 'this is ridiculous.'

'But we are in the right place, yeah?' Dibber asked worriedly. Dibber was flying the *Nosferatu*, while Jack did the fiddly calculations. Even though most of the actual work had been done by the Doctor the previous night, it was still a difficult set of numbers for Jack to wrap his head around. He was a man of action – a smuggler and rogue – not a bloody cartographer.

'Absolutely,' he said, with no real idea at all. As far as his calculations showed, the ship was indeed in the right place.

He just didn't believe for a minute that those calculations were right. He just wasn't enough of a nerd to be good with numbers.

They were out in space some distance from Vandor Prime. Halfway to the middle moon, in fact, and Jack couldn't see why. 'What does he expect us to do out here?'

'Collect the loot,' Dibber said simply. 'That's what he said.'

'He also said he's nine hundred years old and that didn't look too true either.'

'He could be. He *is* a Time Lord.'

'And that's supposed to make me feel better? Knowing that he's a sneaky bastard by breeding?' No wonder Glitz so despaired of training Dibber up properly. 'I wouldn't be surprised if he didn't just send us here out of the way so he could do a runner with the loot himself.'

Dibber shook his head. 'The Doctor isn't that sort of guy. I mean, he's honest, like, but apart from that, he didn't let us down when things got tough.'

'I'll withhold judgement on that one. It's my religion: I'm a devout cynic.' He looked at the ship's chronometer. 'I just hope this Time Lord of yours can tell time.'

The time dams were undeniably impressive, Chat thought, glancing at her watch. They had exactly ten minutes, which the Doctor had said was more than enough for what they had to do. That made Chat just as uncomfortable as wondering what Glitz was going through; even if they were ready early, they had to wait the rest of the ten minutes. As a professional thief, Chat knew that waiting around a crime scene was the worst thing one could do.

Liang pointed to the console that was built into the largest of the time dams. 'That one, Doctor,' he instructed. Chat still wasn't sure why the Doctor had instructed Liang to tell him what to interfere with. It made no sense at all.

All the same, the Doctor seemed to know what he was doing. 'Right, Monty. When I tell you, place the connector just there.' He pointed with a finger. 'Then divert the control system power flow.'

'And that will do what, exactly?'

'Stop me from being fried when I pull out the main phase polarisers and put them back in the wrong order.'

'Right…' Monty agreed nervously. 'Now I remember why I retired. I've never seen technology like this.'

'I'd be very surprised if you had,' the Doctor said darkly. 'It's not exactly local. In fact it's more advanced than should be available to your people yet. Chat, keep an eye out for guards. The alarms may go off when this is done, but it should take them a few minutes to work out where the trouble is.' Chat nodded, stepping back a little to get a clearer view of the rotunda's doors.

'I still don't see why we don't just break into the vault,' Monty whispered.

'Because we'd need a time bridge for that, and I don't have either the equipment or the power available,' the Doctor answered. 'Now concentrate on what you're doing; if you reroute the power supply incorrectly, we will be barbecued.'

'That reminds me, I didn't catch breakfast today…'

'Now! Now!' There was a sudden spark, and Monty quickly started realigning optronic paths and circuits. Meanwhile, the Doctor took a deep breath and snatched the silvered triangular polarisers out of the time dam one by one. He just pulled the last one free before a blue wreath of energy slithered across the gap in which his hand had been inserted.

'I said concentrate, Monty! This isn't a flier engine.'

'Sorry, Doctor,' Monty stammered, pale and sweating. 'It just took me by surprise, that's all.'

'Then remember to expect it this time. Switch the power off. Now that we've bypassed the main supply, it shouldn't show on any security or diagnostic circuits.'

Chat listened especially alertly as Monty did so, but heard no alarms even from elsewhere in the facility. 'Good,' the Doctor muttered. 'Now…' He slotted the polarisers back into the time dam, but in a very different order from which he had removed them. He was left with a spare circuit in his hand. After a moment's thought, he slipped it into a pocket. 'All right, switch the power back.'

Monty did as he was told, and it seemed to Chat that nothing had happened. 'What's happening now?'

'Nothing yet,' the Doctor told her. 'Except that I am about to do something very very clever,' he added proudly. He fitted the control panel back on top of the exposed workings. Liang stepped forward to help, pounding it down with his fist. The panel's fascia cracked slightly, and a few spots of blood smeared across it.

The Doctor operated the controls quickly. 'Time?'

'Fourteen twenty-nine and… forty-eight seconds.'

'Just right…' The Doctor counted down slowly, and stabbed at the 'enter' key.

Which was when the alarms went off.

The officer up in the Security centre did a swift double-take as the vault monitors went red. The facility's prize possession which had been kept under such tight guard just wasn't there any more.

At first he thought it must be a monitor malfunction, but

then alarms started sounding from the time dams as well. Something was very wrong.

'Should be... now,' Jack said. 'But I don't see –'

There was a thud from the cargo hold. Jack and Dibber exchanged looks, and nearly bumped heads as they tried to leave the flight deck at the same time. 'Watch it,' Dibber muttered.

They hurried through the crew room and along the short corridor to the cargo hold. There, lying on a pile of tarpaulins, was the cylinder that Jack remembered so well from ten years ago. Disbelievingly, he picked it up. He lifted it gently, half afraid that it would fade away like a dream. In fact, he told himself, he must be dreaming.

'Is that...?' Dibber asked.

'Yes. Somehow it is. Get the ship turned round, and head for the rendezvous.' Dibber took a last look at the cylinder, and headed back to the flight deck. Jack was still mesmerised. How had the Doctor managed this? Maybe he stole it on his scouting trip... But then why go back? It could be a fake, but it was exactly as Jack remembered: impervious and inscrutable.

'I bet this one wasn't done with mirrors.'

'What the hell?' Monty yelped as the alarms went off.

'That's good news, Monty,' the Doctor said. 'It means it worked. Come on.' He started back for the doors.

'Worked? What worked?'

'Cheer up,' the Doctor said encouragingly. 'We've just stolen the most securely guarded object on your planet. It's now in the *Nosferatu*.'

'How?'

'I reversed the effect of the time field in the vault, so that it would shift the phase there to real time. In conjunction with the time field around the asteroid, it's equivalent to sending the cylinder one hour into the past.'

'But you said it was brought into real time...'

'Exactly, but one hour away in the planet's orbit and rotation. Which is precisely where Jack and Dibber are with the *Nosferatu*. Now we just have to meet up with them again.'

They bolted down the central stairwell, knowing that the lifts would be immobilised when the alarms went off.

'This way,' the Doctor said, leading the group down a set of narrow corridors. A few people passed them, milling around, but no one would stop the SID director, and the security recordings hadn't been checked yet.

Monty started the shuttle's engines even before taking his seat, while the others followed him across the docking bay. Liang knew this was the dangerous part. It didn't matter whether the guards or staff knew what had happened yet, but they would certainly try to stop anyone from leaving, on the general principle that any saboteur or thief would be trying to get away.

He was right: four guards ran into in the docking bay, taking cover behind the scattered crates. Monty opened fire from the shuttle's hatch, the rounds punching through the crates. The Doctor had known better than to prohibit the ue of guns, but he had extracted promises from everyone that they would be set on stun only. A returned shot caught his side, and he fell back into the airlock, the blaster dropping from his hand, and landing on a bench near Liang.

Liang gave covering fire as the Doctor, heedless of the shots buzzing around him, dashed up the staircase to the hatch, and dragged Monty into the ship, Chat following behind. Liang's gun ran dry, and he realised that he didn't even know how long it been since he recharged it. Liang leapt for the bench, shots singing through the air, and landed on the nearest end. The bench tilted like a seesaw, the far end rising and tossing the blaster into the air towards him. He caught it one-handed as he rolled behind the bench, and fired at the nearest guard.

The powerful energy bolt passed through the crate with little resistance, and blew the man across the floor. If he screamed in pain, it was muffled by a faint tinkling sound behind Liang. Something bit hard into Liang's back, and he was pitched forward, the stink of his own scorched flesh stinging the air. He started to turn, firing at another guard. The guard was caught in the shoulder and blown sideways.

The Doctor swung himself round the flight console as Monty collapsed into a chair and Chat hovered nervously behind them. Monty raised his right arm slightly, and winced. A charred trough had been gouged from his side, and a sliver of white rib showed at the deepest part. The wound had self-cauterised, however, and the rib was clearly still intact.

'You'll be all right, there's no bleeding.'

'It's bleedin' painful, though,' Monty said through gritted teeth. The Doctor had grabbed a medical kit from the small bay at the back of the flight deck, and gave him a hefty dose of painkillers. Monty trusted him to get the right mixture – you didn't live long in their chosen line of work without learning something about patching up the inevitable wounds that came with the job.

'My brother!' Chat turned back for the hatch, and the Doctor grabbed her before she could get there.

'Woah!' Liang yelled involuntarily, as he tumbled in through the airlock. The hatch bumped his ankle as it closed. The Doctor shoved the throttle to full without even sitting down, and the shuttle leapt free of the asteroid.

Mandell's lunch was interrupted by Wei's call. Bloody typical, he thought. 'It's happened,' Wei said excitedly.

'The theft?'

'It's gone. Somehow they did it.'

Mandell slapped a fist into his palm. 'Wonderful! Get the ship ready.'

'Yes, *sifu*.' Mandell changed the frequencies happily, and put a call through unofficial channels to the Veltrochni Dragon *Zathakh*. Brokhal's fierce features appeared almost at once, with little of the usual formal delays. 'Yes, *Iirdmon*?'

'Madam Ambassador,' he said smoothly. 'I'm pleased to inform you that your property will be returned to you by dawn. If you'll meet the operatives on Elchur, they'll deliver it personally.'

'My ship cannot reach Elchur by dawn. However, I will despatch the *Thazrakh* to meet you. You will return our property to Pack-Leader Hyskanth.'

Whatever, Mandell thought. 'As you wish, Madam Ambassador.'

The shuttle and the *Nosferatu* touched down next to each other in a grain field far from the city. Once they had retrieved the real – and highly indignant – Professor Hoffman from his cell and deposited him safely in the shuttle, everyone boarded the *Nosferatu*. It blasted off, watched only by some apparently uninterested farmers.

Jack, Dibber, Liang, Chat and Monty all hugged each other

in turn, exchanging stories of their part in the proceedings.

'I don't know how you did it, Doc,' Jack began, 'but it almost made up for the damage to my place. Almost,' he repeated, just in case anybody thought he was getting mushy on them. 'Now we just have to decide what to do with this thing.'

'We do exactly what we set out to do,' the Doctor told him bluntly. 'Return it to the Veltrochni.'

'Are you out of your skull, Doc?' Jack protested. 'If this thing's valuable enough for the Veltrochni to go to war over, it must be worth... I can't even imagine how much it must be worth on the open market. But we've got to find out.'

'No, Chance,' the Doctor snapped. 'That cylinder is the only thing that can keep this war from breaking out. I don't believe that even you would put mere profit above the lives of millions of people.'

Chance started to contradict him; money was money. It couldn't buy happiness, but Jack had found that he could sure as hell rent it for a while. Even so... 'Not millions, no.'

The Doctor took the cylinder gently. 'We'll go to Elchur and hand this over, exactly as Mandell said.'

Chat frowned. 'But what about Glitz and Frobisher? Shouldn't we try to get them away from those bounty hunters?'

The Doctor shook his head. 'Those two are after me. So long as I'm still free, Glitz and Frobisher are perfectly safe. They can't kill them, or else what would they have to draw me in with? At least this way they're also safe from the police, and whatever scheme Mandell is planning.'

'What makes you think he's planning a scheme?' Liang asked.

'Wouldn't you be if you were him?'

Chapter Fifteen

Elchur had been abandoned for centuries. If life had ever attempted to crawl out from the murky depths, it had long since returned to the small equatorial ocean. The land was mostly weathered rock, scoured by dust storms.

The planet used to be an agrarian colony until biochemical weapons in some ancient war or other had sterilised the surface. Some of the original thick prefab blockhouses still remained, empty shells clinging to the foothills in the rocky desert.

Most of the buildings were thick-walled utilitarian bunkers, whitewashed against the heat. At one end of the street, a two-storey building was garbed in long-dead neon signs.

The hot dry wind scraped Mandell's face, but he ignored it, because he felt like a man who had just stepped out on to the beach of a new holiday resort: tired from the flight, but looking forward to the great joys this place would bring.

Word of the theft had been put out on the police frequencies, but with no details other than that the suspects had fled in a government shuttle. Luckily, one of the farmers had the sense to report the unusual landings, and now Kala and Jemson stood by as an outraged Professor vented his spleen on anyone around.

'They're madmen,' he raged. 'Sociopaths!'

Kala had had enough of this. 'Professor, were any of these people among them?' She handed him pictures of Chance, the Doctor, Glitz, Monty, Liang, Chat and Dibber.

'Yes, dammit! That's what I've been telling you! It was

them. All of them!' That was all Kala really needed to know, and she tuned out the rest of the Professor's tirade as they walked back to the police flier. 'Call the station house and tell them I want a ship ready to take us. The farmer says they left in a freighter, and I want to be able to follow them as soon as we get a trace on the registry. We can't let them get out of our territory.'

It would take several hours to reach Elchur, even through the convoluted short-cut of hyperspace. Meanwhile, the Doctor was turning the cylinder over in his hands, peering at it closely. 'Now this is interesting,' he breathed. 'When you first stole it, were you told anything about it?'

Jack shook his head. 'Just a valuable relic. Some sort of art form, we thought.' He frowned. 'D'you know what it is?'

'It's some sort of software-definable crystalline structure.'

'Software-definable? You mean it's a piece of technology?'

'Mmm. And very advanced too.' He seemed quite taken with the thing. 'I'd love to know what it's for. It certainly isn't Veltrochni in origin.' He compared it to the circuit he'd taken from the time dams. 'And it's not from the same source as this either.'

'You mean it's something from before their civilisation? Or they stole it from someone else?'

'That is what I must know myself.'

'Must?'

'That's what knowledge is for: to be uncovered and held up to the light. If there's something here that I don't know about, and I know that I don't know it, then I must find out. You know, there's something awfully familiar about it. I'm certain I've seen this type of technology somewhere before. Of course, that's not much help, given that I've seen just about every type of technology somewhere before.'

A Veltrochni Mage-Dragon was already in orbit with wings
fully spread when Mandell's private cruiser arrived. Mandell
hadn't expected any different, of course; the Veltrochni
determination to get the job done made their actions rather
predictable to his intelligence analysts. The ship was
impressive, he had to admit; its wings were beautiful. They
shimmered like the iridescent scales of a fine fish… In a
barrel, he thought, cracking his knuckles.

He hailed the Veltrochni ship. 'I see you arrived before me,'
he lied. 'If you'd care to join me on the surface…'

'No,' a male Veltrochni replied. 'We will await the arrival of
these thieves.' Mandell was quite impressed by the amount
of venom and revulsion that the alien put into that last word.
He resolved to try that himself sometime.

'As you wish. Their ship is old, so it may be some hours
yet.'

'Not that long,' the Doctor's voice broke in over the open
channel. 'We're just here. I presume there's a landing area
somewhere down there?'

Mandell was ecstatic. He must really be on form today…
'I'm sending the co-ordinates now.'

Jack squinted at the bright sunlight, and wished he'd brought
a hat of some kind. He didn't really feel comfortable in this
sort of climate. He was a temperate-zone man all the way,
ever since he was a boy.

The *Nosferatu* had touched down at one end of the small
ruined town, and her crew now waited amidst the bleached
tumbledown walls.

Mandell arrived next, his lander coming down off to one

side, in what used to be some sort of arena. The thieves watched him distrustfully as he approached. He found that vaguely hurtful, even though they were absolutely right. 'I gather you didn't disappoint me?'

'And I hope you're not going to disappoint me. I want my TARDIS back.'

'Naturally. It's in my lander. The Core?'

'The what?' The Doctor was momentarily thrown, but then recovered. 'Oh, this.' He held up the cylinder. 'Core, eh? For what?'

Mandell cursed himself. Not that it mattered; the word could mean nothing to the Doctor. 'For something, I imagine. Please?' He held out his hands.

'I'll give it to the Veltrochni directly,' the Doctor reminded him stubbornly.

'As you wish.' Mandell was feeling generous now that things were going so well. 'Here comes their Pack-Leader now.' He pointed, and the others looked up into the painfully bright blue sky.

A squat and hunched shuttle was descending. Curved pincer-like legs unfolded from it as it settled on to the dust at the other end of town. A ramp opened, and five Veltrochni in full powered armour emerged. The armour enhanced their already powerful build, and made them look positively lethal. Even Mandell was tempted to flinch as their leader reached the middle of the old town's main street. His bodyguards looked around suspiciously.

'You have our property?' Hyskanth said, without preamble.

'Yes.' Mandell waved the Doctor forward, and the Time Lord handed the Core to the Veltrochni.

'Good afternoon, Pack-Leader. I am known as the Doctor, perhaps your people remember me?' Hyskanth merely looked blank. 'You have a kinsman named Karthakh, I understand?'

'That is true,' Hyskanth sneered. 'He is a bounty hunter, hunting for money. Why do you speak of him?'

'Because he's trying to kill me, and I want to know why.'

'You are a thief, are you not?' Hyskanth said dismissively.

Mandell neatly stepped between them, smiling, before the Doctor could go on. 'It's been a pleasure doing business with you, *Chach-to* Hyskanth. I hope we can do so again some time.'

'Do not presume on your luck, *Iirdmon,*' Hyskanth growled. 'You are fortunate to escape a war you cannot win.'

Mandell shrugged. 'Well, it's the taking part that's important, isn't it?' The Veltrochni Pack-Leader merely hissed, and turned away. Mandell watched the aliens walk the first few yards of the distance back to their lander.

Fish in a barrel, he thought again, and raised the large-calibre slugger that had been concealed behind his back. The handgun fired old-fashioned bullets, which the Veltrochni's energy-absorbing armour couldn't protect against.

The Doctor leapt forward, trying to grab hold of Mandell's arm, but was too late. As the first shot boomed, Hyskanth's head burst in a shower of tissue and quills. Mandell put his smoking gun to the Doctor's head. 'Move again and you're dead.'

The other Veltrochni turned back, raising their KEM rifles, but were immediately picked off by head shots from all around. When the last alien fell heavily to the ground, Mandell put away his gun, and delicately retrieved the Core from Hyskanth's dead hands. 'As I said,' Mandell murmured to the late alien, 'it's a pleasure doing business with you.'

The marksmen Mandell had secreted in the abandoned village buildings during his first landing emerged now. They kept their slugrifles trained on the Veltrochni warriors until they were certain that all of them were dead.

'That slaughter was completely needless,' the Doctor exclaimed, outraged. 'You murdered them in cold blood.'

Mandell looked around at the bodies. So some aliens were dead, so what? Better them dead than his life ruined. 'Yes,' he said simply. 'Necessary for business, though. And it gets better too.' He smiled, eyes glinting.

'Better!?' the Doctor exploded. 'Better! And what's "better" about any of this? Is death better than life to you?'

'Well, it gets more practical, at least.' He tossed his empty slugger to Dibber, who caught it reflexively. 'See...' He looked around, as if seeking a prompt from the ether. 'It's like this. Your gang came here to make this private deal with the Veltrochni. Unfortunately, something went wrong.' He shrugged. 'You crossed them, they crossed you, an adder got in the way, whatever. Anyway, you and the Veltrochni fought each other to the proverbial, and indeed clichéd, last man, who then succumbed to his wounds. In the crossfire, the Core was destroyed.'

'And you expect us to go along with that?' Jack demanded. 'I don't think you've thought this through, you two-faced bastard.'

'I imagine,' the Doctor said pointedly, 'that we are to be killed with the Veltrochni's weapons. After which, we'll be found holding those guns of yours, eh, Mandell?' He leaned forward accusingly. Though he always claimed to be a man of peace, he looked to Mandell as if he was ready to do bloody murder. Not with the troops covering him, though.

'Correct. Having conveniently killed each other, while I

make a getaway with my ill-gotten gains.' Mandell nodded to himself. 'You know how it is, Doctor – if you want something done right, kill the witnesses while you're at it, that's what I say.'

'Then at least tell me what the Core is.' The Doctor eyed him dubiously. 'As you are obviously so fond of clichés, you may as well indulge in the one about revealing your master-plan before we die.'

Mandell laughed. 'Don't be too hard on clichés, Doctor – after all, they're why I'm winning. As for your last request…' He beckoned one of the troops to fetch a portable computer, which he set up on a fairly flat chunk of broken wall. The other troops were busy herding the rest of the gang away from the *Nosferatu*. One man laid a KEM rifle beside Mandell, and received a nod of acknowledgement.

Mandell brought up on the computer an image of a small moon. Bio-domes were clustered here and there, and a gaping crater seemed to be so deep that the moon could truly be called hollow. 'This is the shipyard at Teal Alpha,' Mandell said helpfully. The darkness at the heart of the hollow moon was suddenly split by enormous fusion-powered floodlights. In the vast low-gravity space, a number of large forms were stretched out, surrounded by shuttles and work vehicles.

There were three, all in various stages of construction, from the skeletal to one that was complete but for a few open patches in the hull. Their hulls were the shape of straight sword blades, with engines in place of the hilt, and a large nacelle trailing at the end of a ventral boom.

'Tzun Stormblades?' the Doctor asked.

'Not quite.' Mandell was enjoying this. The Time Lords seemed to think they knew everything, and it was certainly nice to be able to surprise one. There were some differences from the original ships, Mandell knew. Where proper Tzun Stormblades had been so polished that the eye slid off them, these were solid and imposing gun-metal, covered in brightly lit viewports. 'The cylinder here is the last remaining Data Core from S'Arl, the Tzun home planet. The Veltrochni salvaged it during their destruction of the planet.'

The Doctor harrumphed. 'So that's what all this is about, eh? I suppose you're planning to "conquer the universe" with them, eh?' he suggested dismissively. 'I've heard these kinds of speeches before.'

'Nothing so theatrical, Doctor,' Mandell said smoothly. 'I have no particular interest in being a president or an emperor. A fancy title and a crown merely make you attractive to assassins and usurpers.'

'Well, what, then? I'm sure you're dying to tell me.'

'You mean you're dying to be told, surely? It's perfectly simple: the age of Empires is over. Our budgets are being slashed now that we simply have not enough enemies to work against. Before long, I and my employees will be victims of the peace dividend. So I find that we need a new line of business.' Mandell stepped a little closer to the viewport. 'Nobody builds ships like these any more. The masters of gravitational technology are long gone from the universe, and their powers forgotten. To most spacefaring races, this will all be new. A brand-new standard in starship architecture and weapons technology.'

'For you to exploit?'

'Not exactly, Doctor – for me to sell. The SID owns a controlling stake in this shipyard. With the information retained in this Core, we will build a new generation of starships based on gravitational technology. And then we shall sell them, to anyone who is willing to pay the top prices for the latest advances. Already the Draconians have offered thirty billion credit-bars each for those three Stormblades, and I fully expect to be able to beat them up to a hundred billion for the set. I daren't even think what the secrets of RNA memory duplication will be worth, and that's all in there as well.' He stroked his beard, and smiled dreamily. 'When this is over, and the President puts me out to pasture, I may not be the ruler of the cosmos, but I will be richer than Mammon.'

He touched the safety control on the Veltrochni KEM rifle. 'Now, just remember, this is nothing personal; only business.'

The Doctor looked at him impassively. 'They all say that,' he said deprecatingly. 'You're just another greedy little man, aren't you?'

Mandell hesitated. 'Actually, you're right; I lied. This makes me rich, so it's a pleasure. If I'm lucky, the first couple of darts might not even kill you; I've never seen a Time Lord regenerate before, so that could be fun…' He aimed the KEM rifle at the Doctor's chest. 'Bye.'

'I wouldn't be so quick to do that, if I were you,' the Doctor said sharply. Mandell froze as the Doctor continued. 'I have the strangest feeling that you're going to need some strong character witnesses before too long.'

'What?'

'Haven't you looked at the security recordings yet? Very lax of you, that is.'

Mandell began feel a chilly suspicion creep along his spine. He turned to the computer, and tapped into the SID network. From there it took only a moment to access the security recordings he had already had brought back to SID headquarters. On the screen, he saw the Doctor and Monty sabotaging the time dams, while another man, with a beard, instructed them on what to do. The third man looked awfully familiar... The tightly-curled hair and squared-off beard were unmistakable; he was looking at himself.

'So you faked the recordings? We can deal with that?'

'Several guards also saw you with their own eyes,' the Doctor countered happily. 'And just watch the next part.' On the screen, the other Mandell thumped the console, cracking it slightly. Standing out in the sun, Mandell glanced at the little red scar where he'd cut himself on that broken glass in the *Nosferatu*. This couldn't be happening he told himself. It just couldn't. The Doctor nodded slowly. 'Now you've gone and left some DNA traces as well.'

Mandell gaped and shook his head. 'That damned Whifferdill...'

'Actually, no, but it doesn't matter either way.' the Doctor said. He shook his head. 'Doesn't look good for you at all, does it?' he asked in a distinctly menacing tone.

Mandell felt like a condemned man who just heard the trapdoor open beneath his feet. Just as gravity would take over, and hang the prisoner, so it was equally obvious what would happen when this security video got out.

'What,' he began through gritted teeth, 'exactly is it you have in mind?'

The Doctor held up the circuit he had taken from the time dams. 'Let's start with who designed those time dams for you. "A company on Dronid" your man there said.'

Mandell nodded. 'Chronodyne Industries. They're very good.'

'They're also rather too advanced for this century,' the Doctor said acidly. 'What I want to know is, whether they have an office on Vandor Prime, and whether you know who you're really dealing with.'

Mandell laughed. 'Try the Yellow –' he frowned. It was the oddest thing: he couldn't remember off-hand who he had dealt with from the company. There had been a man, but he was just a dark blur in Mandell's memory. 'Why?' Though Niccolo didn't say so, that was as much an expression of his concern at this localised amnesia as it was a question to the Doctor. The possibility that someone had tampered with his mind was most unpleasant.

'Because someone with access to time travel sent two bounty hunters after me from here, and because this company based on Dronid is –' An explosion drowned out anything else he might have said, and bowled Mandell over the wall.

There was a roar, the bow-shock of a vehicle hurtling towards them at high speed. Everyone hurled themselves to the ground, as a heavily armoured gunship thundered towards them on what looked to Jack like a kamikaze run.

It pulled up at the last minute, but a flurry of cannon-blasts ripped through the ghost town. Already-unstable walls shattered, and craters erupted in the sand. As Mandell landed heavily on the other side of the wall, his troopers tried to fire at the gunship.

Their projectile weapons made no impression on the gunship's hull, but its automatic turrets were rather more effective against the unshielded men. Plasma bursts erupted both around and through the scattering troopers.

Blood stained the sand as the gunship dropped to the ground between the humans and the *Nosferatu*. Jack wondered if maybe the VP police force had tracked them here, and it was a strangely attractive idea. This would really put paid to Mandell's plans.

His hopes were dashed, however, when the hatch opened, and the bulky forms of Ogrons loped out with surprising grace. Several Ogrons chased after the SID men, guns blazing, while others grabbed Chat and Liang, and bundled them into the gunship. Monty and the Doctor were next.

Chance looked around at the carnage, wondering what sort of dashing and heroically reckless escape he should attempt. After all, he couldn't let himself be known as someone who was captured by mere Ogrons.

On the other hand, it would be a damn sight easier to pull the rug out from under the Ogrons' hobnailed boots than to do so with the Vandorian intelligence community.

Common wisdom dictated that in a firefight, one should keep one's head down if one wanted to keep it at all. Ogrons had never been great ones for wisdom. Gorrak stood his ground like a tree in the path of an oncoming tornado, blazing away with his plasma rifle.

Somehow he survived. The humans were too frightened to aim properly, and aimed where they thought he would jump to. It didn't seem to occur to anyone that he would just stand and shoot.

An explosion went off in the midst of a group of riot police, and Gorrak laughed uproariously. 'Hurhurhuhr. That gotta hurt.' He opened fire again, driving the remaining Men back. He looked back and saw that the last of the Men wanted by his new partners was aboard their ship. It was time to leave.

'You bastards!' Mandell squeaked, half choked with outrage. He'd spent hundreds of man-hours and millions of credit-bars setting this up, and who'd messed it up? The Ogrons. How in Satan's name had these jumped-up chimpanzees got into this?

Some half-buried corner of his mind that was still connected to rational thought tried to point out that they were most likely the pirates who had been attacking shipping in the vicinity, and had simply got lucky. He wasn't listening to that inner voice, though. People who feel superior often feel that only a conspiracy has the combined power to interfere with them, and Mandell was no exception. It was much easier to fight against a specific enemy than mere chance. It was easier to rage against one too.

He waved to his few remaining troops, indicating the Ogrons and their captives, almost frothing at the mouth. 'Kill them! Kill them all! Destroy! Kill! Kill!'

He was too late, however, as the gunship was already blasting off. 'Godsdammit!' he screamed. 'Get back to the ship. 'Let's go!' One way or the other, he was going to get those strategically shaved baboons for this.

The *Thazrakh*'s Flight Director jabbed a claw at the huge and lumbering vessel which had so recently appeared on screen. 'Pirates,' he spat. 'Power the quantum lance, and bring us about.' Those who attacked others for only personal gain instead of family or honour were vermin, no better than bark-crawlers. Something that knew only how to feed itself and reproduce deserved no consideration.

The flight crew started working furiously.

'Flank speed.' The Flight Director braced himself against the back of the command couch. Even though Hyskanth was on the planet below, and it was his right to hold his leader's place for him until he returned, the Flight Director wouldn't feel comfortable sitting there. He didn't think he'd earned that honour yet. 'Program lateral shear. We will cut them in half.'

The gunnery officer hissed approvingly, baring fangs.

In the *Speculator*'s control room, Borrk whimpered nervously as the Dragon swung about, the quantum lance coming to fiery green life. 'We doomed,' he complained. 'Veltrochni Dragon outgun this ship.'

Karthakh nodded, spines rustling excitedly. 'It is too uneven a match to be a glorious death for us. So we must avoid dying.'

'Bigger guns,' Borrk opined phlegmatically. 'We need bigger guns. Dragon made of hard metal; Ogron guns not hurt Dragon.'

'The hull is built of siligtone,' Karthakh agreed, 'but they have their weaknesses.' If he could just remember what they were…. He had served on a Dragon in his youth, as a gunnery officer. If they had a transmat aboard the *Speculator*, he could transmit a bomb through their shields, since he knew the frequencies.

He wondered if a transmitted signal could do the job as well. Communications transmissions were all electromagnetic signals, so if he could send a stream of energy directly to the quantum lance's program input unit… It should overload, or at least scramble the targeting co-ordinates that the gunner attempted to feed into it.

The *Thazrakh*'s Flight Director pointed a claw at the *Speculator*. 'Fire at will.'

The gunnery officer tapped out a series of quick and practised commands into the targeting console. 'Quantum lance at full power. Target locked –' The console started to vibrate, and the gunnery officer looked at it in surprise. 'Power level now one hundred and fifteen per cent,' he said slowly.

'That is impossible.' The Flight Director dropped into the crew pit to look over his shoulder. 'How can it exceed maximum?'

'Some kind of overload,' the gunnery officer deduced. He started trying to shut down the weapons power. 'I cannot cut the power.'

'Cut all main power,' the Flight Director barked hurriedly. 'Increase the electronic countermea–'

The quantum lance's burning flickered momentarily, then burned more strongly as an explosion burst from just amidships. The Dragon started to list, and the quantum lance shattered. Instantly, green fire enveloped the entire ship, and the segmented hull ripped itself apart.

Borrk looked at Karthakh in awe. Somehow he had destroyed a Veltrochni Dragon without firing a shot. In Borrk's eyes, this was nothing short of sorcery, the greatest sorcery. Truly, Karthakh must have in him the spirit of the canyon gods, who made the ground shake and could topple mountains.

Karthakh watched in silence as the Dragon flew apart, his spines flat. 'It was not an honourable kill,' he muttered to himself. 'They will not rest easily.' Borrk couldn't see what the problem was, but simply tried to look expressionless. This wasn't especially difficult.

Karthakh felt sadness for the first time since his cubs had died in that lightning fire all those years ago. There was no similarity, and yet... They were Veltrochni innocents who had died for a betrayal. If he and Sha'ol had stood by their deal with Mandell instead of allowing the Ogrons some responsibility, this would never have happened. Of course, then the Ogrons would have killed them.

'Get out of my sight.' he finally told Borrk. 'Prepare cells for the new prisoners.'

Chapter Sixteen

Sabalom Glitz was in the grip of utter terror. It the sort of fear that small boys get when sent to the headmaster's office for peeking up girls' skirts. At least, that's what Glitz associated it with. It wasn't the fear of death, since if his captors had wanted him dead, they would have killed him already.

No, this was the fear of wondering what it was that the most fearsome duo in the galaxy wanted with him. In Glitz's worldview, if someone hostile didn't kill you, it must be because they had something even worse planned – unless, of course, they were merely constrained by some kind of moral code, like the Doctor. And Glitz was uncomfortably familiar with the exploits of Sha'ol and Karthakh. Second only to the mercifully deceased Ernie McCartney, they were the two most feared bounty hunters ever to be cursed by the inmates of prison asteroids.

Mentioning their names to a fellow entrepreneur produced much the same effect as asking someone with an endless migraine if he'd seen the results of his neuroscan yet. In some dark corner of his mind, Glitz recalled his old dad telling him how Sha'ol and Karthakh would get him if he didn't do what he was told.

Suddenly the door opened again, and Glitz grinned with relief as the Doctor came into sight, along with Chance, Monty, Chat, Liang and Dibber. They were all shoved into the dorm room which was serving as his cell. Dibber grinned back at him. 'Nice to see you, Mr Glitz.'

'You too, lad,' Glitz agreed with feeling. 'But if only you'd brought a key with you.'

Chat hugged him. 'Never mind all that. I'm just glad you're still alive.'

'Whatever for?' he demanded, pretending ignorance. It was nice, though. He could get used to this, if he lived long enough.

To his surprise she paused, and looked more serious. 'Because there are very few friends from the old days left, and I don't want to lose any more.'

The Doctor cleared his throat theatrically. 'Speaking of losing friends... You seem to have misplaced Frobisher.'

'Not exactly, Doc,' Glitz couldn't help letting some sourness intrude into his voice. 'I haven't lost him, I just don't know where he is.' He hoped that would explain everything.

'There's a difference?'

'He escaped ages ago, and,' he went on pointedly, 'scarpered on his own instead of freeing me!'

'We're on a ship, Glitz. There's not much choice of places to escape *to*.'

'Anyway,' Glitz said with a nod. 'What about you? Didn't you steal the wotsit?'

'We did,' Jack crowed. 'Went like a dream.'

'Where is it, then?'

Everyone fell silent. The Doctor made a face. 'I'm not entirely certain...'

In fact, the Core was resting on a chart table in the *Speculator*'s navigation room. Sha'ol was quite grateful for the Ogrons' instinct to grab anything shiny and expensive-looking. He and Karthakh were consulting their gunship's star charts, which they had uplinked to the *Speculator*'s navigation room, since the colony ship's own charts were over a thousand years out of date.

The door rumbled open, and Gorrak lumbered in, looking ineffably pleased with himself in a simian fashion. 'Prisoners locked up,' he reported.

'Excellent,' Sha'ol said crisply. 'You put them in with the others?'

Gorrak nodded. 'They in cell with other one.'

The two bounty hunters exchanged a look. Karthakh straightened from consulting the charts. 'One? There were two prisoners, surely?'

The Ogron's brows knitted, trying to count that high. 'One human.'

'And the avian?' Sha'ol prompted. 'The bird?'

Gorrak hesitated while the stone cogs that Karthakh suspected passed for the Ogron brain turned over. 'Just one human.'

'Then the avian has escaped!' Sha'ol snapped.

'Maybe not,' Gorrak said slowly. 'Maybe eaten,' he suggested with sudden cheer.

'Eaten?' Karthakh echoed with distaste.

'Food scarce on ship. First bird we see for weeks. Maybe guard get hungry…'

'Ask your clan,' Sha'ol instructed sharply. 'Find out if anyone did eat the creature. Meanwhile, search the ship anyway; the creature is sentient and intelligent, as well as a friend of the Doctor's.'

The Dragon *Zathakh* remained shrouded as she took up orbit around Elchur. If something in the vicinity had silenced one of the newer Mage-Dragons, it could certainly do unpleasant things to an older generation of ship like this one.

Brokhal paced the dusty street of the abandoned town

with uncharacteristic nervousness. There were several craters from cannon blasts, and the bodies of Hyskanth and his bodyguards. Brokhal, however, was more concerned with the three dead Ogrons that her Hunters had found. 'Were there any residual engine traces in orbit?'

'Many,' her son replied. 'This planet is often used as a trading place for smugglers.'

'Weapons signatures?'

'Only one. Quantum lance.' He flexed his claws in frustration. 'It may have been some kind of internal accident aboard *Thazrakh*.'

'No,' she murmured slowly. 'Not with Ogron mercenaries involved. They must be working for someone else. Presumably they tried to make it look like the thieves and Hyskanth betrayed each other, but they botched it.'

'Who?'

'It must be that schemer Mandell. Clearly he never intended to hand over the cylinder.'

'Then we should prepare to bombard Vandor Prime. Their non-cooperation has gone on long enough.'

'Perhaps…' Why had Mandell made this private deal? Why did the President still deny it even to her in private conversations… Unless he himself did not know about it. 'Mandell,' she growled, 'not the President, or the government…'

'Mother?'

She snarled at the heavens. 'We have been played for fools. The Vandorian government was telling the truth when they said they had no knowledge of our property. Niccolo Mandell had kept it secret even from his own superiors!'

She rose, and pointed a claw at the communications director. 'Monitor all transmissions in and out of Vandor

Prime. I want to know where Mandell has gone.'

Frobisher had never been among Ogrons before, and sincerely hoped he never would again. The whole ship stank of rancid food and waste, and the noise they made was barely tolerable. He had originally planned to free Glitz once he had slid himself out under the door, but soon saw how unwise that was. If both prisoners vanished, the Ogrons would turn the ship upside-down looking for them. At least this way, Glitz complained enough to keep the Ogrons busy, and his absence hadn't been noticed yet.

Unfortunately he hadn't found out who had hired Sha'ol and Karthakh yet either, and it wasn't as if he could simply walk up and ask them. Instead he followed them around as discreetly as possible. All Ogrons looked alike to most other races, and Frobisher doubted that either bounty hunter could tell one from another.

Karthakh passed by at that moment. 'You,' he instructed, 'come with me.'

'Yes, Boss,' Frobisher replied in as mindless a voice as he could manage, and fell into step with the Veltrochni. Karthakh led him to the communications centre, where Sha'ol joined them. 'Guard this door,' Karthakh ordered. They went inside, and Frobisher had a clear shot at both Sha'ol and Karthakh, with a plasma rifle in his hands... But that wasn't his way. He was a detective, a gumshoe, not a killer. Besides, if he shot them, he'd never know who hired them, or what was going on.

Sha'ol did something with a band on his wrist, as did Karthakh. The metallic bands glowed. 'If you are troubling me, I hope it is with good news,' a cold humanoid voice said.

'It is,' Sha'ol assured him. 'We have the Doctor aboard our ship.'

'Ah... At last! You cannot imagine what a relief it will be to be finally rid of his insufferable conscience.'

Karthakh spoke up. 'We initiated contact to ensure that we have your wishes correct. For a small extra fee, we can deliver the Doctor to you alive, for you to dispose of as you see fit.'

The voice laughed. 'An appealing idea. We will send a ship to meet you and deliver your payment. Be in the Katana system in twenty-four hours. Only then will I know he is truly dead, and that we can rest assured he will never trouble any of us again.'

'Consider it done,' Sha'ol said. He and Karthakh then filed out past Frobisher, totally ignoring him once more. After all, he was only an Ogron.

Wei had saved his own skin by finding Cronan at the spaceport, and it looked like Cronan knew it. He was shaking from head to foot as he huddled in the least comfortable chair in Mandell's office.

Mandell quivered with rage, or caffeine withdrawal, he wasn't sure which. Either way, he was in a most unpleasant mood. 'This,' he said angrily, 'really offends me, Cronan.' He clamped his hands on to the edge of the desk to stop them bunching into fists of their own accord.

'It was business,' Cronan protested. 'They're only thieves; what did you expect me to do?'

Mandell drew a blaster, and leaned across the desk to shove the muzzle into Cronan's mouth. He heard a tooth break as it went in. 'I expect you to use your godsdammed head. I expect you to check with your betters before you screw up all our lives!' Cronan's eyes were almost popping out of his head in terror. 'Give me one reason why I shouldn't vape your empty head right now,' Mandell snarled. He wished he could allow himself to do what he threatened, because it looked like being a pretty good catharsis. He wasn't so stupid, of course, but there was no sense in letting Cronan know that.

'The Doctor,' Cronan mumbled.

Mandell ripped the gun out, with another tooth. 'What?'

'The Doctor; the one you're after. This Zimmerman is sending me to collect his body.'

Since this merely confirmed what he already suspected, Mandell's rage evaporated, or so he made it look. Such vast mood swings always scared prisoners. On Earth there used to be a saying that one should never ask a question to which one didn't already know the answer, and Mandell liked to stick by that proverb as much as possible 'Ah. In that case, you're about as much use here as a vet in an abattoir.'

Cronan looked even more hunted. 'What?'

'I said you can go. Go on, get out!' To emphasise the point, Wei grabbed Cronan, and physically threw him out the door.

'Nice move.'

'Thank you, Mandell *Io*. The homing nanobots should transmit for several days.'

'Good.' Using the enemy was always somehow more satisfying than using one's friends. Mandell relaxed somewhat. It was nearly time to head home for an evening snuggled up with Kala. There was something he wanted to check first. This Zimmerman wanted the Doctor dead, did he? It amused him to think that by hearing that, he had actually – albeit inadvertently – fulfilled his part of his bargain with the Doctor.

He tapped into the computer system, and searched for 'Zimmerman'. There were several dozen people with that name, and Mandell felt despondent once more – until he caught the word 'Chronodyne' out of the corner of his eye. He scrolled back up. There was a Zimmerman listed as a Director of Chronodyne Industries. No picture on file, but he knew where the VP office of the company was anyway.

Mandell pondered this for a moment, then made a decision. 'Get the flier, Wei. We're going visiting.'

Frobisher returned to the navigation room, but there were too many Ogrons around for him to try altering the ship's course as he had hoped. He supposed he might at least discover something about what they were doing on the ship at all, though the idea of learning anything from an Ogron was something of an oxymoron.

Frobisher started when Gorrak suddenly stamped his foot. Rather than shout with some sort of rage, however, Gorrak continued stamping. Other Ogrons joined in, pounding the consoles with free hands, and from deeper in the ship, Frobisher could hear the constant hammering adopt the implacable cadence that Gorrak was beating out.

'*Born of rock*', Gorrak rumbled, with what by Ogron standards was probably grace. '*With heart of stone,*' he continued. By this time, some of the others were also growling out the words, and Frobisher realised with a touch of culture shock that they were – in their own gravelly way – singing. Frobisher had never thought Ogrons could even grasp the concept of song, and could only mouth a rough approximation of the words, hoping that nobody would notice.

'*From mothering land*
And mountain home

Ogrons we born
Ogrons we die
From rock and stone
Our souls will fly'

The pounding continued as Frobisher recovered himself.

'A gift of stone
Is every breath
To please our masters
With life and death
Ogrons we born
Ogrons we die
In rocks and stones
Our souls will lie.'

The *Speculator* lumbered off into the stars.

Karthakh could feel the ship's deck plates vibrate to the stamping of feet, and his ears swivelled to pick up the simple words being growled out throughout the ship. Perhaps these primitive dirt-grubbing creatures were not so stupid as they had appeared. The Veltrochni warrior made a mental note of that possibility, but allowed himself to be carried along by the raw tide of sound. In a way, it reminded him of the toast-songs that greeted the end of a duty shift on a Dragon.

The words were overly simplistic, though, and didn't stir any sense of pride or joy in Karthakh's heart. That realisation saddened him a little. These were only Ogrons, he reminded himself; an anomaly of the spaceways who by rights should be building stone huts and fighting with spears back on Orestes, or Braah, as the creatures themselves called the planet.

At least they knew the value of song, he decided. That helped make them warriors, in his eyes, because song came from a strong heart.

In the navigation room, Sha'ol tuned out the Ogrons' chanting, as it was an irrelevance. He expected it would distract them from their duty, but this didn't seem to be the case. Perhaps he would compose a minuet once they had delivered the Doctor's head; something truly touching and wistful. He would wait until the job was done, though; that was how things should be done.

Their course was set, and Sha'ol now found himself free to examine the Core. He recognised it immediately as a Data Core from S'Arl. He thought of the planet as his homeworld, even though some part of him knew he had never been there. He had memories of it, though. Ancestors' memories, to be sure, but memories nonetheless.

They were encoded in RNA passed down to Sha'ol, and any other survivors there might be. There were a few, Sha'ol supposed, since the statistical probabilities were against the total elimination of every member of such a widely distributed species. He had never met one, though, and he told himself that he had long been used to being, in all practical terms, the last of his people.

Once it had almost driven him insane. He had been unreasoning for several decades, until the madness simply burnt itself out. Like so many kinds of pain, there eventually came a point where one ceased to register it.

Many members of many species liked to consider themselves unique, but they had no conception of what that truly meant. But Sha'ol knew. It meant always being alone. It meant always being the outsider. It meant knowing that you were a living epitaph to all of the dead. Worst of all, it meant that you belonged to the dead – and were one of them.

Chapter Seventeen

Some over-friendly Ogrons had shoved some rancid meat into Frobisher's fist and dragged him down to the factory floor. There, the evening meal was being served to those Ogrons who weren't on duty manning the ship's controls. After seeing the uncooked cadavers and half-cooked leftovers that they ate, Frobisher wondered if he would ever be able to keep down a chocolate pilchard again.

He slipped away from the Ogron party with great relief. It didn't take long for most of the Nest to get drunk on highly acidic ale, and he had no difficulty in finding his way back to the navigation room.

He had hoped it would be empty, but of course the old matriarch had her little nest there. She and her family were sleeping in a heap in the captain's duty cabin, though, and snoring fit to wake the dead. Sha'ol was also there, but his eyes were closed, and he too seemed asleep.

It wasn't an ideal situation, Frobisher knew, but he might never get another chance to alter the ship's course. Moving with a silence that would be impossible for a true Ogron, Frobisher approached the navigation console. Working quickly, he disengaged the current course, and plotted a new course, back to Vandor Prime. Once that was set, he erased all records of the change in the computer.

'What are you doing?' It was Sha'ol's voice.

'Boss?' Frobisher asked, hoping he could bluff it out.

Sha'ol looked past him at the console, but the disruptor he held didn't waver from Frobisher's chest. 'Gorrak and Karthakh, report to the navigation room. For an Ogron you have done remarkably well,' Sha'ol said slowly, and Frobisher could tell that the Tzun hadn't quite worked out what he was dealing with yet.

There was a growling and snorting from the captain's duty cabin, as the matriarch and her daughters woke. 'What happening?' the matriarch demanded. Sha'ol ignored her, but turned just a hair when the door opened to admit Gorrak and Karthakh. Frobisher acted instantly, puffing himself up into a ruddy reptilian form that oozed with acidic blubber.

Every Ogron in the room screamed in terror, and tried to hide in the nearest cubbyhole, while the matriarch gasped hoarsely and pitched backwards.

Before either of the more intelligent bounty hunters could react, Frobisher had lanced forward, changing into a cheetah as he went. He hurtled out of the still open door, narrowly avoiding a hasty disruptor shot from Sha'ol.

Gorrak checked the matriarch while Karthakh cursed vehemently in his own tongue. The Ogron leader straightened with a dreamy smile. 'Not all bad,' he began. 'She dead. Scare to death by monster.'

Sha'ol didn't curse like Karthakh did. This development simply necessitated an alteration to strategy. 'A mesomorph,' he stated simply. 'A shapeshifter.'

'A Rutan?' Karthakh asked with a hiss.

'Unlikely. There has been no disruption to onboard electrical systems. Also it did not return to its natural state between forms. A Rutan would.' He considered, rifling through generations' worth of memories for any encounters with shapechanging species. There were very few, since such species were rare in the galaxy. 'The most likely culprit is the Xenon mesomorph –'

'A Whifferdill,' Karthakh snarled. 'If there is a Whifferdill on board, it could get into anything.' That was true, Sha'ol was well aware. However, the Whifferdills were intelligent, and this one was clearly on some kind of intelligence-gathering work. That meant it was developing a strategy, and Sha'ol was an expert at strategy. 'We must hunt it down,' Karthakh added.

'Tactically unsound,' Sha'ol snapped. 'We do not have the necessary equipment to scan for a Xenon mesomorph, therefore it is unlikely that we would find it. A search would simply make it easier for him to impersonate the searchers and move among us. To affect our intentions, he will have to attack specific areas of the ship: this centre, life support, the engines, or weapons systems.'

'Or the crew,' Karthakh added.

'Correct. From this time forward, no one will move about the ship alone. Travel in pairs or groups only. Any lone beings are to be shot on sight.' He turned to Gorrak. 'No matter what they look like,' he emphasised heavily, as one had to with Ogrons.

'Even you?' Gorrak rumbled, sounding surprised.

'Especially us.' Sha'ol's unblinking black eyes remained fixed on Gorrak for a long moment. 'Gorrak, set your weapons for stun. It will be to our advantage to interrogate the mesomorph, should he be located.' It was also likely that some mistaken identifications would be made by the Ogrons, and their forces were thin enough already.

'I understand. These good lads, they find mexomuff.' Sha'ol didn't bother to correct him.

Gorrak hurried back down to the main hall of the Nest. Most of his men were there, and some of them could even still stand. Those, he gathered together. 'New orders from mas-

partners,' he said importantly. 'There is shapeshifter on board. Partners say no one to travel alone in ship. Now I tell you; stun any creature who is alone.'

It didn't occur to him that he had walked into the hall alone, until seven different stun blasts hit him.

When he woke up, he knew that at least his men had understood their instructions.

The Doctor had been scouring the room for a ventilation shaft or inspection panel through which he or one of the others could slip out. Without tools, it had taken them some time to unscrew a panel using Jack's belt-buckle.

The Doctor took off his coat. 'If my memory serves me as well as it usually does, this shaft must lead to the auxiliary engineering deck on this type of ship.'

Monty shook his head. 'But this ship's a thousand years old…'

'So will I be fairly soon,' the Doctor reminded him. 'I have been on these things before, you know. Now, from there I should be able to override the door control, or at least make up a key to fit any mechanical lock the Ogrons might be us–'

He broke off at the sound of a scraping from the door. Everyone hurriedly sat down, expecting to be discovered at any moment. The Doctor stood a moment longer, hanging his coat over the open vent. It wasn't exactly a convincing camouflage, but Ogrons weren't noted for their observational skills anyway.

Only the food slot in the door opened, however, and a hairy Ogron hand shoved a tray through. Four covered plates were on it, and a pitcher, which smoked slightly. The Doctor and Jack exchanged glances with each other, and the pitcher. 'Ogron ale.'

'I'll pass,' Jack said, lifting a cover off a plate. There were some chicken drumsticks on it, most likely from the ship's original food processors. He hesitated before biting, though, as Glitz downed the pitcher of ale in one go. 'I take back what I said; you did have guts. Probably not any more…'

'Just something to wet my whistle,' Glitz said, patting his stomach. He lifted another cover off, and saw a soup bowl. A thick hunk of bread lurked in what looked like some kind of primordial slime. 'Now that warms a few cockles!' He grabbed a spoon and started digging at the bread, sure there was some choice meat somewhere in the broth, but it was as if the doughy lump was glued to the bowl.

At which point, the bread opened its mouth and told him what he could do with his spoon. Glitz dropped the bowl in horror, leaping back with the spoon held defensively in front of him. He hadn't thought even Ogron ale would be that strong… The surface of the soup bulged upwards, while the bowl grew stubby legs. In a moment, a familiar penguin stood before them.

Glitz threw the spoon away, unsure whether to be angry or relieved. 'Don't you ever do that to me again, you polar ponce! I thought I was croaking for sure.'

'Don't all thank me at once,' Frobisher said sourly, dangling the door keys in front of them. 'If you don't like shapeshifters, that's your business.'

'I certainly *do* like them,' said the Doctor, warmly shaking Frobisher by the flipper. 'Especially when they've been very clever. It's good to see you again, Frobisher.'

'Look,' said Glitz grudgingly. 'I've got nothing personal against you – I'm just nervous about there being somebody who can be anything, and I wouldn't know about it.'

Frobisher shrugged it off. Not that it didn't irk him, but he had become somewhat inured to such sentiments over the years. 'I'm still flesh and blood like you. Well, flesh anyway. Prick me, do I not... ooze? Wrong me, shall I not come round your house with a baseball bat that's got nails in?'

'There are more important things than revenge, Frobie,' Jack said. 'Not many, I'll grant you; but the one that springs to mind is, why are we here as well as the Doctor?'

'Ogrons,' the Doctor answered, 'aren't noted for their discrimination. I suspect they just grabbed the rest of you according to general principles. The real question is why I am still alive. Sha'ol and Karthakh have gone to a lot of trouble to kill me, so why haven't they done so yet?'

'They figure they can get more money for you alive,' Frobisher told him. 'Personally I wouldn't bet on it.'

'Neither would I,' the Doctor said with surprising warmth. He took his coat down from the vent. 'That money talks I'll not deny, but last I heard, it said "goodbye".'

The freighter used by Chance and the others had finally been identified as the *Nosferatu* and Kala had been thrown by the revelation from central records that it had recently been the subject of a government compulsory purchase order.

Nevertheless, she had managed to get a ship assigned to help her track the fugitives, and so she and Jemson now found themselves standing on the bridge of the *Cobb* ready to pursue the *Nosferatu* to wherever Chance tried to run.

Unfortunately, they had not gone anywhere, and Captain Franke was too busy to answer any of Kala's questions about what was going on. She was getting angry about the whole thing, even though she knew she shouldn't, and strongly suspected that it was stemming from suppressed fear.

Kala had been a cop all her adult life, and faced her fair share of psychos and terrorists, but she didn't like space travel at the best of times, and this didn't even remotely qualify.

She and Jemson were reduced to trying to keep out of the crew's way as a Veltrochni Mage-Dragon faced off against their ship, its quantum lances glinting malevolently. All through the Gamma Delphinus system, Dragons and Mage-Dragons were dropping out of hyperspace, while Wasp fighters buzzed between them, shepherding any ships that tried to leave the orbit of Vandor Prime.

Kala tried without success to tune out the reports of casualties from the surface. There had been no bombardment or invasion – yet – but plenty of looting and people being trampled at the spaceports.

It looked like they had just engaged in a war, and that was something she knew nothing about outside of the history books.

Franke approached with a puzzled expression. 'Officers, it seems your presence is requested in the President's office.'

'Ours?'

'Well, yours at least. There's some sort of crisis meeting going on with the President and the Veltrochni Ambassador, and you've been paged.'

Kala couldn't imagine what they wanted with her. Perhaps it was some mistake, and they'd asked for the wrong Mandell, since Nic would undoubtedly be there.

'We can transmat you directly there,' Franke continued.

Kala nodded dumbly. 'Just don't go anywhere. We'll still have a ship to chase.'

'If any of us are still around,' Franke agreed diplomatically.

In a matter of moments, both Kala and Jemson were being

ushered into the President's audience chamber. The Defence Minister was there, of course, along with the Attorney General, a bunch of politicians and military types whom Kala didn't recognise, and the imposing forms of a group of Veltrochni.

Strangely, Nic was absent. She had been sure he would be here; he was some sort of intelligence adviser, after all.

'Glad you could make it,' Klein said curtly. 'Take a seat; this concerns you.'

'This... crisis?'

'Very much so,' the Veltrochni Ambassador rasped. 'We have evidence that the property whose return we have been seeking was brought to this planet by Niccolo Mandell, without the knowledge of his own government. Furthermore, he is also at least partially responsible for the destruction of our vessel *Thazrakh*, and the murder of her commander on the planet Elchur.'

'Impossible,' Kala blurted. This was nonsensical. The Veltrochni were just trying the old divide and conquer trick.

'It gets worse,' the Attorney General broke in. 'As you know, the Thor Orbital Facility has been the victim of a theft. When we downloaded the security records, this is what we found...'

The recording passed by with the inevitability of death and taxes, and the Attorney General resumed his damning indictment. 'Your husband is clearly in collusion with the very same group of thieves whom you yourself have been watching. We believe that Niccolo may be trying to prevent any chance of the Veltrochni property being returned to them, since that is what was stolen. Not only that, but the previous day a vraxoin lab was found in the stations. The scientist who was in nominally in charge of that section was

234

also seen in the company of Niccolo yesterday.'

Kala sat back, stunned. Nic involved with vraxoin, and political assassinations? Her Nic? That wasn't possible. The sort of man who was happy to talk nurseries and baby clothes wasn't the sort to deal drugs or kill people.

Her brain told a different story, of course, but her heart couldn't listen. Her heart only knew Nic the desk-jockey and loving husband who could never hurt anybody. She knew he was involved with intelligence work and security, but he was an analyst and director, whose place was behind a desk telling all the spies what he wanted them to find out. Not running around killing people for his own gain.

She tried to speak, but couldn't. How could Nic have done these things? How could she have let such a person anywhere near herself, or think of him as the father of her child?

'I want to help,' she managed finally. If nothing else, she wanted to look in Nic's eyes and see the truth when he was asked about these things.

The Attorney General shook his head. 'No.'

Kala's eyes flashed dangerously. 'You have to let me go,' she protested. 'It is my husband we're talking about.'

'Exactly.' He folded his arms. 'Kala, there are laws about personal involvement. Now that Niccolo has been named in this case it would look bad for the department if you were involved. You can see that, can't you?'

'Yes, but –'

'But? There can hardly be a "but" to the fact that you're going to have to arrest your own husband. Whether he's innocent or guilty, the lawyers on both sides would have a field day with that one. The defence could claim you had personal bias in feeling betrayed, and the prosecution would be wondering how long you knew about any of this. The damn thing would never be finished.' He kept his speech soft for the moment, but she heard the underlying certainty.

'Let her come,' Brokhal said suddenly.

Everyone in the room looked at her. 'Why?' Klein asked.

'Because this is a family matter for her. What could be more important?'

The service vents weren't exactly clean, and Monty had the distinct feeling that his hair was no longer white. He wasn't too sure about the state of his joints either; a man of his age wasn't made for crawling through these narrow metal veins. He tried to remind himself that the Doctor was considerably older, but it didn't help much.

They passed occasional grilles, some of which opened on to Ogron-inhabited areas of the ship. Those were not sights that Monty would ever like to see again. Leathery skin and coarse hair engaged in every possible type of organic function from the fairly natural to eating their own dead.

The stench clogged up the vents almost solidly.

None of this seemed to bother the Doctor too much as he led the way. He paused to point down a new branch. 'That way, I think. What time do you make it?'

'Seventeen-fourteen. I hope your friend can tell time.'

'I'm sure Frobisher is used to the idea by now,' the Doctor replied.

Liang studied the others as they all surreptitiously checked their watches every few seconds, his face impassive.

'Cheer up,' Jack told him. 'Won't be that long before you can do your stuff.'

'Just passing the time,' Liang agreed. Doing 'his stuff' was always worth waiting for.

There was a small Ogron nest in the auxiliary engineering section, and the snores from it could be heard throughout this whole deck of the ship. 'What now?' Monty asked in a whisper. 'Go back and try somewhere else?'

'Never look back, Monty,' the Doctor recommended, squinting through the grille. 'Leave the U-turns to politicians. I always finish what I start. Besides, the other areas where we might try this will be even more heavily populated by Ogrons.' He pointed to the open doorway that was on the far side of the dozing Ogrons. 'Ogrons are big, and they have plenty of stamina for distance running, but their reaction times are slow. If we're quick enough, we should be able to get into the auxiliary control room and shut the door on them.'

If they were quick enough? Monty thought. 'Doctor, I'm coming up on retirement age; track and field events are not high on my list of hobbies. Why didn't you bring Jack or Dibber?'

'Because neither of them is qualified to help me make any repairs that might be needed in there. Now, we'll only get the one chance to do this –'

Monty shifted slightly, trying to ease the pain in his ribs and back. 'At least let's find some weapons first.'

'I don't hide behind guns, Monty. Hiding of any kind becomes a habit too easily.'

'Except in these ducts?'

'Especially in the ducts,' the Doctor corrected him. 'So let's get out into the open, eh?' The Doctor swung himself round into a sitting position, and kicked out with both legs. The grille was old and corroded, and fell away the first blow. The Doctor followed through on the kick by sliding right out of the vent.

Monty gritted his teeth as his old bones creaked with the effort of following the Doctor out at a reasonable speed. The sight of three Ogrons shaking their heads as they woke up didn't help his heart rate much either.

Together, both men bolted for the auxiliary control room door. Monty was all too aware of the Ogrons coming to their feet off to his left. His whole body felt as if it were on fire as he ran for the door.

He was convinced he wasn't going to make it, and could just about feel a hairy hand on his shoulder... Then the door slammed at his back, and he propped himself up against a dusty console. While he forced himself to keep pulling air into his painful and resisting lungs, Monty saw the Doctor lock the door control. 'That should keep them out,' he said, as there was a banging of massive fists on the door.

'Yes, but for how long?' Monty gasped.

The Doctor gave him an apologetic look. 'Until it occurs to Sha'ol or Karthakh to cut through the door. Maybe five minutes for them to reach here?'

Monty sank into a rotted chair. 'I might even have recovered my breath by then.'

'Hmm,' the Doctor replied distantly. He had turned to wipe some dust off the auxiliary engineering consoles with his spotted handkerchief, and now experimented with a few switches. 'Now that's a stroke of luck... There's still some power here! In fact it looks like this section is fully operational.'

Monty blinked. This was good news, in a way, but still... 'You mean I did all that for nothing?'

'Yes, luckily for us. Now it's a race between our group and the Ogrons' leaders to get here first. Not having to repair any of this gives us a bit of an advantage.' He started operating switches. Door controls, Monty noticed, and some life-support systems too.

'Hoo-felching-rah.'

Exactly on time, the door to their room slid open. Through it, Glitz could see that every door on this deck had also opened. Then Jack pulled him aside, so that he wasn't framed in the doorway, before flattening himself against the wall beside the door. Chat pressed herself against the wall on the other side, and the door opened.

A pair of Ogrons hesitated suspiciously in the doorway, but that didn't help any. Jack grabbed one by the ears and cracked his head against the wall, while Chat slammed her boot into the other's stomach and clubbed him across the back of the skull when he doubled over. They each took one of the Ogrons' guns.

Outside, pools of light in the distance picked out the edges of thick pipes and walkways that criss-crossed the below-decks area. A narrow walkway with no safety rail led along the row of translucent dorms, an indeterminate distance above an indistinguishable floor. Another Ogron started to emerge from one of the other doors, but promptly slumped back into his chair with a smoking wound in his chest from where Jack shot him.

Glitz immediately checked the other rooms, not at all discomfited by the corpse, and found the small locker for prisoners' possessions. The lock was just a simple magnetic seal, and Glitz had no trouble opening it so that everyone could retrieve their belongings. Frobisher morphed himself into an Ogron, and handed the holosuit unit to Liang.

'How does this work, again?' Liang asked.

'Press there,' Glitz told him, 'and we're laughing.' And the Ogrons, he didn't feel the need to add, would be laughing on the other side of their faces.

A heavy thudding presaged the arrival of three Ogrons into the navigation room where Gorrak had been studiously trying to look as smart as his partners who were going over their course to the Katana system. 'Boss!' the nearest called to Gorrak. He sounded strangely nervous and excitable. 'Prisoners!'

'What about prisoners?' He knew they had prisoners. This was not exactly a proper report.

'Prisoners in second engineering. Old prisoner and one in funny clothes.'

'Second engineering?' Karthakh asked. The Ogron pointed to the place on a plan of the ship that was shown on one of the consoles. 'Auxiliary control!'

Sha'ol was already frantically operating the ship's computer. 'It must be the Doctor. He has shut out all engineering and helm control. He's sealing off all accessways between decks. We must cut our way through to the auxiliary control room. Are they armed?'

'No, they run away from us.'

Sha'ol paused a moment, then fetched his disruptor from the chart table. 'More fool them.'

Chapter Eighteen

'What is this in aid of?' Monty asked, as the Doctor finished his manipulations of the ship's environmental controls.

'I've cut engine power; I'd rather not go to wherever it is that Sha'ol and Karthakh plan to deliver me. I've also increased the oxygen and helium mix in the air. Veltroch's atmosphere has a lot more carbon dioxide than Earth's, and the Ogrons' planet has a higher amount of hydrogen.'

'So this'll suffocate them?' Monty didn't exactly like the idea, but if it would save their own skins…

'No, Monty. There are Ogron children on board as well as warriors, remember. Anyway to do that, I'd have to alter the mix so far that it would affect us as well. But it should impair them a bit, and give Frobisher and the others a chance to beat them here.'

'And if they don't?' He jerked his head towards the door, which was still being thudded by Ogron fists.

The Doctor picked up a large spanner. 'I thought of that.' He brought the spanner down on the console, smashing the controls repeatedly until they were a mass of smouldering junk. 'They're not regaining control of the ship.'

The door to the VP office of Chronodyne Industries opened, to reveal only a vague blackness within. Wei, aware that he would be expected to test the waters, as it were, for his superior, stepped in and looked around.

The place was open plan, and completely devoid of furniture. A few yellowed pieces of paper were scattered on the threadbare carpet, and the air smelled of crumbling rockcrete.

Mandell followed his aide in, nodding to himself. 'I thought so…'

'This building hasn't been occupied in years,' Wei said.

'No, which suggests that the company name is just a front.'

'For who?'

Mandell turned back to the door. 'For this Zimmerman that Cronan mentioned. And what does Cronan do…?'

'Synthesises vraxoin,' Wei answered, trying to follow his superior's lead. 'But I thought this bunch built our time dams…'

'Everyone should have a hobby,' Mandell said with a sort of exaggerated mildness. 'I think it's time Cronan discovered ours. Is the tracer still sending?'

'He's at the spaceport.' Wei said, after checking the signal from the nanotransmitters that Cronan unwittingly carried.

'Good. Let's go.'

Karthakh stopped again, when they reached another sealed door. Gorrak and the other dozen or so Ogrons paused for breath, while Sha'ol started cutting through the door with his disruptor. It took only a few seconds for the sonic weapon to do this job, but Karthakh would have been happier if Sha'ol had let him use explosive-tipped KEM darts. The oxygen levels were rising, though, and none of them wanted to start a fire.

At least the Ogrons' plasma rifles couldn't ignite the atmosphere, which Karthakh found to be a great relief, since they might well have disregarded the danger. He knew he shouldn't blame them for their evolution's slow progress, but the sort of stupidity that endangered their own cubs was difficult for him to bear.

He must be getting old, he thought. This chase was taking

more of a toll than he expected, and he was beginning to get a pounding headache...

Barrand relaxed while Cronan did the pre-flight checks. He watched the activity all around the private pad in the spaceport's executive area. Here, the ships owned by well-to-do businessmen and private security firms were berthed, along with the shuttles for those whose ships were too large to land.

Barrand had barely a moment's warning, a mere flicker of a shadow out the corner of his eye, before a gun was at his temple. The man on the other end was an oriental, with a long ponytail and a smart suit. Barrand vaguely recognised him from his trips to the Thor Facility, and that was not a good sign, considering what had so recently happened there.

The other man was someone he'd never met, but recognised all the same, since people in his business learned to know their opposition if they wanted to stay alive and free. It was Niccolo Mandell. Barrand was surprised that there wasn't a Tac team with him.

'Well now,' Mandell began, 'This is nice and cosy.'

'What do you want?' Barrand demanded.

'Did you say something?' Mandell snapped. 'It's rather rude to interrupt someone else's conversation.'

'As rude as breaking into their ship?'

'Oh, but Cronan and I are old friends.' Mandell grinned nastily, and Barrand began to wonder if he wasn't making some kind of mistake. 'But never let it be said that I'm not a friendly man, so I'm going to invite friendship from you.'

'I've already got a date,' Barrand snapped rebelliously.

'Cancel it. I want to know who your friend Zimmerman is.

You see, he is posing as an official of Chronodyne Industries, who have done some important work for us in the past. But now I find he's a trader in vraxoin, among other things. This is a bit of a problem for me, being so closely associated with law and order. You do understand that, don't you?'

'I don't know who Zimmerman is. I get contacted through a psi-link. It's like some sort of out-of-body experience. You know? I just find myself in this dark place where he talks. I've never seen his face, but I know that there's more than one of them. He's just their spokesman.'

'And Chronodyne?'

'I've never even heard of it,' Barrand admitted.

Mandell sat back in the cramped passenger seat. 'You know something? Incredible as it may seem, I believe you.' He smiled. 'As I said, Cronan and I go way back… At least several days. You, on the other hand, are a bit of a problem. You see, I need Cronan to do something for me, and I'm not too sure that you'll approve. Especially since he'll need your ship.'

Barrand grabbed Mandell by the throat with one hand. 'And how are you going to take it from me?' He squeezed, finding the look of surprise on Mandell's face quite interesting. The SID head's expression hardened, and he wrapped his fingers around Barrand's wrist. Barrand winced; the man was much stronger than he expected from a desk-bound civil servant.

Agony shot up Barrand's arm, the bones of his wrist grinding and scraping roughly together as Mandell pulled him off his throat without apparent effort. Barrand fell painfully to his knees as the grip on his wrist tightened. 'Your ambitions do you credit,' Mandell said, though Barrand heard the cracking of bone more loudly. 'But your grasp on reality needs work.' He released Barrand, who curled into a ball of pain, wanting to nurse his shattered wrist, but fearful to touch it in case it just hurt more. 'I think you see my grip is not a problem.' He turned away, then looked back.

'What *is* a problem is this conflict of interests in those people who happen to work for both of us.'

Barrand nodded painfully. 'I see what you're saying, Mr Mandell... That is our only problem.'

Mandell frowned. 'Did I say it is a problem? Sorry. I'm getting a bit forgetful these days.' He smiled apologetically. 'I meant to say it *was* a problem.' The last thing Barrand saw was a muzzle that seemed as big as the sun, and just as bright.

Cronan could feel Mandell's eyes boring into him, and was glad that in the shadows the SID director couldn't see his face. 'What is it you want me to do?'

'As luck would have it,' Mandell replied, 'exactly what you want to do. Take this ship as you were told, and kill the Doctor. In fact, destroy the ship he arrives in. You can't miss it; it's an old colony ship several miles long.'

'But I was going to do that anyway.'

'I know. But just to make sure, Wei will go with you. I don't want anybody getting lost.'

Mandell rose and left the cramped interior of Barrand's ship. He would return to his own ship, just in case the Doctor got through. The man was foolishly honest, and that meant it wouldn't be difficult to predict where he would go if he got free.

Frobisher and Liang, looking like the most Ogronish of Ogrons, were leading the way through the confused industrial interior of the *Speculator*, the others only a few paces behind.

Although the doors on these lower engineering decks

were all open, it still took the group some time to find their way. The Ogrons were far more accustomed to the ship's layout, however, and the doors blocking their way down from the upper decks didn't slow them that much.

The practical upshot of all this was that Frobisher's group, and the Ogrons led by Sha'ol and Karthakh, emerged on to the ship's central factory floor at the same time.

Both groups hesitated momentarily, then went for their guns. Ogron pups scattered into the ratholes in the ship's walls, as Jack got off the first shot, pitching an Ogron into a pile of spare deck plating.

Ogrons bundled Sha'ol behind cover, and a heavy weight slammed into Frobisher. It was Chat, taking him out the path of a shot that blew metal shards from the wall where his head was an instant ago.

Sha'ol ducked as shots ricocheted around his head, missing him by what felt like millimetres. Ducking behind a large atmospheric pump that had been removed from the freighter the Ogrons had captured earlier, he was relieved to see that Karthakh had also made it to a safe spot.

He activated his subcutaneous communicator with one spindly hand, while firing his disruptor blindly round the corner of the pump with the other. 'All Ogrons report to the factory floor. I repeat, all Ogrons report to the factory floor...'

Liang had abandoned his disguise, since it was only intended to fool stray Ogrons, not a war party led by the two bounty hunters. Frobisher had also reverted to his favoured penguin shape. if nothing else, Jack supposed, it was small enough to make better use of available cover.

There was plenty of that, what with chunks of the stripped

freighter, and the gigantic cogs and chains that were part of the old asteroid-mining set-up.

Jack calmly shot down an Ogron, not willing to let their returned fire distract him. It wasn't that he didn't feel any fear or confusion, but he knew that feelings were only there as a guideline. If a plasma shot hit him he would die, regardless of what he did or didn't do.

Liang pointed through the rapidly thinning group of Ogrons, to where a large portal leading into the next section was set into the wall. That was the section where auxiliary engineering was. 'If we try for that door, we'll be sitting ducks.'

'If we don't, the Doc'll be trapped,' Dibber reminded them.

'Better him than us,' Jack muttered, but then shook his head. He must be nuts, he told himself, but he had an idea. 'Lay down covering fire, and I'll see if I can make it down to the door. Frobisher –' He frowned. The penguin had vanished. 'Where the hell is he?'

The Doctor and Monty exchanged glances. 'They've stopped,' Monty said. 'Think they're on to the others? Or trying to draw us out?'

'Could be either,' the Doctor said slowly. 'Ogrons haven't developed much intelligence yet, but they do have an efficient animal cunning… Only one way to find out!' Before Monty could stop him, the Doctor unlocked the door, and went out, closing the door behind him. Monty was touched by that.

There were no sounds of violence from immediately outside, so he went out too. The Doctor was standing in the middle of the auxiliary engineering floor, listening to gunfire. 'They *are* on to Frobisher and the others!' he exclaimed. He started running, multicoloured coat-tails flapping behind him.

Monty followed at a more sedate pace. In a few moments, he found the Doctor pressed against the wall, peering round the edge of the doorway into the factory floor. Both sides were now well entrenched, Monty saw, but the Ogrons were the ones who could afford to wait.

Sha'ol had been under fire before, so he knew how to cope with the strain, and Karthakh was much the same. However, being trapped while the very environment was being destroyed was quite a different matter; tactically, they were in a very dangerous position.

By now the dead and dying lay between his group of Ogrons, and the escaped prisoners. Luckily he still had control over the emergency doors between sections. 'Pull back,' he hissed to the nearest Ogron. 'We will trap them here.'

'Wrong,' the Ogron said cheerily, and put a gun to Sha'ol's head. He shifted back into penguin form, but the gun remained steady. The Whifferdill looked at Karthakh, who was covering him with a KEM rifle. 'Put it down, or I add to the endangered-species list.'

Karthakh grudgingly obeyed.

'OK, Jack, we're all done here,' Frobisher called out.

In seconds, Sha'ol and Karthakh were surrounded by their enemies, and swiftly disarmed. As a strategist and planner, Sha'ol also knew when a battle was lost.

'Well done, Frobisher!' the Doctor proclaimed loudly. Then he glared at Jack. 'There are a lot of dead Ogrons here,' he said darkly.

'And no dead humans or Whifferdills.' Jack met the

Doctor's gaze evenly. Frobisher didn't want another battle to start, this time between the pair of them, so he tugged on the Doctor's sleeve with one flipper.

'Look.' Frobisher pointed to both bounty hunters' left wrists, where they wore coppery bracers.

'So that's it!' the Doctor exclaimed. He eased the bracers off each wrist.

'What?'

The Doctor held out the bracers, and Frobisher could now see the complex pattern inlaid into them. It was a strange mixture of swirling circuitry and an infinity symbol. 'Time rings. That's how they got into the TARDIS.'

'You mean these are Time Lord technology as well?'

'Exactly.'

'But where did they get them?'

'I should have thought that was obvious – from their employer.'

'A Time Lord?'

'Or Time Lords.'

'Why?

'There are two possible reasons. For one thing, the dismissal of charges at my trial wasn't universally appreciated. I don't doubt for a moment that there are some members of the High Council and the Celestial Intervention Agency who consider me something of an embarrassment.'

'And the other thing?'

'This.' The Doctor brandished the circuit he had taken from the Thor Facility's time dams. 'It's a rather neat copy of some Gallifreyan technology.'

'I thought it came from Dronid?'

'I'm sure it did. But Dronid was once home to a rival faction who left Gallifrey. And I strongly suspect we'll find that this so-called Chronodyne Industries is actually a front for the Celestial Intervention Agency. Someone has been selling off Time Lord technology to other races for their own purposes. Probably the same someone who supplied that ratty little scientist with the details on how to make vraxoin. The secret's been lost for centuries, but a Time Lord could always pop back and collect it.'

That made sense to Frobisher, as much as anything the Doctor said. 'But why draw attention to themselves here?'

'Because infinite age and power doesn't necessarily lead to infinite common sense – a trait most other Time Lords are rather lacking in.' Frobisher wasn't so sure about that 'other' business. 'Apart from that, if they've been keeping an eye on Mandell's plan, they'd know that both Glitz and the Veltrochni know me of old. Presumably they thought there was too much risk that one or other might contact me and send me in the direction of the time dams that they built for Mandell.'

'Shouldn't we tell the Time Lords, then?'

'No need, Frobisher. Everything that I or the TARDIS experience is fed into the Matrix. By now, the authorities on Gallifrey know everything that we know.'

'So we're finally safe?'

'Absolutely.'

A dark and spiky-looking ship hurtled through space on an intercept course.

The tactical computers and navigational equipment clicked rapidly, running through simulated strategies that posited every possible type of resistance that the *Hornet* might encounter from the *Speculator* and its fugitives. It wasn't so much the colony ship that scared Cronan, though, as the gunship that was on board. It was fast and highly manoeuvrable. It was definitely a match for this converted yacht. Even with the yacht's illegal weapons and engine upgrades, it would be a close-run thing.

'The ship with the Doctor and the bounty hunters is in range,' he told Wei.

'Good. Are you ready?'

'Of course.' He sounded offended at the question. Cronan sounded offended a lot of the time, because he took offence at the slightest little thing. Cronan pulled himself upright; he imagined that there was a certain standard of decorum to be maintained when approaching battle. An image that he felt it necessary to uphold, going by the holovids he had seen about space combat. 'Let's kill these interfering scum.'

Chapter Nineteen

The Doctor, Frobisher and the others conferred in the *Speculator*'s navigation room, once Sha'ol, Karthakh and Gorrak were securely locked in the late matriarch's little nest. It had been a slow journey back up there, the group gathered in a circle, but the guns at their leaders' heads had sent a clearer message to the surviving Ogrons than any words could have.

Luckily most of the survivors were the females who did the manual work, and the Ogron pups who fought each other among the disused mechanisms aboard. Neither group showed much interest in trying to rescue their leaders.

'What now?' Frobisher asked, when the Doctor had taken the Core back into his possession.

Jack cleared his throat. 'How about this: we turn this ship around, head for Andromeda, and sell the Core to the highest bidder. Then we all say our goodbyes and retire for a life of luxury.'

'No,' the Doctor said severely. 'The right thing to do is return the Data Core to its rightful owners.

Chat nodded from the doorway. 'The Doctor's right. If the Veltrochni did contact Vandor Prime about getting it back, they'll pay up anyway, and if that story was one of Mandell's lies, there will probably still be a reward for returning their stolen property. Not what we'd get on the open market, but enough to cover all our expenses.'

'There are more important things at stake than profit here. Justice, for one thing.'

'Fine. Ever hear of a little thing called compensation?

Punitive damages?'

'I have,' Liang answered. Without warning, he flowed in to the form of a gorilla, and lunged for the Doctor. Jack and Dibber tried to pull him away, while everybody else yelped in surprise.

Frobisher reacted next, wrapping himself around the gorilla as an oversized python, but Liang then blurred into a large insect of some alien kind, which leapt for the ceiling.

'Another Whifferdill?' the Doctor asked of anyone who was listening.

The insect extended an unnaturally long arm to snatch a gun from Monty. 'Oskar, at your service. Did you really think Mandell trusted you enough to leave you unwatched?'

Chat went white. 'How long –'

'Since your late brother failed to escape from the Thor Facility.' He formed Liang's face, with a malevolent grin. 'I think I played the part rather well.'

'But you're dead!' Jack protested.

'Evidently not. Actors of my calibre never really die, they just play other roles.'

This hadn't been that much of a challenging role, of course. Merely holding a shape was simple enough. Since Liang spoke so rarely anyway, Oskar had less need to think about how to play his voice.

'Actor?' the Doctor echoed. 'I wouldn't have called it that. What is it you want?'

'To return the Core to Mandell,' Oskar answered. 'D'you really think he would trust you lot to keep to your side of the deal? Mandell may be crazy, but he isn't stupid.'

'So you've been keeping an eye on us for him, is that it?'

'It's a living.' If you could call it that. His whole reputation had been a fraud, since he had never used a disguise in life, but merely pretended to do so.

Perhaps if that hooker hadn't OD'd in his motel room, he might have a more artistic career, but he disliked dwelling on the past. Mandell's payments kept him alive, and his name out of the scandal vids, so the change in role wasn't too hard for him to accept.

And if nothing else, it gave him a genuine ire to vent on the targets that Mandell selected.

Glitz had been sidling round, hoping for a clear shot, and now thought he had his chance. Oskar's arm flashed round as he heard the sound of Glitz's gun being drawn.

Glitz's gun snagged on his belt, and for a moment, he knew he was dead. The solid weight of Dibber crashed into him, and both went sprawling to the floor. Jack was already leaping over the console, returning fire.

Blaster bolts blew the locked door to the bounty hunters' prison askew, and knocked charred pits into the walls. The newly revealed Whifferdill dodged easily, but this gave Frobisher the chance to grapple with him again, shoving him towards a panel hit by a stray shot.

'You ignorant screed,' Glitz groaned. 'You could have cracked my skull open doing that.' He wasn't exactly ungrateful, but any response he made was better than the whimper he feared he might have let out. He could always show his appreciation later. 'And I'll tell you something else, you feel as heavy as the Doctor looks.'

Dibber didn't answer, and Glitz shook him. 'Dibber? Come on, lad, you're starting to scare me…' Dibber rolled over, and Glitz saw the cauterised hole that was burned through his back. His eyes were still open, but Dibber wasn't seeing anything with them.

Glitz sat back on his heels, unsure how to react to this.

The Doctor joined in, shoving Oskar forward. Frobisher let go at the last minute, but the Doctor wasn't so quick on his feet. The other Whifferdill reached out an extrusion to steady himself – and touched an exposed power feed.

Sparks arced across him, and his shape lost cohesion. With an unearthly and piercing series of multitonal screams, matter sloughed away from Oskar, until he was little more than a steaming pool of sludge on the deck.

Sha'ol emerged cautiously, and kept his hands in the open as he moved to where the Doctor had been blasted by the power surge. The humans were all covering the Tzun with weapons, and he had no plans to give them any excuses to use them. The Time Lord was lying face down on the far side of the flight deck.

Sha'ol reached out to check both pulses, and straightened. it was a curious feeling... He had expected to feel more triumph at the completion of his mission. He looked up at the others, and motioned for Karthakh to leave the KEM rifle he was surreptitiously picking up.

'Our contract is fulfilled. The Doctor is dead.'

Frobisher lost cohesion, and suddenly he was the little faceless humanoid again, unable to control his own shape, let alone help his friend.

'We bear you no ill will,' Sha'ol reassured the others. 'Our contract was only for the Doctor. With his death, that contract is fulfilled. We need only inform our employer.'

Frobisher was doubtful, but nodded anyway. If nothing else, it would help the rest of the group feel better. That was what the Doctor would want, he knew. There wasn't much point in sacrificing oneself for someone, if those people were then lost anyway.

Frobisher didn't really notice where any of the others were. They had faded from his consciousness, though his brain still knew they were there and trying to comfort him. No such attempt really registered yet, though.

Oddly, the one person whom Frobisher did still see with some clarity through his round glasses was Glitz. There was something of himself in Glitz's expression, yet worse, if that were possible. 'You've never lost a friend before, have you?'

Glitz shook his head. 'Never even knew I had one. I mean, it was just Dibber, wasn't it? Daft nerk who doesn't know to keep his head down.' Glitz sounded as stunned as Frobisher felt. 'I wonder if it gets easier.'

'No,' Frobisher said quietly, 'it doesn't.'

'Glad I ain't got any other friends, then.' Glitz paused. 'I hope not, anyway.'

Sha'ol traced a pattern on his time ring. 'Yes?' a chilling voice asked. Frobisher recognised it as the same one from the *Speculator.*

'This is Sha'ol and Karthakh. The Doctor is dead.'

'He could be faking it,' the voice warned, raising Frobisher's hopes. 'We – he has the ability to stop his hearts, and also possesses a respiratory bypass system. Do you have a medical scanner?'

'Yes.' Sha'ol pulled a compact scanning device from the pocket of his waistcoat.

'Scan the Doctor's brain for electrochemical response.'

Sha'ol did so, and Frobisher watched keenly, hoping something would register, even if that meant they would have to fight again.

'No response. There is no electrochemical or EM activity in

the brain or nervous system.'

There was a long indrawn breath. 'At last…' Frobisher could almost hear the satisfied smile. 'And the telepathic circuits built into the time ring prove it.' There was a longer pause. 'I am a man of my word, for today at least. The hundred million is being transferred into your accounts. You are fine workers,' the voice mused. 'I may use you again…'

The voice faded, and as it did, so too did the two time rings.

'What now?' Jack asked. 'We all kiss and make up?'

'No,' Glitz said darkly. 'Now we go to Veltroch and hand over this bauble like the Doctor wanted.' Frobisher was surprised at Glitz's turn. Maybe he wasn't such a scruff after all. 'Mandell screwed us all over, and that's the one thing he doesn't want.'

Frobisher had to bow to that logic. It was the best way of getting back at the guy who was indirectly responsible for the deaths of the Doctor, Dibber, and Liang. The rest of the gang nodded slowly.

'It's what he'd have wanted,' Jack supposed.

'Liang too,' Chat agreed. Her voice was surprisingly strong under the circumstances.

'I also agree,' Karthakh rumbled. 'Many innocent Veltrochni died as result of Mandell's schemes. It is right that his true aim should be thwarted.'

Sha'ol looked up at him. 'This is most unwise. For a Tzun to enter Veltrochni space…' Frobisher realised that the spindly grey bounty hunter was scared. Terrified, in fact. 'And the Core rightfully belongs to my people.'

Karthakh remained silent for a moment. 'My Pack are your people now.'

Sha'ol looked around, as if he was about to protest. Then he tilted his head curiously. 'As you wish.'

'Well, I'm glad all that's settled!' the Doctor exclaimed with a stifled yawn. He sat up, as Glitz's eyes almost popped out of his head. 'I was beginning to wonder if anything would ever get decided around here.'

'You're alive! Frobisher yelled, hugging the Doctor. The Doctor looked vaguely embarrassed at all the attention.

'Half a millisecond,' Glitz protested. 'You're dead!'

The Doctor grinned cheekily. 'That's twice you've made that assumption, Sabalom Glitz; I wouldn't give up the day job for a career as a coroner if I were you.'

'Our contract,' Sha'ol began.

'Is legally fulfilled. I was, in all the relevant areas, dead, was I not?'

'You were –'

'No heartbeat, no respiration, room temperature skin? And even a medical scanner would have confirmed it?'

'Yes, but –'

'And your employer paid up?'

'Yes.'

'Then,' the Doctor announced simply, 'your contract is fulfilled, by your own logic.'

'It is,' Sha'ol admitted slowly. 'But how are you now living?'

'I was living all along.' The Doctor held out the circuit that he had taken from the Thor Facility. 'A temporal circuit from the time dams, and the power surge. More than enough to put me in complete temporal stasis for several minutes.'

'Stasis?'

'Exactly. I wasn't dead, merely frozen between heartbeats for a few minutes. Your employers don't know that I took this circuit, so they didn't think of that, though I'm sure they had you make certain I wasn't faking it by stopping my hearts.'

Sha'ol looked up at him as he stood. 'How can you be so certain?'

'Because they're Time Lords. Didn't you know? Someone in the Celestial Intervention Agency hired you two to kill me, because they didn't want me to find out that they've been selling our technology, and dealing in vraxoin, for their own purposes. I imagine it's something to do with keeping their local operatives under control – they enlist criminals, get them involved in a lucrative and otherwise impossible trade, and can then threaten to expose them to the authorities. Of course, they probably *do* expose them to the authorities when the other side have something they want. Useful to be able to manipulate so effectively when you're a covert organisation and you don't want to show your hand.'

Glitz stepped between them. 'Pity Dibber was only human, isn't it? The daft nerk isn't going to wake up like you. He should have known better. Mind you, he never was the sharpest knife in the kitchen.' He looked hopefully at Frobisher, and Frobisher realised that Glitz was seeking approval of his acting.

'You're not fooling anybody,' Frobisher told him.

The Doctor attempted to jolly-up the gloomy atmosphere. 'Right,' he said, rubbing his hands together. 'I believe we agreed to return the Core to Veltroch. Since this ship isn't going anywhere now, I suggest we take the gunship in which we were brought here.'

'Your TARDIS is aboard that vessel,' Sha'ol informed them. 'Now that our contract is fulfilled, we will accompany you.'

Frobisher was quite taken aback by the way the Tzun said that, as if there was no question that this was how things were going to be. The Doctor, however, merely nodded.

'What about the Ogrons?' Jack asked.

'The ship isn't going anywhere, so neither are they. We'll let the authorities know where to find them.'

'Acceptable,' Sha'ol agreed. He lifted his disruptor, but this time turned it on the unarmed Gorrak, and stunned him. 'He would have attempted to prevent us. The stun effect will wear off soon.'

Once again, they formed into a circle, this time making their way to the hangar where the gunship was. The few Ogrons they saw didn't know that Sha'ol and Karthakh had made their peace with the humans, and so kept their distance.

The interior of the gunship was as cramped as Frobisher remembered, but at least this time the air wasn't thick with the stench of unwashed Ogrons. When Karthakh pointed to one of the interior cabins, Frobisher was delighted to see the TARDIS within.

'Couldn't we just take the Core in the TARDIS?' he suggested.

The Doctor shook his head. 'The TARDIS' navigational system isn't *that* good, Frobisher. At least this way we know we'll reach Veltroch in the right time period. We can launch any time, on course for Veltroch.'

Monty nodded, and started the engines. The gunship lurched wildly. 'Sorry about that; things weren't so sensitive in my day.' Monty touched the controls more gently, and guided the gunship out of the hangar and away on a long parabola.

Jemson, like most of the other military and legal officials who had come along, was visibly awed by the Veltrochni Dragon *Zathakh*. Its interior was dark and functional, yet also strangely spiritual. The metal walls and buttresses that

261

enclosed the triangular bridge were aged and vaulted. It was like being in a kind of iron cathedral.

Kala never noticed any of this. To her, every chamber aboard Brokhal's ship was just another room like every room anywhere. It was merely a place to stand or sit while she waited to see what truth was held in Nic's eyes.

Nobody knew where he had gone, but it was reasonable to assume that he would either be with the Doctor and the others, or following them. Currently, *Zathakh* was heading for the last known position of the ship which had snatched the Doctor from under the SID's nose. From there, they would track it, as Nic was undoubtedly doing.

Half of Kala wanted more than anything to catch him, and the other half hoped he'd run off, never to return. She wasn't really sure she wanted to know the truth; if he was innocent, then she was joined with his betrayers, but if he was guilty, then her love had been wasted on him.

Neither option was one that would allow her to resist the tears that she knew would come when this was over.

Gorrak was furious when he regained consciousness after a few minutes. Part of it was his general rage at being made a fool of, but at the back of his mind was the matriarch's conviction that his soul was no more solid than wind-blown sand. Even without her taunts, that jibing remained.

At least the Nest was still here. The ship could be repaired, or they would steal another. Then all the members of the Nest would move on. Ogron young grew up quickly, and it wouldn't be long before he had replaced the warriors he lost today.

That was a good thought; he and his mate free from the matriarch's insults...

There was a buzzing from one of the consoles, and Gorrak went to look. Another ship was approaching. He grinned. His luck was changing, if he was to be blessed with a new ship so quickly. His hand had almost reached the intercom switch to call Borrk and tell him to try Karthakh's trick with the communications gear to disable the other ship's weapons when the first torpedo hit.

'What the hell?' Monty yelled.

Behind the gunship, the *Speculator* was reeling. The strain of the badly designed Ogron modifications would have pulled it apart eventually, and the impacts of a volley of plasma torpedoes didn't exactly add to its stability. Some of the constructions that encrusted the vast outer hull started to split. Secondary explosions inside produced flashes of light in the gaping maw that ran through the ship.

Volcanic bursts of burning gases emerged from the *Speculator* as she started to drift. Scrap metal and oddly doll-like Ogron bodies were spat out from the new gaps in the hull. As the ship died, a dark and spiky-looking pirate ship sailed through the debris field which was trailing behind her.

'Mandell,' Jack said. 'It must be.' He sucked air in through his teeth as he looked at the other ship's rate of approach. The new attacker suddenly faded from the sensors. 'So, like, what exactly is the speedosity of this thing?'

'What?' Monty asked

'How fast does it go?'

'I haven't the slightest idea.'

'Looks like we'd better find out.'

'It would be best if I flew the ship.' Sha'ol's calm, precise voice cut through the discussion.

'Yeah, right,' Jack scoffed. 'Meanwhile, back in the real world…'

'Your concerns are understandable, but misplaced. We are all currently in equal danger. It is in all our interests for the best pilot to fly this vessel.'

'Plasma torpedo launched and running,' Chat warned. 'Bearing directly.'

Jack's eyes widened. 'Where the hell did that come from?' On the screen, an incandescent bolt swelled rapidly. 'Are our shields up to thi-' The sudden blast knocked him off his feet and back into the gunship's cramped troop bay.

The ship straightened out again. 'I should say they were up to it,' the Doctor replied. 'How many more hits they can take is quite another matter.'

'You must allow me to take the helm,' Sha'ol urged the Doctor. 'It is necessary to our survival also.'

The Doctor nodded, and rose from the seat. Sha'ol replaced him smoothly.

'Incoming,' Chance announced.

Sha'ol threw the ship into a tight loop without apparent thought. The torpedo blazed past the underside of the hull, missing it by mere yards. 'If the human, Mandell, has been studying Tzun naval architecture, he will have undoubtedly replicated the camouflage field also.'

Frobisher threw him a sour look. 'You could sue them. Your people should have patented that thing.' No one bothered to dignify that with an answer. The gunship shook as the torpedo detonated astern.

'The shield took the brunt of it,' Karthakh said with surprising calm. Glitz suspected that his iciness had become such an ingrained habit that he probably didn't even know how to sound as frightened as he should be. 'It will not hold up to more than one or two near misses. Another direct hit will finish us.'

The Doctor frowned in thought. 'Sha'ol, what's their maximum range, and how long does a shot take to reach us from there?'

'Their firing range is no more than four hundred units,' came the answer. 'It would take a torpedo thirty-two seconds to reach the ship.' The discussion didn't distract him from putting the ship through a series of stomach-churning manoeuvres. Sha'ol cut the engine power, causing everyone to slam forward against their consoles.

'What the hell are you doing?' Jack demanded. 'They'll have a clear shot.'

'Yes.'

'Torpedo launched, bearing directly,' Karthakh interrupted appropriately. Jack glared at the Sha'ol, who merely looked back unblinkingly and slammed the thrusters on full, sending the ship into a full power dive.

The gunship sped over the curve of the planet's terminator as if chasing the night. Plasma flickered around the edges of the shield as it churned through the atmosphere. 'Ninety seconds to impact,' Chat warned, a little shakily.

'This will be the difficult part,' Sha'ol announced calmly. He slammed the controls to port, while pulling up. Everybody grabbed hold of console edges, as the ship lurched not away from the surface, but parallel to it, now heading directly towards the pole.

'They're evading the shot,' Wei warned. Cronan smiled reassuringly, as if the fugitives' postponing of the inevitable merely made the chase more exciting. After all, he was superior, so they could never escape him. Inside, however, he cursed the incompetence of Barrand's crew for missing such a clean shot.

'Follow them,' he snapped. 'Arm another torpedo.' This wasn't as easy as it looked in the holovids...

Sha'ol guided the ship expertly, even though it wasn't a Tzun vessel. If it had been, he reflected, the computer would have sent all the relevant data from the console through his fingertips directly to the brain. He would have been able to feel the ship move with his every thought.

'Nice try,' Jack said coolly, then pointed to a scanner display as they hurtled over the polar icecap, 'but they're following us.'

Sha'ol nodded. 'They are blind to the obvious strategy. That is why we will succeed where they fail.'

The *Hornet* rolled into an orbit in direct pursuit, looping over the planet's magnetic pole moments after the gunship. On the viewer, their quarry hurtled past the equator, but the distance between them was not great enough for them to try the same trick again.

Cronan's eyes hooded over, satisfied at the imminent result of the chase. Even a blind speelsnape couldn't miss this time, let alone someone as gifted as himself. 'Target their engines, we'll blow their reactor core.'

'Locked.'

Cronan held his breath subconsciously, eager for the kill. His whole life had gone down the tubes thanks to at least one of the people on that ship, and now it was payback time. This was going to be so cool, he thought. Another few seconds, and it would all be over. He toggled the communications switch. 'Good try, Doctor, but not good enough! This'll teach you to mess with me –'

'Torpedo,' Wei yelped suddenly, 'bearing directly!'

'What?' Cronan's head jerked up. He called up a tactical display, and felt his throat tighten with fear. It was the last torpedo they themselves had launched, coming round the planet in a slingshot orbit over the equator. Ahead of them, the gunship flashed out and away from the surface, having passed the path of the approaching bolt. 'Evasive!'

Wei tried to alter the ship's angle of attack, to pull up, but the view on screen remained steady. 'We're too deep in the gravity well. You've killed us!'

Cronan almost laughed at the irony, but the breath wouldn't come. He scanned for the torpedo. It filled the screen.

The *Hornet* was struck amidships by her own plasma torpedo. It smashed the ship sideways, blasting a shower of molten wreckage from the engine section. The hull began to crumple with pressure loss as it tumbled in towards the planet. Out of control, it hit atmosphere at entirely the wrong angle, and began to glow with the heat of friction.

A host of possible last-minute pleas and dying declarations crossed Cronan's mind in nanoseconds, until the most appropriate and heartfelt one could find its way to his lips.

'Bugger.'

The crippled ship bloomed. Wreckage was torn from the hull and scattered far and wide, while the fuel and atmosphere ignited in the sort of explosion that was usually only created by firework specialists on drugs, and would have needed a dictionary full of adjectives to describe properly.

'Way cool,' Jack commented agreeably. He slapped the Doctor heartily on the back. 'I like your style, Doc: flashy, but practical.'

'Cool?' the Doctor echoed. 'Cool?!' There were people on that ship, Chance. People who died.'

'Yeah, and better them than us.'

The Doctor glared at him. 'That is a very narrow-minded point of view,' he said disapprovingly.

'OK,' Jack suggested, 'But me, I reckon the Ogron kids on that old ship deserve any sympathy you need to show.'

The Doctor hesitated, then sighed. 'All lost lives deserve that, Chance.'

Chapter Twenty

Mandell's private yacht, paid for out of the SID's budget, was some distance away. Apart from Mandell, there was a small Tactical team on board, just in case. He wasn't going to take *too* many chances where his own skin was concerned. If he played his cards right, he might even get through this without Kala knowing about his work.

He had tried to call to warn her that he wouldn't make it home for a bit, but she wasn't in either. That was unusual, but not unheard of. If she was on a case, she could be on a stake-out. Sometimes he envied her that freedom from secrecy. She could be openly proud of her contribution to the planet's security.

The homing signals that Wei and Cronan had been tagged with had both stopped transmitting, and Mandell could just feel his riches and power slipping away.

He left his luxury cabin, and went along to the yacht's flight deck. 'Increase to maximum speed,' he told the SID pilot. 'This is our last chance.'

Flight Director Trelokh hopped up on to the *Zathakh*'s command balcony to join his mother and the humans. 'We have picked up engine traces from several different ships. There is a great deal of wreckage in the vicinity, and residual plasma torpedo traces.'

'A Vandorian ship?' Brokhal asked.

'Most likely. A second debris field has been detected by the *Khadok* on a landmass on Oblio I. More plasma torpedo traces there. A single engine trace leaves the Oblio system.

From the drive signature we estimate a smaller patrol craft; perhaps a gunship.'

'A gunship was stolen from an orbital tether during this crisis,' Jemson informed the aliens. 'It could be the same one.'

'Where are they heading?' Brokhal demanded.

'Going by the relative positions of the two destroyed ships, we estimate they are making for Veltroch itself.'

'Veltroch? But if they are attempting to prevent our recovery of the Core, then why go there?'

'It is the last place we would look,' Trelokh pointed out.

'There is another possibility,' Brokhal said slowly. 'This Mandell employed a Time Lord to lead his team; the one called the Doctor.'

'So? Even they have renegades.'

'Yes, indeed they do… But the Doctor is known to us as a man of honour. It is possible that he may be trying to return the Core to its rightful place.'

Mandell drummed his fingers on his armrest. He'd get the Core back from the Doctor's hands. Then he could claim the Doctor was behind it all. He was a rogue Time Lord, and between his concerns about the bounty hunters, and Chronodyne Industries, it looked like he could make a good report blaming them for all this.

That could work; he told himself. One way or the other, he'd still come out smelling of roses, and Kala would never know about his more… unofficial methods.

'We're approaching the planet Veltroch,' the pilot said.

'Tell traffic control who we are. Tell them we're on a mission to aid in the recovery of the Core.'

'Doc,' Jack called out. 'I think we got another little problem.'

'What is it?'

'There's a Veltrochni Dragon gaining on us. They'll probably have us on sensors by now.'

'Are they in communication range?'

'Yep. And before you ask, we can't outrun them.'

'As it happens, that isn't what I had mind.'

Jack grimaced disconsolately. 'Dammit, I knew that was coming.'

'Bring us out of hyperspace.' The Doctor sat in the co-pilot's seat, and studied the communications controls for a moment before trying them out. 'I want to speak with Pack-Mother Brokhyth of Pack Zanchyth,' the Doctor called out.

'Mother,' the Flight Director called. 'The gunship is slowing, and hailing us. They are asking to speak with Pack-Mother Brokhyth.'

Brokhal was surprised at this. Brokhyth was her ancestor, long dead. 'I am Brokhal, Pack-Mother of Pack Zanchyth. Who is it who knows my family?'

'I am usually referred to as the Doctor.'

Kala stiffened, looking towards the speakers.

'I know of you. If you truly are the Doctor, that is.'

'I met your... ancestor along with my companions Jamie and Victoria. Brokhyth's daughter Brythal was on board –' It was him! Brokhal knew that instantly. Nobody else could have known these things about her family's contact with the Doctor.

'Very well, Doctor. What is it you wish to speak to me about?'

'I have the Core that was stolen from you by Niccolo Mandell.' Off to one side, nobody took any notice as Kala started to cry. 'My friends and I would very much like to return it to its rightful owners. I want permission to land on Veltroch.'

Brokhal was puzzled by this request. If he was sincere, why not just dock? 'Why there?'

'Because we tried a neutral setting once and you saw what happened. I want to be absolutely certain that is where it is meant to be.'

'Very well,' Brokhal said. 'Veltrochni traffic control will give you landing co-ordinates.'

'Thank you, *Chach-kha* Brokhal.'

Her son switched frequencies. 'Mother, traffic control reports that Mandell is requesting permission to land also. It appears he is unaware of our... interest in him.'

Now that was good news, Brokhal thought. And sweetly ironic too. 'Have him directed to the same landing platform.'

Chat wrinkled her nose. She had never expected to return to this planet again. It hadn't changed at all; the grey vegetation and sweet scent of rot were exactly as she remembered.

The group descended from the gunship on to a platform carved from a single incredibly huge bole on the outskirts of the city of Great Houses. Everyone was fairly nervous, though Sha'ol was most nervous of all. Monty had jury-rigged some parts from the old holosuit to disguise him as a human, and hoped the Veltrochni wouldn't run a bio-scanner over him.

'It is unusual to be here,' Karthakh murmured. 'I had expected to be more relaxed.'

'Humans have a saying for it,' the Doctor said. '"You can never go home again."'

'But I am home,' Karthakh replied. 'What is so impossible about that?'

'It's just a figure of speech,' Jack told him irritably.

There was a loud unnatural howl from behind them. As one

being, everybody in the group turned, to see the battered gunship finally collapse off its strained landing gear. Hull plating popped, crashing into the mossy ground, and some large dark mechanism fell out through the bottom of the hull. It smoked slightly.

Chat was horrified to think that only a few minutes ago, she had been flying through space in that pile of wreckage. She tried to keep her legs from quivering, but gave up as dozens of Veltrochni warriors in powered armour and carrying KEM rifles ringed the landing platform. She was certain that other, shrouded, ones were crouched invisibly among the vegetation.

A Dragon was hovering a few hundred feet above, its spread wings expansive enough to blacken the sky. The only bright spot in the dimness was the green fire of an active quantum lance.

Frobisher was pretty nervous as well. This was not the same as being rousted by a couple of tired cops looking to get an arrest on their records for the month.

He had a distinct premonition that he and the Doctor were going to spend a very long time in a cell here. If they were lucky. And he didn't even have any of his Benny Goodman collection with him to while away the years.

A glow preceded Brokhal's arrival by transmat. She was accompanied by some of the cops Frobisher recognised from the Cafe Terrestriale. 'Doctor?'

'Pack-Mother Brokhal, I presume,' the Doctor said confidently, stepping forward. The sound of so many safety catches being slipped off was like a stampede on gravel. 'This is yours, I believe.'

Frobisher watched in mounting horror as the Doctor

deposited the crystalline Data Core into Brokhal's massive claws. With that, the Veltrochni could wipe out whole planets' worth of people whose only crime was to have been visited by the Tzun in the past.

He knew the Doctor had a fondness for humans, but surely not at the expense of others?

Brokhal's dorsal spines quivered excitedly, and she plugged some leads from her portable equipment into the Data Core. Her spines flattened. 'This is –'

'It's the genuine article, I assure you,' the Doctor said. 'But I took the liberty of purging it.' Frobisher blinked. The Doctor purged it? After all this? 'I think they used to call it *détente*. You can't use it to destroy the remaining Ph'Sor Tzun colonies, but nor can Mandell or anyone else use it to replicate Tzun technology.'

'We never had any plans to attack the remaining Ph'Sor colonies, Doctor. Had we any such plans, we could have done it centuries ago. It is disappointing that you misjudge us so.'

The Doctor winced. 'I'm afraid that I've been rather disappointed myself by people who should know better… But let us say instead that no one in the future will be able to misuse it.'

Brokhal nodded. 'It is still the last relic from S'Arl. As such it still commands great value and respect here.'

'Respect?'

'It is not an easy thing to live with, having committed genocide. This has always been a warning to us, as much as to others.'

The Doctor beamed. 'In that case, the future probably has less to worry about than I feared.'

Kala watched as the Doctor and Brokhal chatted. They

looked... friendly. But they were thieves, she reminded herself.

'Stop!' Kala recognised the voice immediately. It was Nic. Mandell was forcing a way through the assembled Veltrochni, a pistol in hand and a troop of armed Tac officers flanking him. The Tac people all looked decidedly uncomfortable under the circumstances. 'Arrest those people,' he commanded. 'They are thieves and pirates, who –'

He froze as his eyes met Kala's, and she saw a moment of loss in them. He looked like a man who had just seen his most precious possession disappear down a drain.

'Destroyed the Dragon *Thazrakh*?' Brokhal suggested dangerously, when Mandell failed to continue. 'Murdered the crew?'

Mandell started. 'Yes! Them and their Ogron friends!'

Brokhal loomed over him. 'Who mentioned Ogrons?' Something happened to his face then, and Kala wished she hadn't seen it. It was the look of a man who'd been caught out in a lie. And that meant that he was involved, was guilty, just like she had been told.

Compounding his slip, he looked to her for support, his eyes begging her to back him up. In them she saw her truth. 'Arrest him,' she said quietly, not quite able to get the words out properly. It was enough, though. 'For conspiracy to manufacture and distribute vraxoin; for the theft, twice, of the Data Core; for the destruction of the Dragon *Thazrakh* and the murder of her crew; and for...' What was she supposed to say? For lying to her? 'For resisting arrest.'

Every Veltrochni KEM rifle on the platform moved to aim at Mandell and the Tac squad.

And some part of Kala wished they were aiming at *her* heart.

Mandell didn't even see the weapons aimed at him. All that

was in his sight was Kala's face as her eyes iced over. There was no actual physical change, but he saw it all the same. She *knew*. She knew all of it; he could see that in her disappointment, in her loss, in her hatred.

Mandell had always managed to keep guilt from his mind, even when he knew he was breaking laws. If he was doing something with good intent, then what did it matter how he did it? But now fingers of guilt did get a grip on his heart. He had crossed the one line he had vowed never to cross; he had hurt Kala.

The pistol dropped from his hand, and he didn't even notice.

'Was it worth it?' the Doctor asked.

'What?' He was lost now, unsure where his mind was supposed to go.

'All this. All those deaths, and crimes, and it's all for this. But it wasn't worth it, was it, Mandell?'

Mandell knew that right now he should be hating the Doctor more than ever. Try as he might, he found that he couldn't do it. 'I could never hurt her... I thought I couldn't...' The Doctor was gone, though, and Mandell knew that he had answered the Time Lord's question.

As Mandell was led away, and the warriors started to disperse back to other duties, the Doctor took Brokhal aside. 'I'm going to ask a favour of you. Make arrangements to have Glitz and the others released. None of them did any of this willingly.'

'Why should I?'

'Because without them you'd never have got your property back, and there would have been a war. And because a friend of your people asks you. I know that there is a history of passing down exploits in your Packs to new generations of cubs, and I suspect that you know how I helped Pack Zanchyth bring justice to those who destroyed Pack Huthakh.'

'Very well. You have earned that much.'

'One other thing?'

'Do not presume on your luck.'

'I'd like to have some assistance in separating my TARDIS from what's left of the gunship.'

Brokhal nodded, and the use of the human gesture wasn't lost on the observers. 'It will be seen to.'

'You're letting them go,' Kala echoed disbelievingly. She considered the thieves just as responsible for her heartbreak as Mandell. It was guilt by association if nothing else. In truth, though, Kala wasn't too interested either way. Her life had just... stopped, with the revelation of Nic's complicity. He'd betrayed not only the population of their planet, and the Veltrochni, but her and their unborn child too.

'Yes,' Brokhal said simply. 'As Ambassador to the Delphinus group, I must insist that these people are released without charge. They were, after all, merely following the instructions of your government to return our property.'

'But there were no such instructions,' Jemson put in. 'The government didn't know we even had it.'

Brokhal made a strange snorting sound that passed for laughter among Veltrochni. 'You are young, and new to politics. By tonight there will have been instructions to that effect, believe me – unless your President wishes the people to know how he has been duped, he will issue post-dated orders to appear as if he was defusing the crisis all along. As I was saying, this can in no way be considered a crime. However, I do understand your concerns. Family is the thing most important to us, and yours has been damaged by this crisis. Punishing those who were… innocent will not lessen that damage.'

Kala said nothing, and Brokhal continued.

'You may tell your President, as we will, that the Doctor and his associates were just returning our property to us as your government will have agreed.'

'And given how much Niccolo's collusion will embarrass them, they won't complain,' said Kala bitterly.

'Nor should they. Those thieves just saved your planet.'

'Where will you go?' Chat asked Glitz. They were standing on the balcony of a hotel in the City of Great Houses, and he was trying very much to ignore the smell of the jungle.

'Back to Elchur,' he answered after a little think.

'Elchur?'

'My ship's still there, isn't it? How am I going to make a living without it?'

'Does that mean you're going to go straight?'

'Well… I'm an entrepreneur after all. There's always a tidy little earner in some trade, isn't there?' He didn't add that there were more earnings in evading import and export duties. She might take that the wrong way, and he didn't really want her to do that. Nobody else had ever looked at him in quite the way she did, and for some reason he didn't want to spoil that. 'But I can stay for a little while longer, if you want.'

She smiled, and he prided himself on his skills at seduction.

Jack Chance and Monty Kast clinked glasses in the hotel bar. Everything was going on the government's bill, so they were taking the trouble to experiment with as many cocktail combinations as possible – all in the name of philanthropic research, of course.

'Well, I guess we shook things up a bit at home,' Jack commented proudly. He liked the idea that he had that much clout. Already they were hearing rumours that the President might call an early election.

'That we did. Profitable too.'

Jack examined his smoking drink closely, wondering if something in it was making him hear things. It was a Morestran concoction, so there was no telling what was in it. 'Profitable? But we didn't get anything.'

The older man grinned. 'That's because you're young and foolish. And didn't put a bet on with Korled the Terileptil that we'd pull this off.'

Jack put his drink down. 'You did what?' He couldn't believe Monty had done that. More accurately, he couldn't believe Monty had done it without letting him try as well.

'My whole life's savings at odds of four hundred and eighty three to one. Very profitable.'

'You bet your life's savings? That doesn't sound old and wise to me.'

'If we'd lost, I'd be dead anyway, so what difference did it make? So, are you coming back to VP?'

Jack shook his head. 'Who's gonna come to the Cafe with the reputation it'll have after being trashed twice? The insurance is pretty hefty, so I'll buy myself a ship, maybe go home to Earth…'

There was a message waiting for Karthakh at reception. 'An escaped serial killer in the Xotac system,' he told Sha'ol. 'Half a million, dead or alive.'

'Signal them that we will take it.'

After all, what else did they know how to do?

* * *

Frobisher took a last look at the skyline of Veltroch. Leaving any planet was always hard, but he managed because he knew there was always another to visit.

Some visits were more pleasant than others, but Frobisher doubted he would get tired of any of them for a long time. He turned and went into the TARDIS. Rather than remove it from the wrecked ship, the Veltrochni had cleared the ship away from it.

The Doctor was waiting for him. 'Where to, Frobisher?' Now that they didn't have to worry about Sha'ol and Karthakh, there was no need for a random jump.

'Nowhere special, Doc.'

'Nowhere special?' The Doctor smiled slyly. 'I think I recall the co-ordinates for there.'

Watch out for Doctor Who on Video!

The following exciting adventures are currently
available from BBC Worldwide:

THE LEISURE HIVE starring Tom Baker
THE AWAKENING/FRONTIOS starring Peter Davison
THE WAR MACHINES starring William Hartnell
THE HAPPINESS PATROL starring Sylvester McCoy
THE E-SPACE TRILOGY starring Tom Baker
TIMELASH starring Colin Baker
BATTLEFIELD starring Sylvester McCoy
THE MIND OF EVIL starring Jon Pertwee

Coming soon. . .

HORROR OF FANG ROCK starring Tom Baker
PLANET OF FIRE starring Peter Davison
THE ARK starring William Hartnell
THE ICEWARRIORS starring Patrick Troughton